Real Life and Other Disasters

A Britlandia novel

Merren Tait

LOLA PUBLICATIONS

Also by Merren Tait

The Good Life Series

The Year of the Fox

Bluffing for Beginners

The Misdeeds of Sadie Quinn

Odd Girl Roar

The Amateur's Guide to the Art of Running Away: A novella

Britlandia Series

Romance is Dead

Chapter one

J effrey Wainwright's eyes sparkle like a fridge light on cling film.

I want to say it's because he's delighted by the intelligence of my company, but it's probably due to the little bit of saliva he aspirated when I said, "In my next life, I'm going to be a dolphin linguist."

Saying, "In my next life, I'm going to be a dolphin linguist," to your prospective boss is not advisable, but then my ability to gauge 'appropriate' failed approximately half an hour ago when, courtesy of my hunger, my blood pressure dropped so low my heart pumped my thinking juice at a disastrous rate of a quarter of a mile an hour.

Admittedly, I had just arrived and hurriedly explain, "Because of the echo location. You know, the foot traffic. It's like dodgems out there."

Jeff chuckles generously through his bleached smile, so I know I haven't arsed this up. Yet.

A bar is not the kind of place I would have expected to discuss an employment contract, but it is full of suited people, buoyed by release from their London corporate worlds. Jeff looks completely at ease among the other cuff-linked, twelve-tone-saloned-hair white people, and so, I think, it must be how things are done around here.

He sports a black and gold Omega watch. His jacket, slung casually on the stool between us emits the spicy scent of an expensive cologne applied sometime in the past with a little too much enthusiasm.

Whereas I –

I shift from one bum cheek to the other, willing my 99p Primark knickers to unwedge themselves. I would tweezer them out with my fingers, but even I realise that might be considered a little indelicate.

I am in a league so far below these people, you'd need the Hubble Telescope to spot me.

"What can I get you, Sarah?" Jeff leans towards me slightly, the words purred as if he already had a couple before I arrived.

Aware I haven't got this in the bag as I'm yet to sign anything, I settle on a prompting, "Would…champagne be appropriate?" It is 6.25 pm and I haven't had anything to eat since I scoffed the last slice of bread that morning in my otherwise empty kitchen. I'm not sure what a glass of bubbly alcohol might do on a stomach that empty, but it has calories, so I'm willing to throw caution to the howling gale.

Jeff raises an eyebrow and one side of his mouth in one of those smiles that is either cocky or bemused. Or possibly both. The combination of brow and lip makes him look Jokerish. "Very appropriate."

I keep my "Awesome" shriek on my inside, because I am a consummate professional and not fourteen.

He leans forward and pulls the stool with his jacket on out to one side so that our shins are a couple of inches from each other when we cross our legs.

He signals to the bartender, orders two glasses of Veuve Clicquot and I wonder, giddily, if I am seen as a prize asset who requires impressing, or if this is standard fare for a general manager of a luxury hotel.

I want Jeff to be confident in his decision to pick me out of the chef pack, and so I make an effort to string a few intelligent-sounding words together.

"I'm so thrilled you messaged me," I say as he passes over a credit card. "I thought the dynamic in the interview was good, but it's just so hard to gauge those situations, you know?"

"I do know, Sarah." He hands a hissing glass to me and looks me in the eye as we clink a toast. "I can't tell you how *stirred* I was when you agreed to meet." His eyes flicker down to my bare knees and track their way to my ankles.

Ah. So he's that kind of man. The type that thinks wealth and status entitle him to some gentle leering. In this moment, I'll let him. He *is* just about to put an employment contract in front of me.

His eyes return to my face. "You really do have all the right attributes."

I give him the benefit of the doubt that he's referring to my professional prowess and say, "Thank you, Jeff." And a combination of pride and the knowledge that the misery of unemployment has come to an end fizzes in my veins like the bubbles in the champagne. "And anyway, this bar's not that far out of my way." I think of the Tube and bus ride it took to get here and wonder how I will pay for the return journey. Perhaps he could organise an instant advance. Unlikely. Or I could say I forgot my wallet and did he have spare cash for an Uber? "Course, I'd come. This is much more exciting than doing it in an office."

"You'd...?" Jeff loosens his tie and takes a slurp of his champagne. When the bubbles have fizzed their way over his tongue, he leans across the space between us and says, "You *bad girl*. I find doing it in the office *very* exciting."

And that is when I realise something is off. It is in equal parts the "bad girl" comment and the fact that he clearly hasn't brushed his teeth since his last soy flat white.

"Jeff?" I ask, tilting my torso backwards, which only encourages him to lean in further. "I'm here because you have an employment contract with my name on it in your briefcase, right?"

Jeff blinks twice and sits upright. "Um," he says, smacking his lips. "Why would you think that?"

"Because I aced my demo with your food consultant, and you and your HR representative told me in the interview I was a very strong candidate and that I'd be hearing from you soon. Why else would you arrange to meet up four hours after you said, and I quote, 'Wow. You just blew my mind'?"

"Oh." Jeff screws up his nose and flaps one hand around like he is dispelling the fetid air issuing from his mouth. "It's just a job, Sarah. You can get another one. Whereas you and I –" the twinkle returns to his eyes "– have a real connection, a *synergy*."

I remove the hand that has crept onto my knee and place it back on his lap with a little more force than is necessary. It *thwumps* against his thigh. "But I wanted *that* one. And no I cannot just *go and get another one*. They're not lamb kebabs. I've been job searching for three months." My voice creeps up in pitch so that, just to add to my humiliation, the last two words are on the point of cracking.

"Of course you can get another one. You were the top candidate. You'll be hot property if you put your feelers out in the right places."

I peer at him from over the top of my glasses and invite him to employ some thinking about what he's just admitted. "I was the top candidate?"

He shrugs. "Yeah."

"You're telling me, I would have got that job if your penis hadn't told you it had a conflict of interest with your professionalism?"

Jeff laughs. "Ah, Sarah, I believe it was your sustained eye contact and suggestive lip moistening that told my penis it needed to have that conversation with my professionalism."

An iceberg rolls over in the watery contents of my stomach and proceeds to collapse, the frigid backwash splatting against the inside of my rib cage. "It was a job interview. Of course I was going to look at you and smile. I licked my lips because I was nervous!" I run a hand through my hair in an effort to hide the tears attempting to burn their way to freedom. "The only thing I've eaten in the last two days is a slice of bread. *A slice of bread.* I am destitute and you pass me over for my dream job purely for your self-interest?" I stand, readying myself for my dignified exit. "You are a first-class fuckwit, Jeffrey Wainwright."

Jeff throws his hands in the air and leans backwards like I am behaving on the hysterical side of unreasonable. "Calm down, Sarah. I didn't know it meant that much to you." Then he takes a casual sip from his glass and says, "You know, you only have yourself to blame. If you didn't send mixed messages, then..." he spreads a hand in a gesture that he believes indicates his exoneration.

I quaff the rest of my champagne.

Then I reach forward and tug with all my might on his silk tie.

His face slams against the bar with the sickening crunch of splitting cartilage.

Chapter two

"Ms Fulton, you do understand the seriousness of the charges that are probably going to be laid against you? Assault Occasioning Actual Bodily Harm is no laughing matter."

I can't help it. I'm so tired. I'm so scared. I'm so *hungry*. And there's still some alcohol coursing its way through my calorie-depleted system that I can't find any other way to react.

I look down at the blood speckling the front of my gold and purple-striped dress and am reminded of the satisfying feeling of the tie jerking out of my hands as Jeffrey Wainwright's face bounces upwards off the bar.

A fresh cackle burbles up my chest and hits the greasily-lit air of the interview room like the rattle of machine gun fire.

Ha-ha-ha-ha-ha-ha.

The arresting officer, Sergeant Bowman, leans against the wall and peers at me with his arms crossed, waiting for the laughter to play out.

He has a resigned look on his face, like this is not his first I'm-scared-as-fuck-so-my-body-has-decided-the-most-appropriate-thing-to-do-is-laugh-hysterically rodeo.

My diaphragm slowly stops convulsing and I issue a sigh that sounds like it has a question mark after it. *Is this the point where I should probably switch to crying?*

"The duty solicitor shouldn't be far away, but my advice to you? Provocation is not a line of defense that has saved anyone's arse from jail. Regardless of how much the other person deserved it."

A final spasm of laughter shakes my shoulders and I consider him. His weathered fair-skin has creases running the lengths of his cheeks and his stubble shines pale gold when he turns his head. He doesn't look anything like the hard-boiled cop on TV shows. His interview style has been less interrogative and more that of indulging a naughty child.

Given his "regardless of how much the other person deserved it" statement, I think he likes me. At the very least, he has a smidgen of sympathy for my predicament.

"What was the job, then?" he asks, like we are having a conversation in normal, non- impending-incarceration circumstances.

I shift my glasses to the top of my head with one hand and rub at an eyeball with the other. "Executive chef at one of the concept restaurants in that new hotel on Leicester Square."

Sergeant Bowman snorts. "Concept restaurant. What does that even mean?"

"According to the job description, it meant 'a fusion of decadence and avant-garde'."

"So, champagne and vegan oysters?"

In other circumstances I might have laughed. "Something like that."

We fall into silence.

The sergeant opens the flap covering the screen of his phone and peers at it before closing it with a *snap*. "They've got a job going at the station caf."

It takes several seconds for my brain to accept the peculiarity of the man who arrested me for assault suggesting I apply for a job in his workplace.

I answer with, "Sergeant Bowman, I'm a trained gourmet chef with ambitions to open my own restaurant," and immediately feel like an arsehole. He's being nice. And helpful. So I add, "But I do need a job. Thanks for suggesting it." It's a hollow sentiment. I don't need *that* job.

Given the generosity he's shown me so far, I figure I can push my luck a little. "You got any food?"

The sergeant blinks. Then he sighs, pulls a Mars Bar out of his pocket and slides it across the table to me.

My fingers scrabble against the metal of the tabletop in my effort to intercept it. The chocolate is out of the wrapper before my conscious brain computes that its silent half has already issued instructions to my fingers.

I hum and chew, my saliva gathering at such pace that the molten chocolate and nougat slide down my chin before I have a chance to wipe it away with my hand.

There is a knock on the door and the handle turns.

I look up from my double-handed feeding frenzy and into the face of Adam Stringer.

His eyes widen and he says, "Hell no."

Chapter three

Adam stumbles back into the hallway and closes the door. I stare at it.

No.

No, no, no, no, please, fucking no.

Anybody – Trump's hair-dye sweating lawyer, a monkey in a tie – but him.

I do not want Adam Stringer to be witness to this moment, or *God,* to be the one to save me from it.

From the lack of re-entry, neither does he.

I suck at the enormous piece of chocolate in my mouth, because it's the only useful thing I'm able to do, and offer Sergeant Bowman a shrug.

And then the door opens quickly, violently almost, and he strides in, not looking at me.

I jump and blurt, "A-am," and the piece of chocolate falls out onto the table.

I snatch it up and shove it back into my mouth, because even though the idea of swallowing it is all of a sudden nauseating,

I can't leave it there, glistening and half-masticated. Despite appearances, I haven't shed *all* my dignity.

Adam crosses half the interview room in three long-legged strides and stops on the other side of the table from me. He eyes Sergeant Bowman and points at my head. "Don't speak. I want to hear it from him." Then he grips the back of the spare chair as if needing to steady himself.

I don't blame him not wanting to look at me in my chocolate and blood-smeared shame. But it's Adam. So, I choose to blame him anyway, because whatever the narrative, he's always set out to resent me.

The arresting officer frowns. "Ah. She's your client, Adam – Mr Stringer."

"I'll hear it from you first, Sergeant, or she can find another solicitor, which –" he looks at his watch. "– might be problematic at five to eight on a Friday night."

I want to say, "Don't take this out on him," but I have no idea of the calibre of their working relationship. Maybe Adam's a dick all the time to everyone.

The officer flicks his eyes towards me and shrugs. "Okay."

Adam adjusts his grip on the back of the spare chair and the dark skin of his knuckles pale slightly. "Well?"

Sergeant Bowman says, "Alright mate," because men never tell other men to "calm down" and opens his phone to read his notes. "Ms Fulton had a job interview today for the Hatchet hotel group."

"Hachet" I say, pronouncing the last syllable with a silent 't'.

Adam raises a finger to shush me.

"Bloke she clocked was on the interview panel."

The sergeant's statement should at least get a raised eyebrow, but Adam shows no surprise like this is typical behaviour. It is *not* typical behaviour.

I mean.

Launching myself into a metaphorical turd pile? Yes.

Resorting to violence in order to do it? No.

"He texted her a couple of hours later and asked her to meet. He said –" the sergeant looks at his phone again. "– and I am quoting the text he sent. *'I'd like to take the lead after meeting you today and suggest we touch base to discuss your strategic fit. I'm talking an onboarding deep dive. Wink emoji'.* She assumed he was going to offer her the job." Sergeant Bowman snorts. "Guy confused his seduction technique with corporate wank talk." He shakes his head. "Probably all the same thing to the suits." He says, "The Suits" like it is capitalised – a race of people he doesn't understand and has no intention of trying to.

Adam, who is dressed in a suit, doesn't bother to do as much as adjusting his tie ironically, because even irony is an expression of humour too far.

The sergeant continues. "It quickly becomes clear he's meeting her in the hope of sex. He admits she was the preferred candidate, but passed her over so he could ask her out. It is at this point, Ms Fulton tugs on his tie and connects bar-top with nose. He's at the hospital now, insisting she foots the bill for reconstructive rhinoplasty."

Adam raises his eyes to the panelled ceiling before closing them for a second longer than is necessary to convey just how stupid my action was. "That's the full story?"

"No," I say and this time Adam does look at me. It is a glare designed to render the receiver dumb. It works because I know in this moment, as much as neither of us wish to be in it, he is my chance to extract myself from the dung heap and I should bloody well shut up.

I sandwich my lips between my teeth contritely and Adam swivels his head to look at the sergeant.

"She's been out of work for several months, has run out of money and is about to be evicted from her flat. I think that chocolate bar is the first food she's had in a while."

Adam's broad shoulders sag a fraction of an inch and he glances at me before he turns and faces the back wall, his hands shoved into the pockets of his trousers.

I understand. Adam's cold cold heart must be floundering under the wave of pity that has just crested over him.

I take the opportunity of his turned back to lean forward and clean my face with the blood-speckled bottom of my dress and hope I don't end up plowing the chocolate into a wider smear.

I look up from my lap as Adam turns, pulls out the chair and sits down. "Thank you, Sergeant Bowman, I'd like some time with Ms Fulton."

I send Sergeant Bowman a telepathic plea not to leave me alone with Adam, but despite the amount of desperation I project at his thought receptors, he pushes himself up from the table and exits the room.

I eye the closed door and a small, elongated "Nooooo" escapes where a simple sigh of resignation should have sufficed.

This is the moment for Adam to superciliously inform me it is too late for wishful thinking – I'd already done the damage – but instead, he fans his hands on the table and glares at the chewed nails.

I think, maybe, I've broken him.

It shouldn't give me comfort. And I don't like that it kind of does, but at least I don't have to tolerate the lofty heights of his sanctimony *and* my self-loathing.

"My job is to offer you legal advice." His voice is measured, calm. "I don't have to accept you as a client just because you require legal aid."

"Okay."

He looks up at me then, his dark eyes unblinking. "You broke his nose, Sarah."

I don't say anything for a beat. Then, "Yes". Because I did.

"You lost control and slammed his head on a bar."

"I know."

Adam's voice raises itself a notch in pitch and volume. "You're likely up for ABH. You could get jail time, Sarah."

"At least I'll get fed every day."

He slaps a palm on the table, and I jump. "Jesus Christ, what were you thinking? Nothing outside of yourself, as per normal. You think this is going to serve Max well in any way?"

No.

I do not think my breaking a man's nose in a fit of temper is going to serve my brother well in any way. It's probably going to make his life pretty bloody difficult in fact – something I was immediately cognisant of the moment Jeff's face hit wood and half the bar patrons stopped their merry making to stare at me.

The back of my throat burns and the tears that have been hovering for the last two hours push for an ugly release.

I shake my head, hiccup out a "No ho" and collapse into the hollow between my knees and sob.

My longish, brown hair doesn't curtain my face off as effectively as it might due to my fringe, and so my state is not quite as private as I want to pretend it to be.

After several moments, Adam shouts, "Sergeant?"

I raise my head with a sniff as Sergeant Bowman pokes his head around the door.

"Can you please find Ms Fulton some tissues and a glass of water?"

Adam has only ever called me Sarah. His professional distancing shouts volumes. Both of us would rather be anywhere but here.

The door snibs shut and Adam focuses on his hands again. He clears his throat and asks if there's anything else I would like to add to what Sergeant Bowman said.

"Yes." My voice is thick with the effort of stemming tears. "That guy was a douche of the highest order."

The minuscule amount of patience Adam found a moment ago is gone. "Sarah, I'm trying to want to help you here. Is that really the best you can come up with? Because I am at liberty to walk out that door at any point, and I'm very tempted for that moment to be now." He jabs his finger in the door's direction. "Whereas you are not."

"Adam." I lean into the table, towards him. "The arsehole was wearing an Omega dress watch and diamanté cuff links. *Diamanté.* He couldn't see his gross abuse of power for the size of the silver spoon hanging out of his mouth. I have never had a greater sense of injustice in my life."

He looks at me from under his eyebrows. "That would be because you've had the privilege of never experiencing true injustice before."

I want to ask how he dismounts a horse with legs that high, but...he's actually right, I have had that privilege, and I probably shouldn't tempt him to make good on his threat to walk out the door.

Instead, I answer the question he hasn't asked yet – the "how could you?" one. "Look. My rage was fed by literal hunger. It's hard to be reasonable when your body's resorted to auto-cannibalism just to keep from falling down."

Adam glares at me for three seconds, then releases the breath he's been holding. "I will try and get you out of this mess, but you understand I'm only doing it for Max's sake."

Good. He needs to be doing it for Max's sake. I don't need protecting.

My petulance subsides and a surge of gratitude rushes in on its tail. I wipe the heel of my hand across my wet cheeks. "I understand. Thank you, Adam."

Adam's fingers drum the tabletop. I hope it is because he is devising a master plan for extracting me from this situation, but suspect I am about to receive a further dose of disapproval. "I've never understood your ability to behave rashly. Normally it's only accompanied by a level of silliness that was cute when you were sixteen but is ridiculous on a grown woman. This level of impetuousness, however, is unconscionable."

I voice my agreement by not answering, and Sergeant Bowman re-enters with a box of budget-brand tissues and a paper cup.

Adam waits for him to leave and says, "I need to think. Don't make a sound. Don't talk to me, don't sigh like you don't deserve any of this."

I do not intend to sigh in such a manner. I absolutely deserve all of this.

Adam stands up and paces, giving me the brain space to ascend into the vortex of *How could you be so thoughtless?* recriminations and I'm not sure which one I should settle on.

I start with: *I'm going to have a conviction.*

Which prompts: *I might go to jail.*

Then I think of the wider repercussions: *I'm going to ruin my brother's career.*

And move back to self-interest: *Nobody will employ me.*

And extreme self-pity: *I've ruined my life.*

I think of Jeffrey Wainwright. All he gets out of this is a spoiled but completely fixable face and some temporary ego damage.

God how is this fair? Yes, I was unjustifiably violent.

I think.

No. I was unjustifiably violent.

But that fucker was a predatory, power-abusing shitbag, and he won't be held accountable for it. In fact, once he's dusted himself off, he'll probably go out there again to be a predatory, power-abusing shitbag.

I relive the moment of the tie tug and really wish it didn't feel as satisfying as it does. I should not glory in it. It was a terrible, terrible thing to do. Terrible.

Adam pulls his phone out of his back pocket and swipes and types without ceasing his pacing. Then he sits down opposite me and places the phone between us.

"I'm going to call Jeffrey Wainwright. See if we can cut this off at the pass."

"O-kay," I say, because I'm not sure if it sounds more like a scary move or an awesome move.

"You are not to say anything. At all. He must not know you're here. Do you understand, Sarah? If you think you can't adhere to that stipulation, then I will do this in another room."

I totally want to hear Adam kick Jeff's arse. "I will be silent as the grave." I add, "I will not let him provoke me into any kind of reaction," in case Adam needs that reassurance, which I would if I was him. "You have his number?"

"It's on the Hachet website."

"Right. Of course."

Adam taps at the screen and puts the call to speaker.

Jeff's phone rings and my heart jackhammers my breastbone.

He answers with a "What?"

"Mr Wainwright?" Adam says, voice deep and sure. "I'm Adam Stringer. Sarah Fulton's solicitor."

Jeff snorts. "Are you now?" His voice is reedy with nasality like he has a cold, which I would call sobering if being in a police interview room with a charge for assault hanging over me hadn't already maxed out my *hard dose of reality* appreciation. "Well, Solicitor Stringer," he continues, "I have nothing to say to you. I'll have my *lawyer* call you on Monday."

Adam does not miss a beat to do the eye roll I would have. He barely gives Jeff space for thought. "A solicitor *is* a lawyer, Mr Wainwright, and I think we can settle this pretty quickly now."

"Not without my legal counsel present."

"At what? Two hundred pounds an hour? Three? I'm very happy to put up the kind of fight that would tie your *lawyer* up for as many hours as might otherwise buy you a dress watch. I see Beaumont and Walker are running a sale. The Breitling Bentley's a bargain at nine thousand pounds. Or what about a Ulysse Nardin Executive? Has gold –"

"Alright, Solicitor Stringer," says Jeff in an *I'm just humouring you* tone. "Make it quick or I'll hang up. No, you know what? Let's do this over video. I want you to see what she's done." He hangs up and Adam's phone chimes a couple of seconds later with the FaceChat ringtone.

Adam holds up a palm to me and slides his phone towards him in an unnecessary directive to stay out of shot.

Even upside down I can see Jeffrey Wainwright is not in a good way.

He holds his phone so Adam can get a good view of the Accident and Emergency waiting area behind him. It's two-thirds full, which is not a good sign this early on a Friday night. "Two hours. I've been waiting two hours in abject pain and not a single person has made any effort to attend to me."

I wonder at the extent of his ignorance of the public health system and then remember he is very privileged and rather self-important. He's probably never had to wait for anything his entire life.

He tracks his phone down his body. Purple bruising has set in around his eyes. Dried blood rings his nostrils and fills the shadow under his lower lip from a rudimentary clean up. His lower stomach and crotch map the blast radius – a mess of dark brown splotches and streaks.

Jeepers.

I really did a number on him.

Jeff needlessly says, "You see this? You see what she's done to me? If it was the other way around and I'd smashed *her* face against a bar, I'd be locked up, key thrown."

"And yet, the judicial landscape will not only encompass Ms Fulton's actions, there's a whole context of accountability leading up to the point of the supposed assault."

That's right, Jeff. *Accountability.*

"It's not 'supposed'. Did I not give you a clear enough shot? I can't hold the camera any closer to my flattened face without going cross eyed."

Adam continues as if Jeff has not spoken. "You displayed an acute lack of professionalism. In fact, it goes beyond that. You abused your position in denying her a job for your own sexual interest. 'Sexual harassment' is a hot term right now with the Me Too movement, Mr Wainwright. A judge would probably sympathise – a desperate and vulnerable woman misled by a man who has the power to make or break her career. *And*, of course, there's the lack of a previous criminal record. The scales are weighted in her favour."

I don't like to admit it, but *God* he's good. I am very happy that right now he's on Team Sarah. Well, Team Max, and therefore Team Sarah.

Jeff's team looks like it's in need of a sub.

He tries very hard to arrange his features into a look of incredulity, but the rapid onset of swelling around his eyes makes widening them difficult. His thickened lids quiver like a blackberry blancmange as he struggles to force them apart. "She did this!" He gestures to his face and the soiled front of his suit. "No judge can argue with the evidence."

"He or she might if it was self-defense."

"It wasn't self-defense! All I did was buy her a drink."

"You put a hand on her knee, Mr Wainwright. Did she invite you to touch her?"

Gotcha! I have to try very hard not to fist pump. It would be in poor taste.

Jeff blinks. Once. Twice. Then says, "It's my word against hers."

Adam nods slowly, pauses, like he's changing gears and says, "Tracey Martin."

"What about her?"

"She's your CEO, yes?"

Jeff narrows his eyes, which isn't as effective as he might think given they are already little more than slits.

"LinkedIn tells me she did her postgrad at Warwick. Same years as my father."

"Bullshit."

It's not bullshit. I have no idea where Adam's father went to university, but it's too much of a risk for him to hold Jeffrey Wainwright over a lie.

"Now, I can't be sure they know each other – I have yet to ask him – but given they both studied in the same field, there's a very good chance, even if they specialised in different areas."

Jeff purses his bottom lip and gives a series of nods. "That's pretty good leverage."

It's superb leverage. And Jeff should be looking more worried than he is.

He continues, "Well, shaky at best, but you did a decent job of dressing it up to make it look like good leverage. Let me give you a lesson in *excellent* leverage. While we're speaking of fathers, would you happen to know who Ms Fulton's is?"

A sudden chill radiates from my bones like I've been snap frozen from the inside out.

Adam goes very still.

"Didn't think I'd work that one out did you, with her having a different surname? I didn't even need a *lawyer* to do the thinking on that one for me. I mean, *come on*. It was only a matter of time. One of the best fast-paced bowlers the country's produced?"

Adam presses his palms into the table. The tips of his fingers turn pale.

"Maybe a cricketing legend could weather the storm of a daughter up for assault." Jeff places a finger to his lips and I know it's coming. The thing I've been dreading. The thermo nuclear explosion I triggered when I grabbed Jeffrey Wainwright's silk fucking tie.

"But I'm not sure a Member of Parliament could shake it off very easily. Not when it's their sister. I mean," – Jeff laughs – "can you imagine the media circus?"

Adam's fingers retract into fists and I know how he feels. I want to smash Jeff's face all over again.

"At this point, I have no intention of telling the media. But try another stunt like pitting my boss against me again, and that will change very quickly. See you in court." He rings off before my "FUCK YOU, JEFF!" betrays my presence.

Not that it would have mattered. He would have creamed his Armani boxer briefs knowing he was pulling that *Yet again I have all the power mwah ha fucking ha* performance in front of me. Wankface.

We sit in silence for a few moments, Adam staring at his phone, me staring at the top of his head.

So.

That went well.

I am well and truly fucked.

I take a deep breath and attempt to console myself that at least I have Adam on my side.

I mean, on Max's side.

Adam stands, eyes me for ten years like I'm responsible for Jeffrey Wainwright not being a completely useless tit and hamstringing his offensive with very little effort, and I know exactly what's coming.

He's extracting himself from the turd pile before I pull him down into it along with my brother.

"I need to find another lawyer, don't I?"

Chapter four

Fourteen years ago

How? How has this happened?

Three years ago Adam was a spotty stick insect with an instant crush on his new best friend's older sister.

At least, with all the mumbling and quickly shifted eyes when I caught him looking at me, I was pretty sure he had an instant crush. Which was awkward. And sweet. But mostly awkward, considering he spent, and still spends, the best part of his free time at our house.

It's crept up on me.

Adam filling out and up, me –

Noticing. A lot.

Me quickly shifting my gaze whenever Adam catches *me* looking at *him*.

I don't like it. I really do not like it.

And yet.

I want more of it.

Chapter five

Robert 'Bob' Sutton, our family lawyer, pats his breast pockets, the top of his bald white head, lifts up one of the many piles of paper decorating his oak desk, and looks up at me. "Have you seen my glasses?"

I have seen his glasses. They are on his face.

I say, "Yes," and tap my own glasses as he stills and crosses his eyes. "Ah. Here they are. Right where I left them."

He smacks his lips and pulls a piece of paper towards him to read, then pushes it away. "Not that one." He slides another paper into reading range, and away again. "No." On his third failed attempt, he evidently gives up and sits back in his chair, sending it rocking like he has a spring loaded into the supporting column.

It issues a small squeak on the forward motion.

"You know, Sara. I still remember the day your grandfather sought my services in the 60s."

I can't imagine a 1960s Bob. He has an eternally aged look as if he's been pickled and was ancient even then.

"And then your dad in the late 80s. Brought in that teammate of his. West Indian fellow. Could hit a six off a googly. Oh, what was his name?" He flaps both his hands like a child desperate to tell a story, but unable to get the words out fast enough.

I have no idea. Nor do I know it's possible to make a name for yourself by hitting a six off a googly. A six off a googly is a unicorn, as in total fluke.

"It'll come to me. It was quite an event, you know. Never represented a darkie before."

"Bob," I say in the voice I reserve for all things very serious. "'Darkie' is a racist term."

"We got on just fine. Wasn't sure we would, because of the difference in heritage and all that."

"You should never ever say it. Ever."

Bob begins his hunt for the misplaced paper again.

"Don't even think it."

"Ah. Here we are." He picks up a sheet of paper and reads.

His watch ticks loudly and somewhere in the bowels of the building a door slams shut.

Either Bob has not familiarised himself with the content of the paper, or he's forgotten I'm here. Both are a distinct possibility.

I look around the room, run my eyes over the dusty bookshelves, and sit forward in my chair.

In among the leather-bound tomes of lawyery literature is a paperback edition of *The Kama Sutra*. It's just there, hanging out for all his clients to see if they bothered to look.

I snap my gaze back to Bob and appraise him anew. His cabled cardigan has a short trail of egg yolk down the right-hand side and the hair in his ears is several times thicker than the remaining wisps on the side of his head.

Nope. I cannot imagine *Kama Sutra* Bob. That Bob exists one dimension over.

He puts the paper down in front of him and places his palms over the top, anchoring it like it might blow away. "Well. This is a fine to do you've got yourself into, my girl. A fine to do. Any ideas about how you might get yourself out of it?"

Ahh...

I don't really want to point out that there is only one legal professional in the room, who is, consequently, being paid rather nicely for being that one legal professional at this precise moment and the many forthcoming hours, thanks to my parents. So I don't.

"I don't expect to get myself out of it, Bob. I expect to be facing up to the consequences of my actions. I *want* to face up to the consequences of my actions." I add, "I think," because while I'm feeling brave in this moment, I don't expect it to last.

"Right, right." Bob nods and his chair rocks and squeaks. He picks up momentum and after several vigorous backwards and forwards, says, "I think we should probably settle out of court."

If the situation were in any way humorous, I might have laughed at the ridiculousness of his suggestion. "Why? He's not suing me. And I don't think The Crown is down with pay offs."

"Quite."

He stares at me unblinking and I wonder if he's peacefully passed away sometime in the intervening seconds. Then he creakily inhales. "How much have you got?"

I oblige because he is very very old and I have been taught to show deference to my elders. I open my banking app. "Thirteen pounds and forty-three pence."

Bob nods his head as if the amount I've just given him is not woefully and ridiculously tiny for the purpose he's proposing. Or any purpose. "It's probably not going to be enough."

No.

"Have a chat with your parents and your brother. See how much they can rustle up."

"I'm not going to have a chat, Bob."

He blinks at me. His eyes are owl-like behind the magnification of his glasses. "You'll have to if you want to put something reasonable on the table."

"Whatever the amount, it will be unreasonable to me."

He waves a hand. "Nobody likes having to compensate others monetarily for our wrongdoing, but we all do it, Sara."

I choose not to point out the inaccuracies in that statement, and say, "It's unreasonable, because it means Jeffrey Wainwright isn't held accountable for *his* actions. I'm perfectly happy to be held accountable for mine, but he has to face up to justice, too."

"It's your trial, my dear. Not his."

"That's right."

Bob adjusts his glasses. "How are you going to make him face up to justice?"

Christ.

I deserve this. I utterly deserve this. This is the universe punishing me for all my selfish wrongdoing.

I draw a deep breath.

And exhale.

"You are. By exposing what happened prior to me breaking his nose. Having the truth of him heard by everyone in that courtroom and someone much more powerful than him whose job is to judge him for it."

"I am?"

"Yes."

"Right. Excellent." He stares at me unblinkingly again. "How do I do that?"

Chapter six

Olympia taps a manicured nail on her lips before flicking her straightened red hair over her shoulder. "Okay. Here's what we do. *Should* the press get wind of Sarah's arrest, either you deny all knowledge of her existence and hope the family snaps of Mallorca don't surface, which is unlikely. Those shots of her unwittingly banana boating with her bikini top drawn open like a curtain were *pretty hilare*. Or, Max, you claim Sarah bungled a citizen's arrest on the misapprehension that this Wainwright chappy was dognapping Pomeranians for the Belgian degustation black market."

My brother, the fifth ever youngest MP in parliament, does not have a spin doctor. He's not high enough in cabinet, yet, to enjoy that privilege, but our cousin, Olympia, has taken it upon herself to assume that role.

Olympia has a double degree in Theatre Studies and Microbiology. The fact they were awarded at Cambridge makes her slightly more qualified to do public relations stuff than anyone else we know.

"Those photos are not *family snaps*, Olympia," I object. "Nobody puts accidental porn in their family photo albums."

Charging on in typical Olympia fashion, she says, "Everyone loves a hero, Squimpy, even a failed one. And especially if it involves puppies. Introduce a puppy and one's ability to reason flatlines." With a "Hello puppy!" she acts out being presented with a tiny dog and falling into a love stupor.

I mean, she's not wrong. It's everything else she said that could be considered problematic.

Max pushes his bottom lip out and nods his head. "I like the part where Sarah tries to perform a bit of vigilante justice, but I'm not so sure about claiming that Belgians eat handbag dogs as a tasting-plate delicacy. It could be misinterpreted as a bit, I don't know, racist?"

"Oh yes, I suppose it might," says Olympia as she takes the top off the containers of Thai takeaways she brought around, and I find Max's wine in Max's fridge as my offering.

I would like to be able to give more, like a financial contribution to dinner, or a time machine to take me back to the interview where I reduce any confusion about "synergy" by licking my lips less, but the best I can do is retrieval of other people's things – glasses, plates, cutlery – because my things are currently boxed up in Mum and Dad's garage, and because I am officially destitute.

But not homeless, thanks to my long-suffering and incredibly generous brother.

I don't deserve it. But he seems to love me enough.

Olympia spoons rice into a bowl. "Of course, you could always blame it on the Ruskies. When Chelsea Smits-Smythe accidentally married that shock jock from one of those LBC radio shows, I told everyone she was the victim of a spermicide attack."

Olympia is our mother's brother's daughter and comes from several generations of incredible wealth courtesy of the industrial revolution, which means she's been spoilt into well-meaning idiocy, despite having an IQ of 137.

I love her very much. Even if she does insist on calling me a completely nonsensical pet name.

"Apparently, he shags like a champ. Make anybody do something very silly."

Max places a hand on her shoulder. "Olympia, spermicide is actually a thing, so it doesn't work as a Russian intelligence-flavoured metaphor for being shagged into stupidity."

"Is it?"

"It's a contraceptive."

She screws up her face. "Sounds awful."

I ladle tofu green curry on top of my rice and say the thing that needs to be said. "Max shouldn't lie to cover my mistakes."

"Damage control, not lying," says Olympia. "No one lies any more. They just apply an Instagram filter over the truth. Everyone. All the time. It's perfectly normal."

"I don't want to be normal. I want to have integrity and...stuff."

Max leads us, bowls and wine glasses in hand, from the kitchen island to the dining table. "The problem is, Sarah, being virtuous, even being accountable, tends to land people in the public eye in a steaming pile of media fallout, even if it's the right thing to do. All you learn from the process is that telling the truth is a much greater risk than being found out for fudging the truth."

Really? God. No wonder people don't trust politicians.

"Thankfully I've never had to do it," he adds.

"Until now," adds Olympia.

"It may not come to that – having to make a statement to the press." He takes a large mouthful of his curry and I take a large mouthful of my wine.

I really, really don't want it to come to that. My brother is a very good person who chose one of the hardest careers in order to do right by other people. He shouldn't have to navigate unnecessary difficulties on top of the ones he already has because his sister's an idiot.

For once, I agree with Adam. I'm a self-centred person who never thinks of consequences for others.

I plonk my wine glass on the table and grip his forearm with both hands. "I am so unbelievably sorry. Me and my stupid, stupid..." I flail around for an adequate noun and come up with "stupidity" because, apparently, I need to prove the truth of my words. "I was so outraged, my brain stopped. I can't believe I did it, that I'm *capable* of doing that."

"I can," says Olympia. "When you were four, you 'washed' Uncle Alistair's Jag with stones from the driveway because he said pretty little girls like you would only ruin a game of lawn cricket, remember?"

"That's not helpful," I say.

Max extracts his forearm from my grip, places his still-loaded fork back in his bowl, and wraps an arm I absolutely don't deserve to be wrapped around me, around me. "Do you know it's easier to be a gay male in politics than it is to be a woman? Even a *white* woman who has the privilege of colour, but not of gender? And I'm not just talking about the knuckle draggers typing their vitriol with bravery behind their faceless online personas, I'm talking about the intelligent, educated men on the opposing benches, and even some of the men on the supporting benches. It's appalling the disrespect shown to women in leadership. The art of misogyny is alive and well three decades into the 21st century and it's utterly shameful. I understand why you cracked." He gives me a squeeze. "We'll weather it if we have to. The press may never find out."

"They're like drug dogs," I say. "They'll sniff it out. A different surname isn't protection enough."

Our mother, being the black sheep of the family, turned her back on the lifestyle of having everything, and kept her name when she married a modestly-paid sportsman.

When I was born, she didn't see why I had to automatically inherit my father's name. Especially when 'Fulton' sounded far less ridiculous with 'Sarah', a name she'd always wanted for a daughter, than 'Sawyer'. Sarah Sawyer would be a laughing-stock. My father agreed.

When Max was born, he got 'Sawyer' and that was that, fair and square.

Of course, I'd closed all my social media accounts to make it a bit harder for the press to sniff out the family connection, but there's always traces left behind, so at best I've probably stalled the discovery.

Max already sensibly curates all his social media feeds to exclude family, but if the connection is made, the outlook is –

Not worth thinking about really. Mostly because the press delight in hounding politicians into a corner and exhausting them so the opposition can go in for the kill.

Olympia swallows a mouthful of wine and asks, "I still don't really understand why you couldn't have asked your parents for some dosh when you lost your job."

My eyes meet Max's. He knows why.

Max is the golden child and I can do every wrong in my mother's eyes. I wasn't prepared for what it would have cost me if I'd come cap in hand. Of course, in hindsight, my mother's criticism would have been a rosy alternative to what I now have to pay.

"Or me," Olympia continues. "I'd have given you some money."

"Because our mother instilled in us the virtue of being self-made. Nobody deserves handouts. Whether you have money or not is the result of the luck you have made for yourself. Supposedly." So naturally I believed, rightly or wrongly, I deserved to be in a position of destitution, and I absolutely couldn't face the shame of holding my hand out. To anyone.

"She's a complicated woman," says Max, which is a diplomatic way of putting it. What he omits to say is, "Who fails to see her own privilege."

"You know," says Olympia, "I've always thought your outrageous behaviour was a rebellion against her disapproval of you, Squimpy. You are such a clown. I think it's delightful. You can be so very silly and I think Aunty Amelia should be happy to have a daughter with so much verve and colour."

"Yes," I agree. "Though breaking a man's nose is not the kind of outrageous I wanted to get her attention with."

I change the subject, because my relationship with my mother is not one I like to dwell on if I can help it. "You know Dad's insisting I use the family lawyer?"

Max's dark head jerks around to face me. "Bob Sutton? Is he still alive?"

"Almost. Though he can't remember my name. Calls me *Sara* like I'm some bourgie-girl. Sorry, Olympia."

"Quite alright, Squimpy."

"But he's an estate lawyer. What use would he be?"

I shrug and say through a mouthful, "Dad's paying. Bob says he's watched *Law and Order* and *Boston Legal*. So that and the fact he passed half the bar in 1873 qualifies him, apparently. It's the excitement of the imagined courtroom drama that's put life back in the old dog. Who knows? He might...do alright."

Though at this point in time, even "might" seems generous. "He says I should settle out of court."

"Well, that would solve the media ish."

It takes me a couple of seconds to realise Olympia has dropped a syllable, no doubt due to some verbal fad that favours confusion over effort.

"But can you even do that?" I ask.

"I don't really understand how the legalese works," Max says, "but people can drop charges against other parties, so Jeffrey Wainwright certainly can."

"How much do you think it would take for him to do that?" asks Olympia.

"I told Bob I'm not paying Jeff anything." I look at Max and I know I can't do it to him. His career is so new and so bright and he's so good at it. This country needs politicians like him. "But I've changed my mind. It's probably for the best, for all of us." I have no idea how much it will take or how I'll ever pay him or Mum and Dad back, but if I don't want things to get ugly for Max, all this needs to go away.

Max looks at me for a long moment and eventually says, "I'll support whatever you decide," which we both know means, "Actually, I agree. A payoff is the only option". At least it took him several seconds to grapple with what it means for me, because he's a decent human.

I'm going to be rewarding Jeff for his unethical behaviour and losing my chance to stand up for the sisterhood, but it's the right thing to do. Well, okay, it's the wrong thing to do, but it's for the right reason.

"I think that's a sensible decision, Squimpy. Hand over some dosh and you won't have a conviction, or trouble getting a job, securing finance, travelling overseas. You won't make Max look like he's a member of a criminal dynasty."

"How do you get 'criminal dynasty' from his sister breaking one person's nose?"

Max ignores us both and says, "For now, we need to try and get your name withheld in the courts. Check with Bob tomorrow that he's making an application."

"Okay, but I don't think they make exceptions very often."

"I know. It's worth a shot, though."

"Look on the bright side," says Olympia. "If Jeff refuses to be paid off, I hear they now make ankle bracelets in pastels."

It's utter nonsense and not at all bright side-y, but I can't help asking, "Where'd you hear that?"

"Lolly Bagshaw's brother got done for embezzlement. His is duck egg blue."

"Figures." I can't stand pastels. They make my fair skin look washed out. Just my luck.

"Of course, none of this would have happened if your ex-boss wasn't a total piece of work," continues Olympia. "Blacklisting you from all the decent restaurants in central London."

It's true. When I fell out with the owner of the Michelin-star restaurant in Soho I worked in because I didn't appreciate her bully brand of management, she set about making sure it would be very very hard for me to progress my career, or, in fact, have any career at all. Not only did she do "arsehole" with a dedication that was breathtaking, she was also, unfortunately for me, incredibly well-connected in the industry.

"I don't really want to think about her right now, Olympia. I'd rather we talked about literally anything else, like the surrealness of how I'm going to be working at the staff cafeteria in the police station I just spent a night in."

Olympia sits up straight. "Are you? Oh, jolly well done, Squimpy."

I am. Because I still haven't worked my way out of my ongoing state of desperation, and because I am a big girl and able to swallow my chef's pride.

"I want to say 'You have to laugh, really' but I'm not finding much humour in it."

Max lays a hand on my arm. "I'm sure it will be fine. You'll enjoy the challenge of revolutionizing the standard fare. Bringing haute cuisine to the City of London Police."

"Yep," I say, knowing very well I will not have the opportunity to do any haute cuisine-ing. Not least because cops want food that is hearty and affordable on their very modest salaries, but also because I've been employed to do front counter duties.

"Speaking of which," continues Max, "there is one benefit for me out of all this drama. Having home cooked meals. I can't remember the last time I ate anything other than a frozen meal for one on a weeknight. Getting in the door at 9 pm tends to dampen the will to chop onions."

Home-cooked meals were undoubtedly within my skill set, and it was the least I could do to earn my keep.

"Can you do my washing, too? In fact, can you be my magical house-elf and bring some semblance of a normally functioning home to the place?"

"You want me to be your Dobby?"

"Yes please. But with clothes, and less obsequiousness." He sips his wine. "I mean, that last part's up to you, but all the grovelling might wear a bit thin after a while."

"I could...try a little obsequiousness if it pleased you, though my curtseying skills are a little rusty."

"Oh, I'll teach you," says Olympia. "Four years of etiquette classes. Do you know, I can glide across a room without using a single muscle above the ankle?"

Max sensibly doesn't comment on her dubious claim and says, "Poor Adam's not going to be pleased about you being here all the time, though," instead, which is a shit non sequitur.

Yes. *Poor Adam.*

He and my brother reconnected properly a year ago, more than a decade after they went to different universities and in different directions, only bumping into one another now and then. Adam has spent that year barely hiding his irritation at my presence whenever Max invites us to the same social occasion.

Olympia says, "I just don't understand it. How can two really top people, whom I like, not get on at all? You know, Squimpy, it makes social engagements a bit tedious if you have to be in the same room as each other."

It was a reasonable question.

Max had a fair idea, but the heart of the matter was unknown to anyone but Sarah Fulton and Adam Stringer.

Chapter seven

Fourteen years ago

Max, Adam and I lounge in the attic, a space that was converted to 'the play room' as soon as we were old enough to be reliably independent in our activities.

Max and I have long since stopped lobbying our parents to cease calling it 'the play room' now that we are older and definitely and defiantly not children any more.

Max tells us about a boy at school he likes, while I wait with sweaty palms for Max to then ask who we like.

If he does, I could always say "no one".

But then, Adam might be hurt. I don't want Adam to be hurt. I want him to still like me. I want him to have nurtured his crush until it's this pulsating monster suffocating him and he can't think of anything else but how much he likes me.

I have one of those monsters.

And if I say "no one", he'll think I don't have a monster like him, and his monster will slip away.

Max doesn't ask who we like. Max has to "have a piss" instead.

He leaves the room and Adam and I are alone.

We lie on beanbags that have been slung so that they touch and our heads are only inches from each other, and look up at the plastic, glow-in-the-dark stars stuck to the ceiling.

There's not much to see. The curtains are open to the afternoon sun, so the stars are keeping their magic for later.

Adam's arm rests on the floor between us.

As does mine.

I slide my hand towards his and my stomach is a murmuration of starlings, whirling and separating and converging.

The monster takes over and I am powerless to its need to touch him.

My little finger shakes as it bridges the small gap between our hands and rests up against his little finger.

He goes very still.

Then he wraps his finger around mine and the bean bag *scrunch*es as he turns his head.

I roll mine to the side so I can see the small, hesitant smile on his face.

"I like *you*," I whisper.

"I like you, too," he whispers back.

Chapter eight

I adjust my virtual reality goggles as my Darcy avatar – Mister D'Arsy – comes online.

Mister D'Arsy is my avatar name because I am very clever and very witty. And also because a few people found the game before me and I was forced to be very clever and very witty.

Now there are so many Mr Darcys, people have to run a series of numbers after the name.

The Elizabeth Bennet who suddenly appears opposite me got in late to the game judging by her Lizobeth2000 moniker. She's told me it's a nod to the 1988 sci fi film *Cherry 2000* featuring an ass-kicking female bounty hunter, or tracker, or something.

I'll have to take her word for it.

I say "she", but given that the attractive female fighting characters are always played by men in the gaming world, I'm fairly sure she is, in fact, a "he". It's pretty much the only phenomenon where cis straight men unanimously would rather be a woman. Mostly because the characters have all the strength attributes of men, but with boobs.

She sits straight-backed, ignoring the prop cup of tea on the table between us, as one might while the alien hordes rage outside, and says, "Good evening, game master."

The game, *Pride and Prejudice and Aliens*, is an adaptation of the book of the same name, one of many derivative works of Seth Graham-Smith's, frankly spectacular, *Pride and Prejudice and Zombies.*

And while *Aliens* might not have garnered any literary merit, the game has attracted a large and dedicated following, because who wouldn't want to wear an ankle-length dress and do battle with extraterrestrial invaders? I mean, there are lasers. If you're good enough to procure one from an enemy.

"Hello, Liz. How might I be of assistance this evening?"

This is not the first time Lizobeth2000 has booked a game master session with me to ostensibly receive tactical advice from a veteran player. It's not even the twentieth. I stopped counting after we hit thirty.

"I have a pressing question that's been plaguing me since our last chat."

Our last chat was twenty-one hours and thirty-four minutes ago.

"What pose would Lizzy B, the alien killer, have if she was a superhero?"

I say, because I am Mr Darcy and I have a duty to cast derision, "She'd have her hands on her hips, looking at us down her nose like the self-satisfied, righteous, judgy person she is."

She replies with, "Super Darcy would be a poseur of such superior quality, I can't actually think of one. All the dick poses are already taken."

I laugh, because while my answer is mostly off-truth, hers isn't. And it's funny.

God I love my sessions with her. They are a wonderful balm for my anxiety about my arrest.

I have an urge to reciprocate, to make *her* laugh, so I tell her I did something radical on my Tube commute to work.

She says, "You slurped the end of an iced drink through a straw very loudly and for the entire journey."

"God, no. That would have been horrifying."

"You pole danced on one of the poles and shimmied down from the top using only your thighs?"

"That's tomorrow's rebellion."

"Which line do you take and what time?"

The software generates a male or female voice when you talk, depending on the character you're piloting, so it's no indicator of the person behind the avatar. Nor is it sophisticated enough to add accent, which means all I can say for certain is this player is middle-class English.

Initially it's pretty weird speaking in a female voice and hearing a male voice give the same inflection and tone on the same words a split second later. But you get used to it.

"I asked people sitting around me how they were."

Liz gasps. "No! That's truly anarchic. People must have been terrified."

"Most of them pretended I hadn't spoken. They couldn't even bring themselves to raise their eyes to meet mine. So, I said 'hello' to everyone coming down the escalator on my way out of the station to see if I could cause a panicked stampede."

"Did you?"

"No. Startled looks and frowns only, which I'll take as a small but significant victory."

"You, Mister D'Arsy, are an agent of chaos. I've never once tempted chaos. It's not in my genetic make up."

"What did you inherit instead?"

"A strong aversion to acting outside of societal expectations and the uncanny ability to fall asleep mid-sentence."

"I bet that goes down well in the boardroom."

Three months ago, Lizobeth2000 appeared in the chatroom needing help locating a target she had to rescue. I gave her some tips without making it too easy for her, and then a couple of weeks later she wanted advice on how to coordinate a defense on a besieged York.

The following week, she asked for help on something that required a short answer, and stayed, because I said the answer was simple and she would have worked it out if she wasn't distracted by her own cleavage.

She laughed and asked if I'd got pneumonia yet from all the swimming and staring at myself in the mirror. I've seen the Colin Firth version, and I absolutely would risk pneumonia to get another eye full of that.

We carried on from our smack talk starting point and the rest is history.

Liz says, "Actually, speaking of work, I need some advice."

I invite her to recline on the Georgian chaise lounge behind her, which we both know is a metaphorical invite because we're in a twenty-first century VR chatroom and not some sci-fi Hollywood imagining.

What I *can* do is steeple my fingers because of my hapgloves and say "Pray, impart your troubles, child," which sounds more like a priest than a Regency period shrink, if they had them, but Liz laughs anyway.

"I've been head-hunted for a much higher paying job."

I hold up a finger. "Please halt your whining for a moment while I set my synth to violin." It may sound mean, but she knows I am low salaried. Because I've whined about it to her.

"It could be a game changer for me."

"Game changer, how?" I could guess, but this is Liz's couch time, so my job is to prompt, listen, and if I have solutions, offer them diplomatically.

Okay, mostly diplomatically.

"It would mean I could probably afford to buy a property at some stage in this ridiculously overpriced market. Have a secure home."

"Right. So why are you bringing this to the problem table?"

"It would mean working in corporate."

"And?"

"I'm not really values-aligned with corporate. I'm more about working for the little guy, rather than propping up the big folk at the top."

"Ah." I already like Liz. A lot. But this new information elevates my estimation of her to a whole new level of respect that makes me want her to like me a lot, too. I hope the fact she's brought this dilemma to me means she might already.

Thankfully, I'm able to deliver and already have the answer. "Are you single?"

"Yes."

"Do you want to stay single?"

"No."

"Then don't compromise on your values. Wait for the double income to buy the house."

"But I might never meet someone."

"But you probably will. Most people do."

Liz's right hand, which hovers above the tabletop because the one she's sitting at in real life is higher, curls around something and moves back and forth rapidly, like she's idly playing with the computer mouse while she thinks. "I really want the certainty that I can buy a home in the not-too-distant future."

I do understand. It's a big carrot that's being dangled in front of her. "What's better? Being miserable in a soul-sucking job that pays a shit tonne of money, or being moderately poor and waiting on a dream that will probably happen anyway? Both scenarios lead to buying a house."

"Except, I'm more likely to attract a partner with a better paying job."

"Are you wanting to enter a 'science of attraction debate', or a 'nature of all women debate'? Because I'm up for either. Be prepared to have your arse handed to you."

She pauses before saying, "You're...assuming it's a female partner I'm after?"

"Yes." Because it's time we dropped the pretence that we don't know each other's real gender. Of course, she could be gay, but after the hours she's committed to chatting with me and the amount of banter that edges into flirtation, I don't think so.

After a couple of seconds, Liz says, "Okay."

"Good. So, the question *then* is, which person do you want to live inside? The corporate money chaser, or the socio-serving humbly guy? Because whichever you choose, you have to be comfortable in that skin."

"I...could do it for a little while?"

"You could. Just be sure not to burn out or get to the point of hating yourself before you go back to your old job."

Liz counters this with, "They want an answer by tomorrow."

Right. In that case, I guess Mister D'Arsy has to perform his magical problem-solving duties.

I take a deep breath to buy some time to think about how I might help.

I mean, I'm not a psychologist or whatever, but I do want to help Liz because the fact she keeps asking for it means I can't be terrible at it and because of the whole liking her thing.

"Close your eyes and picture yourself on your average day at work."

Without the invention of a haptic balaclava that might detect facial expression and eyelid movement, Liz keeps staring at me, but I know the pilot has closed their eyes, because she is very still.

"Imagine a good day."

I pause.

"And a bad day. How does doing that work make you feel? You don't need to tell me. Just hold on to that emotion."

I wait several seconds.

"Now imagine yourself as the person in the corporate position. Picture what the job will ask of you. How does doing that work make you feel?"

Liz barely pauses for reflection before sighing. "It's no competition."

"Didn't think so."

"Thanks. I knew what my decision was, I just felt pulled in the money direction."

"As we all are. It's very difficult to walk away from it when we're sold it as an ideal."

"Yeah."

We descend into a short silence. No doubt Liz is lost in her thoughts, contemplating her lucky escape.

"You know, for all your arsy-ness, you're very good to talk to. You always reposition my perspective after my day pulls it out of alignment."

And there it is. The crowning high I always chase when I talk to Lizobeth2000. There are others – the flirt high, the banter high, the 'you understand me' high, the 'I just made you laugh' high, but this is the best one, because it makes me feel as if I'm not living a life that's all about me.

For once, I feel kind of good about who I am.

Liz continues, "Though, I feel this is an unbalanced relation-ship. I wouldn't want us to forge a damsel and saviour pattern given that I'm an Austen woman who can handle a sword better than most men and mostly choose whom I marry."

"Would you like me to break out the 'how ardently I admire and love you' line so you can feel less insecure, or crack straight into the sword handling jokes?"

"Wow, that's a tough one. I choose...the love declaration, but in the voice of a Welshman who says 'w' for 'l's."

This is what we do. As soon as we get too close to...getting close, we pull away again with flippancy.

Because despite how much I like her, how much I anticipate my chatroom sessions with her, I have to be careful. As does she.

It's kind of the unsaid etiquette of the chatroom to protect your identity, to never reveal who you are. So we haven't.

Even though I sort of want to.

There are too many trolls in the online world and too many girls – and boys for that matter – groomed by dodgy men. It's kind of a shame it's come to this, but you just never know who you're communicating with.

Lizobeth2000 could be a thirteen-year-old girl, or a sixty-five-year-old bored by retirement.

But I don't think so.

We've talked enough for me to feel confident that the pilot is not a perve or belongs in an inappropriate age bracket.

I'm also reasonably confident I'm not a fool and haven't been suckered in by a Nigerian con-artist.

At the end of the day, it doesn't matter. It's not like we're ever going to meet.

Chapter nine

"The downpour was so heavy, it literally soaked through my clothes and started funnelling down my arse crack." Jas turns and mimes the water-corralling properties of her bum cheeks and Ian punctuates his wheezy laugh with a snort.

I've only been working in the police station cafeteria for four hours and already I love these people. The job is one of those you'd describe as 'character building' and is woefully paid, yet this team approach it as a convenience to celebrating the small wins in life, of which they manage to find many.

It took one hour for me to be promoted to till duties because of my "bubbly personality", but really because the rest of the team can't be arsed making polite chit chat with people they see every day but know nothing about.

We are all required to wear a pale blue shirt and a white hair net, which naturally makes me look like I've suffered catastrophic blood loss.

I am not feeling awesome about having to wear it.

Jas, on the other hand, with her dark skin, black eyebrows and round cheekbones, makes it look like a new season accessory.

I have defied the other uniform stipulation of black trousers and black shoes, by wearing my orange trainers with turquoise laces and rolling up the bottom of my black trousers to reveal my panda socks.

Jas sighs deeply as if now the 'being caught in the rain without a raincoat' story is told, she can die happy, and sprinkles grated cheese over the large tray of lasagne.

Simone, a blonde, white woman in her late thirties, wipes tears of mirth from her eyes. "You know what I want to know?"

"What's the little hollow at the base of your thumb when you splay your fingers called?" says Ian, and drops the knife he's holding to peer at his red-freckled, tattooed hand. "Question's been bugging me since 1974."

Ash, who's black, straight out of school and speaks like he's acquired the wisdom of half his lifetime already, pushes a tray of dishes into the steriliser. "You have had fifty odd years to find the answer, Ian. It's not like it's a rhetorical question."

"I forget. By the time I've done the wondering about it and I'm anywhere near knowledge tools, my brain's on to the next thing."

"You know, that is an excellent question, Ian," says Simone, "and not one that I have an answer for, I'm sorry. Mine's as equally elusive." She frowns at the milk caked onto the frothing arm of the coffee machine and rubs at it with a cloth.

Ian pivots and props himself against the bench, arms crossed.

Ash turns his head as if cocking an ear.

Jas leans over her station, places her chin in her hand and looks up at Simone.

Simone stares down at her cloth and blinks. Then she flares her nostrils in a stifled yawn.

Jas says in a monotone, "I think I just aged a year."

"What?" Simone looks up.

"We're, like, dying from suspense here, S. What's. The. Question?"

"Oh, right. Sorry. You guys been watching that sci fi show that's massive on Netflix?"

"Um. That question's completely quantitative, Simone," says Ash. "You know what 'elusive' means, right?"

Simone flaps a hand in front of her face like she's shooing a fly. "No, that's not my question. You know the main character? That massive alien guy?"

"Is that your question?" asks Jas.

"No! The question's coming."

"You're asking a lot of questions. It's confusing as to which is the real question."

Simone sighs. "I'll *tell you* when it's the real question. So, you know how he's all bald headed, and has no nose and ear lobes?"

We did, because it was a show trending so hard nobody wanted to miss out.

"So my question is –" she drops her voice, "– What does he look like underneath his clothes?"

"O-kay," says Ash with raised brows and a bemused smirk.

"He's kind of –" she glances over the top of the coffee machine to check for approaching customers "– weirdly sexy, but judging from his lack of protruding parts, I just can't imagine him with bits designed for –" she raises her pointer finger, pokes the air with it and whispers, *"interlocking.* It's probably all, you know, Ken doll smooth down there."

"Gross," says Jas. "I do not want to think about alien sex."

"I kind of do," I say. "I bet those Kassiling things could teach us a thing or two. All those naughty little mouth tentacles."

Simone sighs. *"Mouth tentacles.* I bet they get it right first try."

Jas eyeballs the two of us from under her eyebrows, then mimes holding a pen and crossing something out on the bench top. "Great, that's alien cunnilingus off the agenda. Next item of business?"

Ian pulls a roasted cauliflower from an oven. "I've got one while we're on the topic. How do you have sex in zero gravity."

"How many years has that question been bugging you?" Ash asks.

"I know, right?" says Jas. "No traction. How do you, like, create the needed friction when you're both on the same float trajectory?"

"1983," says Ian. "Sally Ride. First female NASA astronaut in space. Gets you thinking."

Jas puts the lasagne in the open oven and slams the door home. "And what happens to the aftermath? No one wants to be ambushed by a floating bubble of spunk. That shit is grim."

Ian cackles and Simone slaps a hand across her mouth, laughing out a "Oh ho, my God," through her fingers. "That is so repulsive."

I wipe at my upper lip and scrutinise the clear protection plate in front of the till. "I think I just sprayed snot over the perspex divider."

"You know, Jas," Ash says, "for someone who protests about thinking about space sex, you seem to have done a lot of thinking about space sex."

"I said *alien* sex. Astronaut sex is a *totally* different thing."

I process a payment for a sports drink and a sandwich, thank the customer, and turn back to the conversation. "I also have a pressing question about the show. How does Rid, the Ny Mercenary, pee? I've looked closely at that suit. There's no trap door or retracting crotch flap. She has to go sometime."

"You know," says Simone, "I bet distant-future incontinence pads would be super absorbent."

I express my dubiousness with a "Fft. Rid is *way* too cool to be wearing nappies."

"Catheter?" says Ian. "I've had a couple of those in me. Separate times, mind. Best convenience device I've ever experienced. Apart from pockets. They're pretty handy."

Jas grunts. "She probably just pees in her suit like all dirty wetsuit wearers. It'll get absorbed by the suit's regulatory system and is, like, recycled for cooling or something."

"No way," says Simone. "Rid does not look like someone who would use their own urine as a coolant."

I raise a finger. "Urine, I'll have you know, is an excellent coolant. We've all peed our pants and regretted it ten minutes later when a breeze gets up."

Ash raises his eyebrows. "That's a *childhood* memory you've just tapped into, right?"

"Nope. Didn't leave my gaming chair in nine hours last night."

I am met with a range of disgusted expressions, which is fair enough.

I tell them I was joking and hope they believe me. They don't know me yet, after all.

Jas clucks her tongue. "I wouldn't put it past some gamers. Those hardcore dudes can be rank."

Simone's jaw slackens. "What, they just pee where they're sitting rather than pause the game to take a bathroom break?"

"When you're live gaming no one's going to wait for you while you tap a kidney." Jas shakes her head. "Meatheads in meatspace."

"In what?" asks Ian.

"The real world," I say. "As opposed to the virtual world of all things online."

Simone says, "You know, I shouldn't be grossed out by that? I've been covered in every fluid it's possible for a small body to produce, and yet..." She raises her hands in a shrug. "I'll tell you one thing for free. You know you're alive when snot hits your eyeball."

"Ah. You know you have a defense mechanism for that, S?" says Jas. "It's called eyelids?"

"Never underestimate the power and velocity of a baby sneeze, Jasmeena."

With no customers waiting, I leave the conversation to do the other task I've been assigned as the new kid on the block – wiping down tables and retrieving trays from the 'resource recovery station', which houses a bin for rubbish, recycling, and compost.

Not all customers buy their food from us. The large dining area is also a space for staff to eat their lunch.

One such man sits at a table with a spine so straight you could run a plumb line down it and forks salad into his mouth from a metal container. In front of him is a book.

Ah.

I wondered when our paths would cross, but I honestly didn't expect it to be on my first day.

I need to let him know I'm here. And give him a piece of my mind.

I stand in front of him. "Adam. Hello."

Adam Stringer looks up at me, his eyes bulge and it takes several seconds for his chest to reanimate, as if the breath has been sucked out of his lungs in a sudden and fierce vacuum. He looks like he's concentrating on peeling the planes of his lungs away from one another to draw in air.

It shouldn't give me any satisfaction, but if I said it didn't, I would be lying.

"No." He places his thumbs on his eyeballs. "This is not happening. No, no, no, no."

I mean.

It is.

Actually happening.

But it's probably unnecessary to point that out to him.

His book has fallen closed with the removal of his hand. It's an Austen novel. *Persuasion*.

Go figure.

He draws a deep breath and removes his thumbs from his eyes, but before he can make his protest, I say, "Oh no. You don't get to be all indignant. I spent a night in the cells on a mattress that smelled like semi-digested vindaloo because of you."

Adam sits back in his chair and crosses his arms. "You spent a night in the cells because of *you*. Your decision to break a man's nose."

"But it didn't have to happen. Maybe I deserved it, but you abandoning me at one of the most vulnerable times in my life made sure it did happen. Why? Why did you decide to be that person, Adam?" by which I mean "traitorous arseface".

Eventually, I'd found the courage to call my brother, confess, and ask him to pick me up after I was released pending the Crown Prosecution Services' decision to charge me, but not after suffering one of the darkest nights I'd ever faced.

"Because, Sarah, I didn't want to play protector in a game I couldn't win and that you don't deserve to win. You have a unique knack of bringing a pile of shit into my life and rubbing my face in it. This time I had a choice as to whether I was subjected to it or not. I extracted myself before you brought me down with you."

"And deserted Max in the process."

Adam's nostrils flare. "I didn't do it lightly. There are other, better lawyers, you can bring on board to protect Max, and if it goes to court, you're going to want a barrister anyway. I didn't leave him out to dry. I just chose not to get involved."

I wait a second before saying, "When the going got tough."

"Yes. Because it would have been detrimental to me. You are exhausting, Sarah, and because of the emotional attachment I have to Max, the whole process would have been utterly depleting. So, don't tell me your right to be incensed about my decision trumps my right to be angry about your presence ruining my lunch hour. This is the only down time I have from the crap I have to face out there." He jabs a finger towards the door. "It's sacrosanct."

I fold my arms across my chest. "The police station cafeteria...is sacrosanct?"

"I get twenty minutes away from my work each ten-hour day, to eat my lunch and recalibrate. Yes, it's sacrosanct."

"Couldn't you eat your lunch at a park or something, like a normal person seeking escape from their workmare?"

"Where, Sarah? The closest green space is a ten-minute walk. By the time I got there, I'd have to turn around and walk back."

I focus on the crease between his eyebrows and dig around in my chest cavity for any sympathy. I can only find a grudging obligation to respect his reason for walking out on me after the phone call to Jeffrey Wainwright.

However, I can probably make an effort.

I suppose.

"Okay. I'll...make sure you don't have to see me," I say and don't bother to keep the resentment out of my voice.

"How?"

Because I know it'll get a reaction, I whisper, "*I'll be invisible*," and wave finger-splayed hands over my face, crossing them in front of each other like I'm conducting a magic trick.

Adam's answer comes out surly. "I'll still know you're present, lurking in the background. Just because I can't see you doesn't mean you won't be corrupting my down time."

I frown. "I am not doing this to punish you, Adam. I needed a job and I could start this one straight away."

He crosses his arms. "They hired you despite being arrested by someone in this very building?"

"No. I didn't tell them, because all I was required to disclose was previous convictions. As yet, I have none. Besides, management believe in the rehabilitation process. Most of the staff have convictions of varying degrees."

Adam flicks his eyes to the food service area and I see his mind jumping between conclusions to settle on about management's approach. All he says is, "Good," which is brief, but nice, I suppose, and then ruins it by saying, "You shouldn't have withheld your impending charges, though. It's unethical, Sarah."

He's absolutely right. I just don't need him of all people to point out what I already know. "I'm aware. But right now, I have run out of options. So, I'll just have to live with it."

He eyes me for a beat. "You are...something else." There's a tightness to his words, like he's reigning in his disgust. Then he shifts to a different chair so his back is to the service area and I take that as my cue to get busy on the invisible.

I collect the trays and return behind the service counter to find the half packet of A4 paper and roll of sticky tape I'd seen on the desk in the small staff room and start on my invisibility project.

Eight minutes later, we are swamped with a short rush on hot food.

Four minutes after that, a lull descends, which means I have nothing to do but the other part of my job of keeping the cafeteria floor clean.

Adam is still there, doggedly sticking to his twenty minutes to prove this space is not up for compromise, though his shoulders sit closer to his ears.

I know I said he wouldn't have to see me, but it's going to be pretty difficult when I have to actually be in his field of vision to do what I'm paid for.

"I don't suppose there's any costumes stashed out the back?" I ask Simone.

Jas says, "What, for all the Christmas pantos we stage in here?" and Ash laughs.

"For being anonymous when a customer would prefer you didn't work here."

"Your arresting officer come in?" asks Ian.

"Something like that."

"Fuck 'em," says Jas. "Wear your face loud and proud."

"I could...or...not." I ignore Jas' disapproving eyebrows and go out to the staffroom to pick through the lockers. I find blue overalls, a bikini top, compression socks, and a white hockey mask.

I choose the overalls and the hockey mask.

Creeping on tiptoe out onto the cafeteria seating area, I squeeze the trigger on the spray bottle as quietly as I can and begin wiping tables.

I get to table six without incident and wave at the team behind the counter. Simone and Ian wave back, Jas turns her palms to the ceiling in a *What the fuck?* gesture, and Ash stares at me open mouthed.

"What are you doing?" asks Adam.

I freeze, finger trigger poised over a table behind him. "You know it's me?"

"Yes, I know it's you!"

Right. Who else would be out here wiping tables? I should have thought this through better. "Sorry. Costume options were limited."

"You look ridiculous."

I turn to try and look at myself in the mirrored wall designed to make the cafeteria seem more spacious, just as a man steps back from closing the drinks fridge door and pivots into me.

He yells and jumps backwards.

"Sorry," I say.

He clutches his drink to his chest. "Jesus. That is truly frightening."

"Sorry," I say again.

"Who are you? Mrs Jason?"

Um. "Mrs who?"

"Friday the 13th?"

I say nothing. Because I have no idea what he's talking about.

"The horror movies?"

I turn to Adam. "I look like something from a horror movie?" I face the mirrored wall behind the drink refrigerators.

The cherub lips I'd painted on with red lipstick and the black Betty Boop-esqe curls around its top edge I'd drawn with permanent marker might, on reflection, look a little creepy.

I tip my head to one side.

Okay a lot creepy.

I remove the mask.

"I was just..." I wave the mask around as if that might explain my intentions, and settle on, "trying not to be Sarah."

"All you did was *amplify* the Sarah." Adam shifts in his seat so he faces me squarely. "It's always a one-woman show with you."

I sigh. Yes. Indulging my inner clown brings me joy and, most of the time, other people joy, but right now I see it through Adam's eyes. Glib and childish.

But because it is Adam, I am obliged to protest anyway. "I'm not an exhibitionist."

He points to the short, paper castle wall I taped to the perspex screen in front of the till in the previous several-minutes-long lull. It has an arrow slit so I can look out at the cafeteria floor.

"I have to watch for customers without you seeing me. It seemed like a fitting solution," I add without any intention of backing up that statement if Adam calls it to question.

"Why is it only as tall as the till?"

"So that when you leave, I can stand and pretend I'm pacing the parapet."

Adam's laugh is humourless.

Probably.

He turns back to the table and pulls his lunch box towards him. "Right now, Sarah, you are my least favourite person. And I deal with sociopaths on a weekly basis."

I know I'm his least favourite person. But I am surprised at the "right now" qualifier due to the years of him letting me know how little he thinks of me.

Picking up his fork, he chases a lonesome mini tomato around the container. "I had resolved not to have anything to do with you ever again after Max's birthday." He spears it, looks at it, then drops the fork into the metal container with a clatter. "You can't even allow me that."

I move a couple of tables away and pull the trigger on the spray bottle. It issues a soft *fft fft*.

Adam has forgotten there's one small detail that could potentially tie us in some way for the rest of our lives. "I'll always be Max's sister. Can't do much about that, I'm sorry." *Fft fft.* "Unless I die," I add with a ridiculous little giggle that is entirely unsuited to the morbidity of my words and will not in any way help the situation.

So, I say, "And I'm sure even you wouldn't want that," to invite him to make this whole exchange worse.

Adam chooses to neither confirm or deny, which is understandable, or unsurprising, or both, and I move off to decrumb the next table.

Once it's sterilised and I start on another one, Adam says, "You're jinxed," and I give a little jump. "Whenever things are going really well in my life, you come along and mess it up."

I continue scrubbing. I do know.

It isn't intentional.

But yes, it is unfortunate.

"And you always come out of things smelling of roses."

Not this time.

"It's like we're forever doomed to ride a luck see-saw. When you go up, I go down. *Christ* it's unfair."

I turn then. "Adam. I'm sorry I've ruined your *me time* in the cafeteria. But I am scrubbing tables for less than a living and have an assault charge pending, which may well land me in jail."

So.

Stop your goddam whining.

"Knowing you, you'll be absolved somehow. Or your parents will have you exonerated."

Adam hasn't turned around to deliver his complaint to my face. He directs his words to the empty chairs in front of him and people at a couple of other tables stop their conversations to stare at him.

"All you had to do, Sarah, was swallow your pride and ask your family for some money to support you while you found employment. Maybe then you wouldn't have been in a condition to descend into lunacy when you were presented with an injustice."

Firstly, asking for money from my parents would never ever be an "all you had to do" thing.

And secondly, *descend into lunacy*? Adam is only ever supercilious with me. The expression of his disapproval through the use of superior language should be amusing if it wasn't so incensing.

I could walk away now without him knowing and leave him to look unhinged, enjoying a rantathon for one.

I don't. I say, "A *gross* injustice," and continue wiping.

Adam turns then. "It doesn't matter –"

And I straighten up to look at him. "It absolutely matters!"

"Yes, okay, Jeffrey Wainwright should be held accountable for his actions, but not by you meting out violent retribution. Nobody. Nobody is ever deserving of that."

Hitler might have been. Or Idi Amin.

I don't say this, though, as I know Adam's head is now in a place in our past that is painful to both of us, and despite my unwillingness to behave respectfully when I'm around him, I treat this place like the kid gloves it deserves.

So, I say, "No. I know. Jeffrey Wainwright didn't deserve what I did." I do mean it. "And I do deserve what the law hands down to me."

Adam opens his mouth and I rush in with an "I am sorry, Adam".

Maybe he knows I'm talking about more than what happened in that bar a few days ago.

Maybe he doesn't.

Chapter ten

Fourteen years ago

Adam and I have talked about this. Doing this.

We've talked about doing this a lot.

And now it's time.

Adam's had to visit the bathroom to throw up and do a toothpaste mouth rinse, and I've had to pace and flap-shake my hands, and now it's time.

The barbecue's in full swing below. Everyone – my parents, Adam's parents, family friends, neighbours – is busy enjoying the July heatwave, and talking loudly and drinking beer or wine out of plastic glasses because of the pool, and not noticing Adam and I are missing.

Max knows something is up and is leaving us to it.

We stare at each other across my bedroom.

Adam's in his underpants. I'm in my bra and knickers.

His chest heaves.

Behind him, the closed sheer curtains flap against the open sash window.

Then I walk to him and we are kissing. Just like we have been lately, with hungrier and hungrier mouths.

I cannot get enough of his skin against mine. Feel enough of it beneath my fingers and palms.

I push his underpants down his thighs and he frees them from his legs and I am on fire.

I press myself to him. I lean all my weight against him, needing all of him with such a fierceness I am overwhelmed by it.

He steps backwards, off-balance, and then I am off-balance too and I fall into him and he takes another step and the window frame catches him at the back of his knees and –

He's falling out the open window.

Chapter eleven

I do the house elf thing and have miso risotto accompanied by stuffed smoked aubergine on the table in time for a respectable hour for eating, because Max calls to say he is coming home early.

'Early' doesn't actually mean early. It means 7 pm, which is earlier than the usual 9 pm.

And because I've made enough for four, I invite Olympia around to help us eat it.

She marches in the door, plonks a bottle of probably very expensive wine on the table and after she kisses us both, claps her hands. "I've got a fun game."

"Eating's a fun game," I say, because I am very hungry and dinner smells very good.

"We can play while we eat." She pulls out a chair and sits at the table. "It's just a talking game. Not as fun as strip polo, but I'm not sure eating and playing strip polo is advisable."

Max agrees as if he has actually played strip polo.

Olympia's idea of 'a fun game' is to outdo each other in the "who's had the shittest day" stakes. Except she says "awfullest" because she's posh and "shittest" isn't part of her vernacular.

"I'll start," she says. "You know how I do a lot of freelance stuff – brand advice and what have you?"

We did.

"And you know Jonty Hargraves, who was in my year at Cambridge but got kicked out due to salting the ol' rim with a bit too much dedication?"

By which she means "cocaine habit", and no we don't know Jonty Hargraves.

"Well, his family own some farms up in Lancashire and Jonty's investing in cattle, like Angus, for the prime meat market, and he asked me for help with the branding of his business, which he decided to call Jonty's Angus, because he's never had much imagination. So, I do my thing, and send some advertising material to as many Michelin star restaurants as I can Google, only I didn't proof it, did I? I ended up sending gorgeous-looking prime meat info packs to top nosh houses for Jonty's *Anus*."

I do my very best to spray the table with rice via my nasal passages.

Max chokes on his wine and has to thump his chest.

"Quite. I haven't told Jonty, yet. Seems like he might have to set his sights a bit lower than three-star restaurants now none of them want to cook his anus."

I look at Max and we break into fresh laughter, and Olympia says at least someone's finding the positive in her "abs disaster", by which she means "absolute" and not some catastrophic sit-ups failure. "Right," she beams. "Who wants to have a go next?"

Max loosens his already loosened tie and issues a sigh. "My proposed bill failed at its first reading."

As Olympia says, "Oh, well done, Maxy. You kicked my whoopsy out of the ball park," I ask, "The pay equity one?"

He takes a large gulp of wine in answer. "I want to say I'm not surprised. The politicians in this country will make stupid, completely unnecessary decisions out of racism and xenophobia that have a hugely adverse impact on our economy and claim they didn't see it coming –"

Olympia contextualises this with a "Brexit, Squimpy" in case I missed the subtle clues.

My phone vibrates in my pocket and I pull it out and look at it. Mum's calling. I put it back and wait for it to silently ring out.

Max continues, "So, of course they'd refuse to back a bill that ensures pay parity for women between sectors. Apparently, the 2010 Equality Act is enough, even though it only ensures parity within the individual workplace, not across sectors. The racism and xenophobia, sadly, doesn't surprise me, but the misogyny gets me every time. There were *women* in there who opposed it. It should have at least got through the first reading. We have a majority."

"A slim majority," I say. "A slim majority created through a coalition with an unpredictable centre-right party."

"Are you saying I *shouldn't* be surprised?"

"I'm saying…you have every right to be disappointed."

"But, Sarah, how, this far into the modern age, can we be dumb enough to depreciate half of our population? To fail to see they need protecting and a bit of extra leverage to have every opportunity a man gets? Do they not recognise that women, despite appearances, are not on an equal footing with men?"

Olympia says, "Bring back the matriarchy," and I say, "What matriarchy?", and she says, "Take your pick. Boudicca, Queen Victoria, Beyoncé."

Max continues as if nothing, not even something sensible, came out of our mouths, "It would pave the way for all industries that are female dominated to achieve pay parity with similar industries that are male dominated. Why wouldn't anyone want that?"

My phone stills, then rings again.

"Because it's too expensive," I say. "The neoliberals will do anything to protect the best interests of business."

Whatever Mum's calling about, it's not worth ignoring her over.

"But a lot of those jobs are civil," says Max. "The vast majority of money will come out of local and central governments' pockets."

"But it'll have a flow on effect to business and it gives them something to crow about when they do the whole 'protecting the rate and tax payer' thing." I stand. "Sorry. Mum's calling. I better take it." And walk into the lounge.

Behind me, Max says, "I just really thought they wouldn't make women have to fight so hard, Olympia. Pay equity is still achievable, it's just going to be a longer, more drawn-out shift driven by the unions," and I tap my phone to accept the call.

"Hi, Mum."

"I have a letter from the Crown Prosecution Services in my hand, Sarah."

My insides freefall.

"Shall I tell you what it says?"

I don't need her to tell me. It is very evident from her tone what that letter says. I curse myself for giving Mum and Dad's address on the night of my arrest when I knew I wouldn't have my own address for much longer.

"No, Mum." My voice is low. I do not want Max and Olympia to know what is unfolding. Not yet.

Mum tells me anyway. "You've officially been charged with Assault Occasioning Actual Bodily Harm."

Well fuck.

It shouldn't be any great surprise, but the confirmation of it has my stomach listing. I clamp a hand to my mouth and will my system not to evacuate my dinner through my nostrils. My knees give way and I collapse onto the couch.

"Do I need to tell you how heartbroken your father is over this whole thing, Sarah?"

I am tempted to say, "Yes. Apparently you do," but I don't have the energy. "Nobody's more disappointed in me than I am, Mum."

"Oh, I wouldn't bet on it. You have been –"

I cut her off with, "Thank you for telling me, Mum," and hang up, because she has already made it very clear on numerous occasions how disappointing I am to her, and it's entirely unhelpful to have it repeated in this moment when I am officially on route towards having a criminal conviction.

I press the phone to my ear again while I draw in several deep breaths and compose myself for re-entering the dinner conversation. Then I force my lips into a smile, stand and say, "Thanks for ringing, Mum," and return to my seat at the table.

"Everything okay?" asks Max.

"Yep," I say as brightly as I can manage. "She just wanted to congratulate me on getting a job."

"That's nice, Squimpy." Olympia waves her fork at me. "Now. Can you top Max's humdinger?"

Yes.

I probably can.

But Max's failed bill is of much more importance and has far bigger consequences than my charge. I'm not going to eclipse any sympathy he needs from us, especially because I'm not deserving of anybody's sympathy.

"No, sorry. I had an uneventful day." I stab a piece of aubergine. "Totally normal. Nothing even remotely shitty." I look up and smile at them both. "Not a thing."

"Oh shame," says Olympia. "It's a better game if we can all play."

Indeed.

God. The debt I'll owe to my parents to make the charges go away will be far greater than the money I'll have to pay back. But it will be worth it, because Max is a rising star and the little people need politicians like him on their side.

Max stares at his plate and pushes the contents around. Then he releases his fork so it clatters against the porcelain and looks up at me. "You know what, Sarah? Fuck misogyny. You have to do this thing. You have to go to court and find a way to make a stand against Jeffrey Wainwright, because there are so many Jeffrey Wainwrights out there. They need exposing. Even if he's never held legally accountable, what he did needs to be shown to the world. He still needs to receive judgement."

It takes me a moment to answer. "You do know what this could mean for you, right? Your life could get very difficult very quickly. You could have your portfolio removed."

Max bats away my concern with a flap of his hand. "I won't have my portfolio removed. I've already told the PM about it. She understands it won't look good if it gets out to the press, but the controversy isn't over anything I've done. So."

"So? Politicians bow to pressure. The pressure placed on politicians by the opposing benches, by the tabloids, by mob public opinion is phenomenal, which means she's still an un-known entity. I wouldn't count on her word, yet, Max, even if she has integrity coming out her ears. *You* could bow to pressure for that matter. It might get so bad you're forced to fall on your sword. It would kill me if I did that to you."

"*If* it came to that, and I doubt it will, it won't be you who did that to me." He reaches across the table and nudges my hand with his pointer finger. "Look, Sarah, if I deprived you of this opportunity to stand up for all the women who have been exploited by men in positions of power, it would kill me, too. So, I think it's worth taking the risk. Please take the risk. Don't give that fucker a thing."

I look him in the eye and wait three seconds before saying, "Okay," like I've deliberated about it.

Because there is only one possible course of action.

In a day or two, when I'm feeling brave enough, I'll ring Mum and Dad and see how much they're willing to lend me.

Chapter twelve

Sergeant Bowman, my arresting officer, leans against the cafeteria's front counter by the coffee machine.

Simone slides a cup of coffee towards him and beams. "I made a leaf!"

She has been on a barista course and is testing out her new skills on today's customers, all of whom have been very polite about the unidentifiable patterns in the tops of their lattes.

Sergeant Bowman peers down at the cup. "It looks like a baby's head crowning."

Simone gasps and pulls the cup back towards her. "My froth does not look like a surprised vagina!"

I slide down the counter towards her and eye the coffee.

It kind of does. I tell her it kind of does and pass the coffee back to Jas for her opinion.

Her opinion is she likes it, because, "Leaves and hearts are so 90s."

They aren't. I wasn't drinking coffee in the 90s, but I'm fairly sure coffee art came in at least a decade later. "Remember the 90s well do you?"

"No. I wasn't even a scrotazoa in the 90s."

"Do you mean protozoa?" says Ash as he brings a tray of plates to the front counter. "Though technically you were never a protozoa, even when you were one cell. By definition they always exist as single-celled organisms."

"No. I mean scrotazoa. Think about it."

"I don't want to," I say as the words "Jas' dad's ball sack" swim into my mind. "No, too late." I give her a double thumbs up. "Thanks, Jas."

"I made a pavlova once that looked like Margaret Thatcher," offers Ian. "Perfect replica of her hair. Put me off making one ever again."

"All pavlovas have Margaret Thatcher hair, Ian," I say. "Pavlovas and a Thatcher bouffant are almost synonymous. Next time you make one, imagine Nancy Regan instead. Or the late Queen or something."

"Who's Nancy Regan?" asks Jas as Adam walks into the cafeteria. His gaze is on the tables in front of him and I duck down behind my paper castle.

Sergeant Bowman, who has reclaimed his coffee and, unfazed by the prospect of placing his lips on a surprised vagina, sips at it. "What are you doing?" he asks me mildly.

"She's hiding from that tall, black guy in the blue suit," says Jas. "The hot one."

The sergeant swivels his head, looks for the hot, tall, black guy in the blue suit, says, "Ohhhhh," and swivels it back again. "Say no more."

"What?" says Simone, looking at Sergeant Bowman like he has delivered a great injustice. She shifts her eyes to me. "Please say more." She looks at the sergeant again. "She hasn't told us anything."

"I think it's a kink," says Jas. "She gets off on spying on fit, unsuspecting men. That arrow slit is metaphoric."

"It's not a kink! And can we stop bringing up vaginas, every-one?"

"I didn't bring up any vaginas," says Ian. "Though, it's not the worst topic of conversation I can think of."

"What would that be?" asks Simone.

Feeling we've already fielded the worst conversation topic, I try not to think of Jas as a scrotazoa again as Ian says, "Verb conjugation."

The sergeant asks for sugar for his coffee and I remember I should be entertaining a suspicion. "Why did you say 'Say no more'?" I ask him.

"Because I have a fair idea of why you might not want Adam to know you work here."

"Do you? How?" I say. Then, "He knows I'm here. I'm vol-untarily hiding to make his lunchtime more...relaxing."

"I bet."

"You bet what?" asks Simone. "Tell us what you know."

I narrow my eyes at him. "Yeah, what do you know?"

Sergeant Bowman draws a deep breath, says, "Well," and Jas, Ash and Ian stop what they are doing and move towards the counter.

I don't want to hear. But I do.

It's like licking the hot tap in the bath back when baths had two taps. You still do it even though you know it's going to send a reasonably unpleasant electrical charge straight to your brain.

"The night you were arrested, Adam storms up to my desk and begins pacing. He says things like, 'I'm not going to help her. I am *not* going to help her,' and 'She got herself into this mess. It's not my responsibility,' and I say, 'How do you know her?' and *he* says" – the sergeant pauses to draw a large breath – 'She's my friend's sister'."

He takes a sip of his coffee.

Simone says, "That can't be it."

Sergeant Bowman says, "My coffee's getting cold," and has another drink.

I peer at Adam through the arrow slit, knowing he's too far away to hear the conversation, but check again anyway.

"Adam tells me how Sarah has always turned up in his life when he's at a high point and brought disaster for him, while she rides off in a better position."

"The luck see-saw."

Everyone turns to look at me.

"That's what Adam calls it," I say defensively, though I'm not sure why I have to be defensive. "He says I'm jinxed."

The sergeant continues, "He tells me about this one time he was skiing in Austria with his new girlfriend, who he thinks he's falling in love with, and he hears this shouted 'Adam. Watch this!' and he looks up to see Sarah snowboarding towards the edge of the track he's on and she crouches down to jump the lip, but..." The sergeant looks to me.

I sigh. "My board edge caught a lump of ice and my jump was more of a directionless tumble. Look, I didn't know he was there skiing. I just happened to spot him and he was someone I could show my new trick off to."

"But what happened?" begs Simone.

"She took him out and they had to be choppered off the mountain because she broke his leg and gave herself a mild concussion and a fractured wrist."

Simone gasps and I say resignedly, "Yep."

"That's awful," says Ash helpfully.

It was, but that's not the end of the story. Unfortunately.

"It gets better," says Sergeant Bowman. "He spent the next two days trapped in hospital waiting for an operation with Sarah in the bed next to him. 'Torture' and 'Hellish' were the adjectives I believe he used."

Jas grimaces. "Awkward."

Extremely.

"And to crown it all off his girlfriend, who he thinks he's in love with, remember? dumps him because she's a competitive rock climber and had an eight-week circuit through Europe and

North America coming up that Adam could no longer join her on."

"No!" says Simone.

"And Sarah got off with the doctor."

All eyes turn back to me. No one says anything because no one really needs to. It is truly as awful as it sounds.

"He was a registrar," I say as if that somehow makes everything alright. "*And* we had a nine-month, long-distance relationship," with fantastic sex until the whole 'hardly ever seeing each other' thing wore thin, "so I didn't just 'get off with him'."

After a beat, Ash says, "Wow. That is truly terrible."

More terrible than I realised. I never knew about his girlfriend dumping him.

"He must really hate you," says Jas.

"Yes, I think he does."

"Poor Adam," says Ian.

"Look." I move to push myself to standing, then remember I'm meant to remain hidden. "Adam's been a judgy, sanctimonious arse since almost all the time I've known him. He doesn't deserve all your sympathy. You can give him a little bit, because that's fair, but that's it. And him telling you that –" I point a finger at the sergeant "– was totally unprofessional."

"But very entertaining."

Everyone looks out at the cafeteria floor to watch Adam.

Simone clucks her tongue.

"Who is he?" asks Ash.

"One of the duty solicitors," says Sergeant Bowman.

"Really?" says Jas. "He can solicit my attention any time he likes."

"You want to borrow my arrow slit?"

"No thanks. I have a better view from here."

"You know what?" says Simone. "I'm going to make him a complimentary coffee."

"Don't put a vagina on it," says Ash, who has returned to his workstation along with Ian.

"I'll put a heart on it. The poor man could do with more love."

I try not to roll my eyes. "The poor man could do with a heart."

Sergeant Bowman drains his cup while the coffee machine grinds and whirs.

I take nine pounds forty for a roast vegetable and quinoa salad, and an orange juice, and Simone carefully pours foam into a latte bowl.

She plonks the metal jug down and quietly says, "Oh," and then, "Ohhh no."

I scoot along the counter and join the sergeant in staring into the cup.

The bottom point of the heart is fat and the top two curves are over-rounded.

This time there is no debate. Even Simone accepts she's spectacularly failed on the sleight of hand.

"I've made a cock and balls," she wails and a group of three people approaching the counter exchange alarmed and then amused looks.

There is a scuffle behind me as the rest of the team race to view it.

"It's more like a nubbin and balls," says Jas.

"On the plus side," says Ash, "you didn't make a vagina."

I dish the first customer up their roast chicken and chips, while he looks between me and the cluster at the coffee machine with a twitching mouth.

"You can't waste it," says Ian. "You just did that course. It'll be good coffee, that, despite the genitalia garnish."

"I can't give him that!" says Simone. "It's offensive. It'll offend him."

"Yes, you can," says the sergeant. "And I'll deliver it for you." He gingerly picks up the cup and the surface shivers. "It'll amuse him. He could do with a laugh after all the trauma Sarah's given him."

I couldn't imagine anything amusing Adam. It has to have been fourteen years since I've heard or seen him laugh.

"I really don't think you should, sergeant," I say, but Sergeant Bowman gives me a wink because Simone has just handed him a big spoon to stir the pot with and he knows this is an opportunity for more entertainment.

He makes his slow way towards Adam, holding the coffee with both hands.

I take the customer's money, dish up a second lot of chicken and chips for the next person in the group, and will the sergeant to exude a charm and charisma that will win Adam over.

The third person is a black woman in a pants suit who looks like she might be important. She wants the cheesy vegetarian pasta bake and a cup of tea.

As I place the plate on her tray, Sergeant Bowman delivers the coffee.

"Tea for one," I call to Simone.

The sergeant says something to Adam and points towards the cafeteria service area.

Adam's head whips around.

I am right. He is not amused.

The team wave at him, but Adam looks straight at me.

I have to give the pants-suit her change, so I can't point to the real culprit, who, if Adam had any powers of deduction, or just eyes, would see standing behind the coffee machine. I am several metres away doing an entirely different task.

But such is the narrative he's been telling himself over the years that I have made it my singular objective to make his life miserable, he has automatically jumped to an illogical assumption.

Sergeant Bowman spreads his hands in a 'come on mate, it's a laugh' gesture, and Adam whips back around, his shoulders hunched.

Pants Suit walks through the space on the left-hand side of Adam's table and, as she nears him, he stands and turns to his left because Sergeant Bowman is on his right, and collides with her.

Her tray flattens against her chest, and his coffee tips down his front.

They look down at themselves, their respective messes dripping onto their shoes.

And then Adam erupts.

"You," he shouts, finger extended in my direction. "I mean –" he looks down at himself. "– what the fuck?" His voice rises several notes on the fuck. "It's like you engineered this to happen. What is *wrong* with you?"

Pants Suit takes a step back as Adam sluices himself down with his hands, calmly places her tray and the remains of her lunch on the table next to her, and delivers a "Mr Stringer" in that commanding, collected way that has had naughty school children clamping their sphincters shut for generations. "Just because you have the privilege of being waited on by others, doesn't give you the right to disrespect them in such a violent way, or any way." She shakes her head. "You surprise me. I would have thought better of you."

She heads back towards the counter where Simone is already dishing up a second meal and Ash has wet some cloths to help with mopping her up.

Adam stares daggers at me.

I shake my head and spread my palms in a futile attempt to make him understand I had nothing to do with it.

He picks up his book and lunchbox and storms out of the cafeteria.

Sergeant Bowman throws me an 'oops' look that is mostly sincere, and I narrow my eyes at him, because as funny as he thinks this is, he's just made my working life a whole lot more complicated.

Chapter thirteen

T he chatroom has a soundscape of muted lasers being fired and the occasional explosion in the background.

It's relatively discordant with the laughter that peppers our conversation, but I've long since tuned it out.

I say, "I see you challenged WickedWickhamOG to a duel. Did he dare to threaten your dignity?"

Liz "Ffft"s. "As if I would let him anywhere near my numerous petticoats. He was just being an arrogant, boastful dick, and continually moving in on my plays. I wanted to remind him there is one monarch of the alien-killing Austen world, and she is Queen Elizabeth."

"And how did that go for you, then?"

"Bastard gutted me. My intestines flumped out on the flagstones. They really make the graphics graphic these days, don't they?"

"Had you come to me before your pride forced you to make a rash decision, I would have counselled you against taking on the expertise of WickedWickhamOG. There's a reason that dude has 'Original' as part of his name. I mean, you'd think the fact he had no numbers in there would have been a bit of a clue."

"I didn't think he'd want to hurt a lady."

I laugh. "His whole character arc is about hurting ladies. Haven't you read the book?"

"I have. And I've seen the Colin Firth and Keira Knightley versions."

"You should have known better, then."

"But he's a cretin, and I really wanted to deliver some femme justice. It's Darcy who metes it out in the story. We're not under the social restrictions of that era in this game, because it's not authentic in any way and it's played by people who live in the twenty-first century. It's time to take the power back."

I pause. "But you didn't."

"No."

"He skewered you like a pig on a spit roast."

Liz sighs. "He did."

"What was the viewing number?"

"Just under seven thousand."

I laugh. "That'll teach you to go all ego during live streaming."

"It absolutely did. He has a rabid following of frothing fans."

"So what's your next genius move?"

Liz doesn't miss a beat. "Change my name or get a kitten."

"I...completely see the logic in both those choices."

"A kitten will teach me there is more to life than beheading invaders from space."

"Or you can dust off your skirts and continue the game as Lizobeth2000 like the big woman you pretend to be."

"Yes, I could. I might just wait a day or two first. For the sake of my dignity." She sighs. "Why can we be such dolts when it absolutely matters that we shouldn't be dolts, and have our shit together in a totally meaningless simulation? Sorry, I'll clarify that statement. When I say 'we', I'm mostly just referring to me."

"I don't have my life sorted out there. In here I'm Mister D'Arsy, game master extraordinaire. Out there it feels like I'm barely scraping by."

She doesn't say anything for a moment and I hope what she is about to present is something I can give advice about, because I like being this person. The help-y one. At the moment, it feels like all I do is ask others to prop me up. It makes me feel less useless, like I actually have some agency.

"Have you ever had a famous friend?" asks Liz.

Friend? Thinking of my father and brother, I say, "Kind of. You do?"

"I have a friend who's...moderately renowned. Their public image is growing and it's hard. I'm finding it hard and I feel like an arsehole for finding it hard."

"Why?"

"Because I feel like I'm being unsupportive."

"But why is it hard?"

"Because if we want to spend time together anywhere public, it's impossible to relax. There's always someone – a fan, or somebody indifferent who wants to make a joke in front of their friends, or someone who's...not a fan, or there's media. I've been making us hang out at home and it feels, I don't know, selfish."

I know exactly where Liz's head is at. "To not allow them to lead a normal life? To kind of prevent them from leading a normal life?"

"Yeah. Exactly."

"How does your friend feel about the attention?"

"He says it's part of the job. He accepts it, or at least, he behaves as if he does. I think if he struggled with it, to articulate it would allow resentment to creep in, so he's not willing to admit it. But I don't really know."

"Do you know what? I think you're a really good friend to be even having this dilemma. And I also think he would understand."

Max does. He knows exactly the potential negative effect constant attention, especially the bad kind, could have on me. We haven't talked about it, either, but I know he does. "Your friend might be willing to wear his fame and all it entails, but he won't be willing to let it affect those he cares about who haven't asked for it. He'll know you're uncomfortable. Has he asked or passed comment about you guys always hanging out in private?"

"No."

"I bet you anything he's fully cognisant of why you're doing that, and he's okay with it. Just talk to him about it."

"What? With words and stuff?"

"You could always communicate through the medium of Pictionary, though it's probably less efficient."

"I prefer interpretive dance. But then, anything I attempt on the dance floor could be considered interpretive. That's the beauty of it. You don't need a sense of rhythm to absolutely nail it. In fact, the more tempo-challenged, the better."

"I'm really gutted affordable VR tech is only at headsets and hap gloves."

"You want a demonstration?"

"I need a demonstration."

"Imagine a new-born foal. Now imagine that new-born foal negotiating a catastrophic machinery failure at the ball-bearing factory."

I laugh. "You're lying. No one's that uncoordinated on the dance floor."

"I am lying. I actually have an excellent sense of rhythm, but I love to hear the dulcet tones of a simulated D'Arsy laugh too much, so I had no choice."

I grin. I'm stupidly, utterly delighted. "My laugh is such an addiction, you have to wildly misrepresent yourself? What else have you told me that's total fabrication?"

"Addiction might not be an accurate description, but I enjoy it very much."

And we're into this Flirtland we've recently discovered, which is exciting but a total waste of time seeing we'll never meet.

Still, I can't help myself. "Enjoying something to the extent of compromising your integrity to get it might actually be considered an addiction, and I know for a fact you have a lot of integrity and value it pretty highly, so, ergo, I stand by my claim."

"You don't need 'so' and 'ergo' in consecutive word sequence. They mean the same thing. It's tautological."

"Nice redirection to avoid agreeing with me. Also, say that last word again."

"Tautological."

"I just got a shiver down my spine. Polysyllabic words have never had that effect on me before."

After a pause, Liz says, "If you have a partiality for me being grandiloquent, please asseverate your desideration."

Wow.

I think my knickers just caught fire. Though I can't let her know that.

"Those aren't real words. You can't just reel language that sophisticated out of your brain on cue."

"And yet, I did."

"What are you? Some kind of Oxford scholar?"

Liz, sort of, giggles, which is probably the result of the vocal processor throwing the pilot's voice into a higher register, and which should probably be unbecoming on a ruthless alien slayer, but is in fact, strangely becoming. "I am not an Oxford scholar, though I'm flattered you might come to that conclusion."

After a pause, I say "Can you do it again?"

"What? Confabulate with sophisticated locution?"

God yes. "I can only guess what you just said from the context, but I've just reached the conclusion everyone else is wrong."

"Wrong about what?"

"French isn't all that."

Liz laughs. "By 'all that', I take it you mean 'sexy'?"

"I...might do."

"You think I sound sexy when I use unnecessarily complicated language?"

"The 'unnecessarily complicated language' is the sexy part. That it just happens to be coming out of your mouth is of no consequence."

She says, "I see," but I hear the humour in her voice.

I've certainly never found it sexy before. Adam's academic patois has always seemed superior, like he has to prove his intelligence and in order to do that, must make everyone else feel dumb.

Lizobeth2000 just makes me feel, kind of, turned on.

"Though, I would appreciate it if you kept it to a minimum, because I don't actually understand what you're saying even if I admire your superior word usage."

"We could do a knowledge exchange. You give me game advice, I teach you the meaning of polysyllabic words that aren't in common use."

"That'll take the mystery out of it and it'll lose its appeal. Half the reason people go weak kneed over French is because they don't know what's being said. I once told a guy my gynaecologist was a crying mushroom and he had his tongue down my throat in under a minute."

"Did you mean to tell him your gynaecologist was a crying mushroom?"

"I might have mashed a few phrases from my *French in a Minute* phrasebook I bought for the school trip to Paris I never went on. I've been since, but not with the phrasebook."

"They have conversation starters about gynaecologists in French phrasebooks?"

"Hey, you never know when you're going to have a vaginal emergency."

Liz is quiet, like she's either laughing on the inside, or trying very hard not to imagine a vaginal emergency.

So I say, because I am suddenly flummoxed over my choice of conversation thread and her silence, "I've never had a vaginal emergency." But I don't leave it there, because I am a moron. "Except for the usual fungal stuff, and that's pretty easy to deal with, so I suppose it's not really an emergency." I finish with, "actually."

My display momentarily pixelates like its shuddered.

Somewhere in the Regency background, a church bell tolls sombrely.

An alien clears its throat.

Eventually, Liz says, "I'll have to take your word for it."

"Yep," I agree, because words are finally failing me after I've already done the damage with them.

Liz laughs.

I laugh.

"That was awkward," she says.

"Nothing like a bit of thrush talk to kill the conversation."

"No, no. I enjoyed that. Discussing other people's fungal infections is my other favourite pastime."

"After interpretive dancing?"

"At the very least, it made me forget for several seconds what a total numpty I made of myself in the game last night."

"Well, in that case, you're very welcome."

"I couldn't help noticing that back *before* we talked about how you've never had a vaginal emergency, you mentioned something about troubles in your real life. I also can't help noticing we always end up talking about me and solving my problems. So, tell me. What's troubling you, Mister D'Arsy?"

Ha. Big fat ha bloody ha.

I wasn't laying that out for her to see. No way.

"Nothing. I misrepresented myself. My life is perfect."

Chapter fourteen

Fourteen years ago

Adam rolls down the roof of the first storey verandah and off the edge.

I lean out the window and yell, "Adam!" as he hits the water of the swimming pool with a *slap*.

The startled barbecue attendees look from him to me and back again.

And my dad, standing next to Adam's dad with barbecue tongs poised, has a face that melts from an 'O' to thunder in the space of my heartbeat.

I can't see Adam, but Dad yells, "You little shit," at the swimming pool and I know Adam is alright.

Except.

Dad drops the tongs, Mum yells, "Ethan!" and Dad jumps in the pool.

The wet crack of knuckles connecting with face is very loud in the sudden quiet.

And then all hell breaks loose.

Chapter fifteen

I step on a diagonal to avoid colliding with a texting pedestrian and answer my phone. "Hi, Max."

Max doesn't bother with pleasantries, which is a sure sign he's not particularly happy with me. "I've just been on the phone to Mum."

Oh.

My duplicity is probably out of the bag then.

"When were you going to tell me you'd been charged?"

"Um." I hadn't thought that far ahead. "When I felt brave enough to tell you they'd also been dropped?"

I stop at the edge of the footpath and wait for a car to merge into traffic before crossing the road.

"No, Sarah. Please don't do this."

"It's too late. I'm on my way to meet with Jeffrey Wainwright's lawyer now."

Max is quiet. I imagine him counting to ten or breathing diaphragm-deep to find his inner calm. "Why are you taking this route? It's so far beneath you, I –"

"Because I can't do it to you, Max. I'm not going to be responsible for hamstringing your career before you've had a chance to fully prove what you're capable of."

"It won't hamstring my career, Sarah. It will be an unslightly blip for a while and then it'll be forgotten."

"And I have other...obligations," I say over the top of him.

"Mum gave you the shaming the family speech, did she?"

"Among other things."

"Where are you? Are you meeting at Bob's offices?"

I don't answer, which we both know means "yes".

Max says hurriedly, "Don't do anything until I get there," and hangs up.

I peer at the traffic. It's moving the kind of sluggish one would expect for this time of the afternoon, so I doubt Max will make it in time if we reach a quick agreement.

I increase my pace anyway and get to Bob's offices with five minutes to spare before the appointment time.

I spend that five minutes alternatively glaring at the large clock on Bob's wall and the bright reflection in Bob's spectacles as he finalises our version of the proposed agreement with single-finger jabs at his computer keyboard.

There's no point in me saying he should have had it ready well in advance for me to read over, and not be placing commas with seconds to spare. Because he hasn't. And at 104, he's unlikely to change his work habits now.

By the time the printer whirs into life, it's been just under fifteen minutes since I spoke to Max, and just over two minutes since Jeffrey Wainwright's lawyer was due to be shown in.

A bead of sweat tickles the skin under my left armpit as it rolls towards the fabric of my bra, and I clamp my arm against my body to halt its progress.

I've already tried to put a stop to my knee jiggling, but as soon as my mind shifts to willing Jeff's lawyer to walk through the door, or for Max to be stuck in a traffic jam, it starts up again.

There's a knock at the door and it swings open to reveal the practice's receptionist gesturing for a three-piece-suited white man to enter.

He takes one step and Max dives past him and closes the door in his face with a, "Won't be a minute."

"Max!" I stand and he holds up a finger before bracing himself on his knees to catch his breath.

Bob's magnified eyes blink in alarm behind his thick spectacles. For all I know, he could be imploding on the inside like I am.

Eventually my inner panic reaches the motor-control part of my brain and I collapse back into my chair and grip my hair. I let out a "Fuuuuuuu–" and Max cuts me off with, "How much does he want?"

He straightens and his chest rises and falls with his heavy breaths.

"We haven't got to that part yet, Max. You barged in before numbers could be placed on the table."

Bob's chair squeaks as he leans forward. "Are you wanting to up the bid? Your sister's only got fifty thousand in the pot. Might need a bit more if they play hard ball."

"*Fifty thousand*?" Max eyes the door and lowers his voice. "You're borrowing fifty thousand pounds off Mum and Dad?"

"It's what they were willing to lend."

Max places his hands on his hips. "No. Just no. I won't let you do it. I won't let you be saddled with a debt that big because you think the right thing is protecting me and saving Mum and Dad the embarrassment of having a child with a conviction."

"It's the right thing to do."

"No, it's not and you know it. I'm willing to deal with whatever fallout *might* happen, so if you take me out of the equation, it's just Mum and Dad's agenda you have to consider. Fifty thousand pounds and letting Jeffrey Wainwright get away with sexual misconduct is too high a price for you to pay to save them some humiliation."

"Max," I whisper, "I couldn't live with myself if it ruined your career."

Max throws his hands up into the air. "It's not going to. You'd have to be selling state secrets or be having an affair with the Prime Minister herself. Yes, it might get difficult for a bit, but it's a storm I can ride out. Other politicians have weathered far worse."

He walks towards me and squats in front of my chair. "What if it's not enough? What if Jeffrey Wainwright, knowing you descend from a very wealthy family, tries to fleece you for as much as he can get?" His eyes pinball between mine and he grabs my hands. "You need to be prepared for that. I wouldn't put it past someone like him to further his exploitation."

The door bursts open and Max stands as Jeff's lawyer strides into the room. "I'm not sure what's going on, but our appointment was at four-thirty. If you'd like a resolution to this situation, I suggest we proceed."

He sits in the chair next to me and crosses his legs as Bob stutters, "Q-quite."

Max shifts to stand behind my chair. He places his hands on my shoulders and even though they are only resting on me, I feel the full weight of them.

Bob looks at me.

I look pointedly at the printed agreement in front of him and he says, "Oh yes."

He turns it around and slides it towards the lawyer who doesn't bother to look at it. "We can worry about the details later. What we need to establish first is the financials. My client won't settle for anything less than one hundred and fifty thousand pounds."

My head is filled with static.

One hundred and fifty thousand pounds? I couldn't raise that money. And even if I could, how would I ever pay it back?

Max's hands tighten on my shoulders and I hear myself say, "I don't have one hundred and fifty thousand pounds."

"You're a Fulton," says the lawyer. "You'll be able to find one hundred and fifty thousand pounds."

Bob, who I'm vaguely aware should be leading the negotiating, says, "It's not an unreasonable amount, Sara."

Not unreasonable? The static turns to a high-pitched whine.

I can't think. I can't *breathe.*

"Sara? What do you say?"

Max squeezes my shoulders again and the whine thins into nothing.

I look at the lawyer. He is far too young to be as confident as he is. He looks fresh out of whatever public school rounded his vowels so perfectly.

I grab Max's hand and he squeezes my fingers.

"Ms Fulton?"

"Yes?"

"What's your decision?"

My decision –

Someone else with my voice says, "My decision is…"

I stand, pulling Max behind me and we are running out the door.

Chapter sixteen

"**I**s it really necessary to wear your stab-proof vest in the cafeteria?" asks Simone as she hands Sergeant Bowman his cup of coffee.

He glances at me before saying, "Yup," and taking a sip.

I huff and before I can shape my indignation into words, Jas says, "Fair call. Sarah does have a liability factor that some might find charming and others, scary as fuck. I, myself, am all for nurturing it, because I like to laugh at others' misfortune."

"I am *not* a liability!" I eye Sergeant Bowman, "The most dangerous thing I handle is a fish slice. Jas has more chance of stabbing you than I do."

"Except I'd use a double-bladed knife to stab someone, not a kitchen knife," says Jas. "Less resistance when both sides are sharp."

Ash turns and looks at her. "You do know you work in a police station, right? And there's a police officer standing within hearing and arresting distance?"

"It's not a confession, Ash," says Simone, with a laugh. "It's an opinion for a hypothetical situation."

"Or is it?" says Jas.

"Stab-proof vests," says the sergeant, as if Jas and Ash and Simone have said nothing, "protect you from more than just stabbing. I'm also not too keen on having my ribs broken. Or the knobs on my spine scraped. It really hurts when that happens."

"Oh my God, yes," says Simone. "When you knock the scabs?"

Jas nods. "Painful AF." She looks over at Ian. "That means 'as fuck', Ian."

Ian nods solemnly. "Back in the 80s it meant Air Force. Or audio frequency. I can't remember if anyone referred to their Athlete's Foot as AF, but it probably stood for that, too."

"To be fair, Ian," says Ash. "AF could still stand for all those things."

As Simone adds, "Amniotic fluid," to the list of things AF could stand for and Jas says, "Anal fissure," I exit the kitchen area to collect the trolley the cafeteria users place their dirty dishes on.

Sergeant Bowman eyes me warily as I walk past him, but doesn't move from his ankles-crossed, cup-poised-in-front-of-mouth position.

I narrow my eyes at him in return and carry out my duties without anything happening to prove a stab-proof vest worn in my vicinity is warranted.

Once Ash has emptied the trolley, I wipe it down and set about returning it. Without the weight of the crockery, the wheels glide effortlessly over the polished linoleum.

"How many of these have we got?" I ask.

"There's one in the chiller," says Ash. "For wheeling out heavy stuff."

"You guys ever think about having a trolley derby? Make the tables into a course and have one person riding and one person pushing?"

"No," says Ian. "Though in 1979, I thought about surfing a skip bin down Clearview Street."

We wait for the rest of the story, but evidently, thinking about surfing a skip bin down Clearview Street is as far as Ian got.

"I'm up for it," says Simone. "Can't be much harder than racing around the supermarket with a screaming toddler in your trolley, trying to put everyone in the store out of their misery as quickly as possible."

"I'm one hundred percent up for spectating," says Sergeant Bowman. "I might even be tempted to place a wager on who wins."

"I'm not convinced," says Jas. "I think you should demonstrate the derby qualities of that trolley before any of us commit to holding one."

I'm not fooled. I know Jas is being provocative, because as she's already admitted, she's entertained by my willingness to court disaster.

I am also happy to rise to the challenge, because in my head, it will be a lot of fun, and I've evaluated the risks. There's not *too much* that can go wrong. "Alright. I'll perform a perfect glide to park the trolley home. Behold."

I push the trolley out to the cafeteria floor and line it up with the space on the side of the wall where it sits. Then I run three steps and leap onto it belly first so that I can assume a Superman pose, one fist on my hip, the other punching the air in front of me.

My trajectory is good.

My propulsion is not. I've totally overcooked it.

I collide with the rubbish, recycling and compost station as Adam rounds the corner into the cafeteria.

Behind me, there is an explosion of laughter and the scramble of colleagues disappearing.

Once the small swing doors to each of the station's compartments have slowed their furious *fwap*-ing to a casual *fwap*-ing, I dismount.

I had aimed for graceful, but the trolley is higher than my leg length and I miss my footing. I topple sideways to land on my back.

Another wave of laughter rolls around the cafeteria.

I peer up from my prone position at Adam who has stopped walking to channel all his energy into rolling his eyes.

I grunt my way to standing and straighten my shirt. "You're early," comes out as an accusation. Because it is. How am I meant to pretend I don't exist if he doesn't stick to the rigid itinerary he's set himself?

"I was hungry. I also have a reasonable expectation of not having to come in here to eat and witness the staff riding the equipment in a flagrant disregard for health and safety regulations. But, of course, I should have known better."

Once upon a time, I thought I was in love with this person.

I've never congratulated myself on my escape, but perhaps this is the moment I should.

"You know, it is possible to have fun without being reckless, Sarah. Frankly, I'm surprised it's taken you this long to end up with a conviction, considering most convictions are the result of some degree of stupidity."

"I'm not stupid, Adam."

"Then act like it."

I throw out a cutting, "*You* act like it," because only I'm allowed to think I'm stupid and hearing it from someone else has withered my reserve of decent come backs down to the ones last heard when I was seven.

Adam sighs and says, "So I hear you were given an opportunity to settle out of court and you chose not to."

"That's right. Bribing him into dropping the charges is not something that sits very comfortably with me."

Adam shrugs. "It happens."

"It's *unethical*. You're seriously advocating for it?"

"I'm advocating for you to consider options that result in an outcome outside of your self-interest."

I take a step backwards and am then angry at myself, because it looks like an acknowledgement that Adam is right. "I'm not being self-interested. I'm making a stand against men who abuse their positions of power. I want to make things as uncomfortable for that man as I can. I can't do that if I accept all responsibility for what happened and pay him off for the privilege."

"But there's a very likely risk you'll expose your brother to the kind of venomous rhetoric that forces resignation. If you'd stopped to look outside of yourself, you would see that."

"I do see that. Max is happy for me to take that risk in order to bring about justice for women. You don't recognise Jeffrey Wainwright's behaviour as entrenched? As something that needs to be fought against and stopped?"

"Of course I do. But there are compromises one has to make to protect the people they love. Surely you see that."

Someone steps between us to unload the rubbish from their tray.

"Look," continues Adam, "if you're intent on doing your usual show boating, for goodness sake, ask the judge to withhold your name."

Usual show boating? Making a stand against abusers of power isn't *show boating*. It's refusing to be yet another victim. It's being empowered when so many people don't feel they can make a stand, or that they'll be listened to if they do.

Isn't it?

I march back to the staff area, crouch down behind the castle and announce, "Adam doesn't find me very funny," in response to their questioning expressions.

"Understandable," says Sergeant Bowman.

"I find you funny," says Simone. "And my opinion matters more than his, because you actually like me, so you can just ignore him."

"But that was funny AF," says Jas. After a pause, she adds, "The fact that he's clearly dead inside doesn't make him any less fit, though."

"No," says Sergeant Bowman.

"And that thing with the coffee the other day was prime comedy gold," Jas continues. "Really bad. But also really funny."

"It was like watching a car crash in slow motion," says Ian. "You know it's going to happen and there's nothing you can do about it."

"A clown car crash," says Simone.

"You'd think the poor bastard would prefer to eat his lunch in the stairwell," says Ian.

"I didn't actually do anything. You do know that right? I literally had nothing to do with the sequence of events that led to Adam getting his arse hauled over the coals by Pants Suit woman."

"You must have conditioned him with your luck see-saw to think you did have something to do with it," says Ash. "That kind of accusation comes from a deeply traumatised place."

Deeply traumatised.

Okay, maybe a little traumatised.

"*Or,*" I say, "it could have everything to do with him just being an arse."

"You can be an arse who's traumatised," says Ian.

"Just because you're an arse, doesn't lessen the validity of your trauma," says the sergeant.

"Please tell us, Sarah," says Simone. "Why does he think you've set out to ruin his life?"

I hold up my hands. "I will tell you on the condition you believe that I haven't actually set out to ruin his life. He's completely neurotic. I might have, however, had a few...run ins with Adam that haven't ended very well for him."

"Like the skiing incident," says Ian.

"Like the skiing incident," I confirm.

"Is this one better or worse?" says Jas.

"Depends on whose point of view you sympathise with."

"I'm not sure. I like you and all that, but he is fi-ine, and I can be fairly shallow on occasion."

I shrug my shoulders. "I can cope with your fickle rewarding of sympathy, Jas. I'll keep it concise." I glance at Adam through the arrow slit and take a deep breath. "So, there was this time I had been out all night celebrating an incredible review we got in the *Sunday Times* and I'm doing my walk of shame home and I bump into Adam who's on his way to do his bar exam and I'm still drunk and still high on our success and I give him a hug that he doesn't want and...vomit down the front of him."

"Jeez," says Simone.

"I know. It was awful. He didn't have time to go home and change and so just washed it off, and then he failed the exam. Apparently the smell of it put him off."

"He must have been pretty bloody angry," says Ian.

He was. Very angry.

"So, that's the happy story of how Adam didn't become a barrister and I got a promotion on the back of the review."

"What's the difference between a barrister and a solicitor?" asks Ash. It's the first time I've heard him seek information from us instead of giving it.

"Barristers do the dramatic stuff in court. The ones with the wigs," says Ian.

"That's terrible," says Simone. "It's like tripping someone up and kicking them when they're down."

"It's like *accidentally* tripping someone up and and then *accidentally* kicking them when you're clumsily trying to help them back up again. I didn't mean for it to happen. For any of it to happen."

"Couldn't he redo the exam?" says Jas.

"Exactly! He seems pretty happy in his career path. It's like he was looking for a way out of barrister-dom or something. Not that he would ever see it that way. He'll always choose to see me doing rash, stupid things that have a negative impact on him and hold it against me and call me selfish and inconsiderate."

Nobody rushes in to reassure me I am neither of these things. Instead, Ian says, "I think maybe you should keep your flak jacket on, sergeant."

Brilliant.

I peer out the arrow slit at Adam and a wave of heat rolls over my body as I replay the words he just threw at me.

Christ. Am I really doing the right thing?

Max might be being all noble now, but he could truly regret it later.

I feel suddenly and furiously resentful that after all the debate, all the second guessing and soul searching, my brother and I have come to a decision that sits right with us, and in just a few choice words Adam has scuppered all confidence.

I make myself shift my thoughts by focusing on the team resuming their duties.

Sergeant Bowman runs a finger around his empty coffee cup and licks the foam off his finger. And Simone says, "What was the review for?" as she stacks take-away cups on top of the coffee machine.

Ah.

I haven't told them what I did before police stations became a daily fixture in my life. Mostly because if I was employed as a cafeteria cook and knew there was a gourmet chef on the team, I'd probably feel self-conscious about my abilities, or intimidated, or something.

"It was for, um, a restaurant I worked at?"

"Which one?"

"The Trading Post."

Simone shakes her head. "Never heard of it."

"Isn't it all posh nosh?" says Sergeant Bowman, "with prices that make your eyeballs bleed?"

I answer, "Yeah," and charge a customer for a Chicken Tikka Masala sandwich and a Coke.

"Ooh," says Simone. "What did you do? I bet they tip well in those swanky restaurants."

I wait for the receipt to print out and hand it to the customer before saying, "I worked in the kitchen."

"Like as a kitchen hand or something?"

"Sarah's a chef," says Sergeant Bowman, because of course he would. "Aren't you, Sarah?"

There's three long seconds of silence before Jas says, "You are shitting me."

I turn. Everyone's staring at me, as well they might.

Jas points at me with her knife. "You're a chef who's worked in gourmet restaurants and you say nothing like this whole experience is too beneath you to bother mentioning it?"

Um.

Yes. I can see now how it might look that way.

"I'm not employed to cook, so it seemed unnecessary to mention it. It wasn't a snobbery thing. I just...didn't want you to feel like I was judging you."

"Except by you not saying anything, it feels as if that's exactly what you've been doing this whole time."

Right. She's right. God I'm an idiot.

"Do you mean to say we could have been chatting about the joys of food this whole time and swapping trade secrets?" says Ian. "I feel a bit robbed, I have to say, Sarah."

"Cheated, is the word, Ian," says Jas through narrowed lids.

As per usual, I've behaved out of my self-interest. Out of the discomfort *I* feel and not anyone else's because I didn't bother to check. "I'm sorry. I thought I was doing the right thing, but I can see it was very presumptuous. I would actually love to talk food and swap trade secrets."

"Well, don't bother to start yet," says Jas. "I have to do some mental manoeuvring from seeing you as a right twat to a just a partial twat first."

"Fair enough."

A customer steps up to the counter and tells us there's spilled juice or something on the floor between some tables.

Everyone looks at me.

"What? I can't do it. Adam will see me."

"Yes, you can," says Jas with a grin that is positively demonic. "Clean up the spill, Sarah."

"Ash, can you do it?" My voice isn't quite a wheedle, but it's not far off.

He says, "Sure," and wipes his hands on this apron.

"No," says Jas. "Anything out on the floor is Sarah's job. Sarah has to do it."

"I also think Sarah should do it," says Sergeant Bowman.

"Your opinion doesn't count," I tell him. "Being you are not cafeteria staff. Simone, you don't think I should have to do it, do you?"

"I don't know. I want you to do it, to see what happens, but I feel bad about wanting you to."

"That counts as a 'yes' vote," says Jas.

"An 'I don't know' has never counted as a yes vote, Jas," I say. "Ian?"

He throws up his hands. "I'm Switzerland."

Jas grunts and rolls her eyes, then settles them on me. "Here's one way of looking at it. The spill is behind where Adam's sitting. As long as he doesn't turn around, he won't see you." She picks up a pair of tongs from her workstation and glares at everyone else. "The other way of looking at it is that if any of you volunteer to do this job for Sarah, I will insert these in the closest orifice to hand and release the catch." She gives them a snap.

"I change my vote to a 'yes'," says Ash.

"Which makes a majority of me and Ash to Simone's one," says Jas.

"What about my vote?" I say. "I get a vote. And it's 'no'."

"You know," says Simone, "on second thoughts, I think I also want to see what happens. I'll fill the bucket for you."

"Traitor," I say to her disappearing back, but accept the inevitability of the situation and begrudgingly offer my thanks when she returns.

The mystery liquid does indeed appear to be orange juice. It is also within a table's distance of Adam, which would have meant I'd have had to master the art of wetting and squeezing a mop in complete silence if Adam hadn't chosen to block out any Sarah-related noise by wearing ear buds.

So this shouldn't be too hard to avoid fucking up.

It takes three passes to make sure the surface of the floor isn't sticky and as I raise the end of the mop and place a "Caution" sign over the wet section, the crash of several metal objects hitting the kitchen floor sends me spinning towards it.

The end of my mop hits something with such force, I lose my grip on it and it clatters to the ground.

Oh God.

I hunch my shoulders and imagine knocking Adam face first into his salad de jour and don't want to turn to face whatever new shitty reality's just descended.

When I do, I find I am wrong.

It's far worse.

I'd managed to time the swing of my mop with Adam standing to leave.

Beneath his glassy eyes and pale face, a large, wet patch covers his crotch like he's lost his bladder control and I know without a shadow of a doubt there's no coming back from this.

Chapter seventeen

"Do you ever not like yourself when you're around certain people, or a certain person?" asks Lizobeth2000. "Like, they somehow make you behave in a way that is not who you think of yourself as?"

"Yes." I think back to Adam's angry accusation I mopped his crotch on purpose, despite my profusely apologetic assurances. In the end, I lost my temper too when I probably should have been more understanding. The man was in a reasonable amount of pain, after all. "I know exactly what you mean. How do you behave when you're around that person?"

"Completely reactive. I think I have a mean streak – just sometimes – but I'm mortified it rears its head and I am definitely not proud of myself in those moments."

"Can you take a step back, a few deep breaths before you choose your reaction?"

"I know I should, but it's like the behaviour's entrenched."

"Then avoid them. Do you have to interact with this person?"

"Sometimes."

"At least you're aware of your behaviour. That's a start."

"In other words, I'm not trying hard enough."

I say, "Do *you* think you're trying hard enough?" and feel this is a question I need to ask myself.

Liz says nothing, which means "no".

There's nothing else to add. She knows what she needs to do, but I can't help feeling I've failed her somehow. I haven't soothed out her concerns, been able to give her the magic bullet I think she expects of me.

There's no usual gratifying conclusion to this conversation. No, "You're so insightful, Mister D'Arsy," no "You see me," or whatever.

I feel sort of empty to have led her up the *Take a cold hard look at yourself* path and left her there. I want to be able to provide some kind of comfort or reassurance, and it might be for the sake of my own ego, but I think it's more likely because I care about her. Very much. And I don't want her to be feeling shitty about herself. "Do you believe in star signs?"

"No. I believe in science."

I laugh. "Right. That's the end of that conversation, then."

"What were you going to say?"

"Something deeply meaningful and profound and reassuring, but it doesn't matter now that you shat all over it with your, frankly outrageous science...upholdery."

"Upholdery?"

"Upholdery. As soon as a word enters the sphere of hearing, it's valid."

"That logic sounds as tenuous as someone's personality being determined by a constellation. What other words have you validated by giving voice to them?"

I have to think about it. "Mansoon," I say after a couple of seconds. "As in waiting for the mansoon after a dry spell of involuntary chastity."

"Got it. Mansoons and vaginal emergencies. I feel like I'm getting to know you well." Her tone is teasing, and I grin and imagine myself blushing becomingly were I a blusher.

"I also gave birth to the term 'cravvy'. You know, when you're craving something so bad it makes you crabby. Like, 'I'm all cravvy for a Big Mac right now'."

"So...like hangry, but much harder to understand without an explanation. And less catchy."

"Yes, okay. *Now* it's the poor cousin to hangry, but I came up with it first. Those hangry creators stole my word meld approach. I should be acknowledged for its genius."

Liz laughs. "You're right. Combining two words to make one that covers both meanings definitely didn't exist before you thought of it."

I love it when she teases me. I laugh and wait, hoping for more.

"How wide was the dissemination of 'cravvy'?"

"Not a single concentric circle. I had to explain what I meant every time I said it. I tried for a whole year to bring it into common usage, but the Oxford Dictionary weren't interested. Even after the fifteenth phone call."

Liz pauses before saying, "You are joking, right?"

"I might be. You know anyone who works there? I'm thinking of seeing how open they are to adding 'upholdery'."

"The 'U' section is a little slim to be fair. I'll have a thumb through my contacts."

"Thank you."

She shifts in her seat and her avatar wobbles. "You know, a thought struck me the other day that I'm not sure my ego is comfortable with. Anybody who's paying attention to who attends the chatroom probably thinks I'm a really shit player who needs an extraordinary amount of help."

I only give a split-second pause. "Yes."

"Brilliant."

"Take comfort in the knowledge it's useful for our egos to be uncomfortable on occasion." I feel clever and sage-like after I've delivered those words, then try to ruin it by following it up with, "A thought struck me that this whole chatroom situation is like a twenty-first century version of pen pals. But with instant gratification."

"How so?"

"In that you have no idea who you're communicating with, but you make the commitment anyway."

"That is true. I've missed a whole season of *Love Island* due to the time I set aside for our sessions."

"It's good to know I hold more appeal than waxed bodies gyrating in a hot tub."

"They do hot tub gyrating?"

"Probably."

Liz withholds her opinion on this, so I am forced to ask, "Are you mentally reviewing your priorities?"

"I wouldn't dream of it. Metaphorically. There might be a chance I dream of gyrating bodies in hot tubs literally. Actually, that's not true. I don't get enough sleep to waste energy on dreaming."

"You don't get enough sleep?"

"Not on nights I talk to you."

I am very happy that the system doesn't have the sophistication of portraying the fluttering of my heart or the self-satisfied expression that I'm sure is radiating out of my face. I mean, I shouldn't be surprised, given this is not the first clue Lizobeth2000 has given that her life outside work maybe orbits a little bit around her visits to the chatroom, but I can't help but be thrilled anyway.

And while her meaning is only inferred, I have no qualms about being completely candid. "Liz, you are, by a lead of light years, the best thing that happens in my life each week." And with my commitment to a court case, I really really need good things to happen to me on a regular basis.

She doesn't reply. I hope, like me, she is basking in that knowledge.

"I take it by your silence, your ego *is* comfortable with that piece of information?"

"My ego is...very content."

My level of happiness rises to a position on the joy spectrum that feels disproportionate to her level of words.

Liz says, "So, you're saying, you want to remain twenty-first century pen pals but with instant gratification for some time longer yet?"

"I don't want to sound needy or anything, but God yes."

Chapter eighteen

"What's this for?" I ask Simone, pointing at the short microphone sticking out of a panel set into the counter. It's been there the whole time I've been working at the cafeteria, and today, finally, I've thought to ask about it. It has two depression buttons next to it that read *Talk* and *Lock*.

"It's for the loudspeaker system."

That much I had worked out. "But why is there a loudspeaker system?"

"From the days when people used to place orders, I think. It was before my time. I guess this place got big enough and busy enough to warrant a move to a more efficient system. Counter food or nothing."

I look out over the cafeteria floor. There are only a few customers and I am too curious to worry about whether I might be disturbing them.

Pressing the *Talk* button I say, "Spilt milk hazard in aisle 3. Aisle 3. Can Jerome in frozen goods make quick with the mop please?"

My voice bounces off the surfaces of the cafeteria's seating area and most of the heads of those sitting at tables turn to look at me. I say, completely unnecessarily, "Still connected."

"Yep," Simone agrees and tips a bag of coffee beans into the grinder.

Jas shouts over the sizzle of frying mince, "Show us your beatboxing skills."

I answer, "No," because I don't possess any and am not prepared to try to find some now.

"Ash," says Jas, "you do it."

He answers mildly, "Just because I'm black doesn't mean I'm hip hop-flavoured."

I offer, "I can do a good impression of one of those heart imploding moments when you've sat in the airport lounge too long drinking chardonnay slammers?"

I pinch my nose with my fingers and say in a nasal voice, "Calling passengers Reverend Josie Wilkes and Duchess Eleanor de la Croix, please make your way to gate 13a immediately. Your plane is ready for immediate departure and your bags are about to be off-loaded."

"As if," says Jas. "A reverend and a duchess would never be seen doing chardonnay slammers together."

"But they would have 'reverend' and 'duchess' on their boarding pass. Have you ever noticed the ridiculous list of honorifics?"

"Honor what?" asks Simone.

"The signifier before your name, like Mr and Mrs. I once travelled to the States as General Sarah Fulton. I was hoping to at least get a salute from the air stewards if not a free G and T, but the one who checked my pass when I entered the plane just looked at me witheringly like I was taking the piss or something."

Ian clucks his tongue. "How very dare they?"

"That's what I said to him, but it didn't go down particularly well."

"If I was going to have an honorific," says Jas, "I'd be Empress."

"I'm not sure it's an option on the booking form."

"It'd sound good though."

"I think Reginald sounds good," says Simone. "I wouldn't mind that one."

"Ah," I say. "It's actually a name, Simone. And a man's one. It's not an honorific."

She stops dishing up cannelloni for a customer and looks at us. "Is it? It sounds like it could be a military title. Or a clerical one for that matter. The Reginald Simone Clay is here to see you m'Lord."

"I agree," says Ian. "We could petition to have it recognised as a title."

Ash says, "I think we should do away with honorifics altogether. It's pretty archaic to demand a woman indicate her marital status. And it renders non-binary people invisible. Like usual."

"And who on a plane needs to know if you won the privilege jackpot and were born a peer," says Ian. "You're just another sardine in the tin can. Being a duke isn't going to save you from being eaten first when the plane goes down in the Andes."

"Grim," I say as I notice Adam is sitting in the cafeteria now a table of two have departed and revealed him. I'm not sure how long he's been there.

I honestly don't know why he keeps making himself miserable.

Actually, yes I do because I've known him a very long time. Stubbornness coupled with pride and self-righteous determination to make a point.

It must be exhausting being him.

I crouch, because I've made a promise to Adam, and tell the customer her two-course meal and drink comes to sixteen pounds fifty. She stands on her tip toes to give me the cash over the top of the perspex screen.

I can just reach her fingers without revealing my head above the parapet.

I retrieve her change and we do the whole just managing to reach each other routine again in order for me to hand it to her. "Thank you. Enjoy your meal."

Jas peers at me from where she leans over her workstation, her head propped up in her hand. "That must be really humiliating."

"It's not humiliating. I'm not humiliated."

She raises her eyebrow.

"I am in control of this situation and I choose for it not to be." I'm making doubly sure there can be no courtship of any Adam/Sarah disaster. If I don't exist, it can't happen.

The team continue their tasks, glancing at Adam and then at me from time to time as if expecting a nuclear explosion at any moment.

"Can you guys stop it, please?" I ask once the customer I finished serving walks away.

"Stop what?" asks Simone, her eyes wide in feigned incomprehension.

"Willing a disaster. It's not going to happen because I have the situation completely under control."

"But do you?" asks Jas.

"Yes. As long as I don't have to move from this spot, nothing can happen."

"That method didn't work so well with the coffee incident," says Ian.

"It worked fine. It was Sergeant Bowman moving from *his* spot that caused mayhem."

"Or the mop incident."

I don't say anything, because the only reasonable response is to agree and I don't particularly want to acknowledge that event actually happened.

"What I want to know," says Ash, "is why the universe keeps you both on a path of collision. I don't believe in fate, but if I did, I would attribute it with being the reason for your continual run ins with each other."

"Fate," says Simone. "That sounds romantic."

"Except it isn't," I say. "There isn't anything remotely romantic about vomiting on somebody the day they fail a career-making exam."

"Or breaking their leg and making their girlfriend dump them," says Jas.

"I didn't make her. She made that decision all on her own."

"That can't be the sum total," says Ash. "That dude carries too much resentment for it to be based just on those incidents."

I don't say anything.

"Tell us," says Jas.

"No."

"Please?" says Simone. "You're the best thing that's happened in this cafeteria in months."

"Yeah," says Jas. "Don't deny us our guilty pleasure."

"While my heart bleeds for you, the answer's still 'no'."

The four of them stare me down, then Ian says, "Go on," and I find it very very difficult to not do anything Ian wants me to do, so I take a deep breath.

"Last year, I was exiting Max's flat when Adam was arriving and he pushed in the key code to the door at the front entrance as I pushed the 'exit' button, and then he pulled the door as I pulled it because I forgot which way the door opened. The door locked shut and wouldn't reopen and then the fire alarm went off and everyone in the building arrived in the foyer and couldn't get out."

"Oh my God," says Simone.

"Yeah," I say. "Smoke started to appear on the stairs and people started panicking and Adam shouted at us to stand back and disappeared. Then his car came round the corner and rammed the plate glass."

"Cool," says Jas.

"Not really," I say. "The fire brigade arrived after that. Turned out the smoke was from a malfunctioning smoke machine in an absentee DJ's flat. And that there was an override of the door system just above the skirting board that we probably would have spotted if I hadn't put my handbag there when Adam and I tried to jostle the door and argued through the glass about who broke it."

"Ah," says Ian. Then, "Yep. All electronic doors have an override for emergencies."

"What's the really bad part?" asks Ash.

I peer at the ceiling. "Adam's insurance company refused to pay for the damage to his car and replacement of the door, because the situation was avoidable."

"And you got off with a fireman," says Jas.

After a pause, I say, "Not right away."

"That's awful," says Simone. "He gets punished for being a hero."

"And you get rewarded for being a total muppet," finishes Jas.

"That's not fair. I wasn't a *total* muppet." I flap a hand. "Look, it all worked out in the end. It took a couple of probably very stressful months, but Adam managed to legal his way into getting his insurance company to foot the bill."

"But you still capitalised on the situation," says Ash.

I shrug. By which I mean "yes". Then I remember I'm meant to be hiding and crouch again.

I look out the arrow slit.

Adam stands to leave.

He hasn't seen me the entire time he's been here. Disaster-aversion objective complete.

I pluck the cloth and spray bottle from the shelf under the bench and sling them onto the counter, ready to hit the tables once Adam has disappeared.

"I think there's still something romantic about it," says Simone.

"Well believe it or not, there was a time I used to like him. Very very much, when he used to be a decent human being and before he got all uppity and used words like 'crude' and 'repartee' and then argued they still had verbal currency like a complete tosser."

I stop. And watch the tide of dawning realisation roll in, like I'm having an out of body experience, and wait for the horror to hit.

Because that entire monologue sounded as if it was spoken in stereo.

I look at the team.

They are not looking at me. Their faces are tuned to the cafeteria floor, expectant.

I hoist myself to my knees and peer through the arrow slit.

Adam is almost at the threshold of the cafeteria exit. He's very still.

And he's staring directly at me.

I shift sideways, as if he can actually see me through the narrow gap in the paper, and pull the spray bottle and cloth away from where I put them.

Both the *Talk* and *Lock* buttons are depressed.

Oh.

Oh shit.

"Um," I say and when I pull my tongue away from the lack of saliva glueing it to the roof of my mouth, it makes a cluck, which reverberates around the cafeteria. "Adam. I'm...really sorry. You weren't meant to hear that. Obviously. You're not...*that* much of a tosser. I was using hyperbole for the benefit of a good story." I grimace and say, "Sorry," again.

I shift my position and look back through the arrow slit.

Adam is gone.

"Alright!" says Jas with a glee that is incredibly unsuited to the situation that has just unfolded. "You shamesters owe me ten pounds each. I will thank you to pay up at my closest convenience, which is today, because I have my eye on a fumazing dress at Missguided. You know, with the hood and everything?"

I push myself to standing and say, with gritted teeth through the pain of blood flowing back into my legs, "Why do they owe you money? Did you guys have a wager going?"

"To be fair," says Simone, "Ian, Ash and I were backing you not to act in any way that would belittle, embarrass, or anger Adam."

"*To be fair*? How is that something you can say when you're betting on whether or not I do something arsehole-y?"

"Again, to be fair, you didn't *mean* to do something arsehole-y, and I would argue a lack of intention should render the outcome void."

"We didn't bet on the intention," says Jas, "we bet on the outcome."

I say, "And I would argue all of you have absolutely *intended* to do something arsehole-y by betting on my completely accidental ability to bring misery to Adam's life. That's a truly horrible thing to do."

"It was Sergeant Bowman's idea," says Ian.

Bloody Sergeant Bowman.

"And you happily participated. Just because it was his idea, doesn't make you devoid of responsibility."

"And yet," says Jas, "I have no qualms of conscience."

I walk past them towards the break room. "I'm having a time out in the back. I would appreciate it if, while I'm gone, you could think of how I can make this whole thing better without making it worse."

As it turns out I don't have a chance to make things worse first.

When I'm heading home for the day, Adam intercepts me, stepping out from a doorway near the cafeteria.

I jump. "Jesus! How long have you been waiting there?"

Adam folds his arms. "There's a betting ring, Sarah. Half the station's in on it."

"What?"

He rocks back on his heels and peers down his nose at me. "You're the favourite, of course. Odds are three to one. I've been told to relax and be a good sport, it's only a bit of fun."

Oh.

This is bad. I haven't anticipated the betting being anything other than what I'd put a stop to in the cafeteria.

"They're all laughing at me and laughing with you. Naturally, because the universe wills it, they think you're a crack up. You've probably orchestrated this whole thing so you can make some quick cash."

I say as mildly as I can, "No, Adam. I haven't orchestrated anything. I had nothing to do with your...moment in front of the power-suited lady, and today was just unfortunate. And I definitely have nothing to do with any betting ring. Sergeant Bowman set it up."

I push my glasses up my nose. "Look. I think it's truly horrible. *Really* horrible, but I doubt *half the station* are involved. It'll just be his mates. And everyone in the cafeteria."

Adam's arms drop to his side and he laughs at the ceiling. "Once again you've turned me into a public joke. I just..." Running his hands down his face, he continues with growing ferocity, "Honestly, Sarah. You could have got a low paying job anywhere. The only reason you picked this one was to torture me."

"Get over yourself, Adam. My decision to work here had nothing to do with you. I am truly sorry for today. I didn't mean to say anything through the loudspeaker at all, let alone something hurtful. I feel awful, but it was an accident. Nothing else."

"It's always an accident. There can only be so many accidents before it has to be intentional, Sarah." He drops his face so he's looking at me from under his eyebrows, and lowers his voice. "This is *my life*. You're making a mockery of it and it's unbelievably unfair. You think you're the victim of unfairness? That you have to be the poster child for sexual harassment in the workplace? What you're doing is undoubtedly harassment in *my* workplace." He jabs his chest with his finger and raises his volume. "I love this job. It's really challenging at times, but it's the best thing that could have happened after you lost the last job for me and you're ruining it with your thoughtless, self-absorbed...bullshit!"

He marches off back into the bowels of the building, too angry to notice the stares and stopped conversations that have happened as a result of his outburst.

But I do.

And with a sinking feeling I know he's just made a few people several pounds richer.

Chapter nineteen

Fourteen years ago

Max has to go around to Adam's now, because Adam doesn't want to come over to our house, which means Adam and I don't get to see each other much, because I don't really want to go to Adam's house.

His parents have never said I'm not welcome, but their son is sixteen and has probably been led astray by a promiscuous older girl, so they've never said I'm welcome, either.

In all honesty, the shame and humiliation and guilt is just too big for me to face up to them.

And then word gets out at school. Somewhat ridiculously, I'm a 'cougar' and the boys start to look at me differently, like I'll give them a blowie at lunchtime, and the girls look at me with grudging admiration or respect or something they feel they should be reluctant to give.

Being Head Girl I already have a high profile, and I desperately wish for this new-found attention to be temporary. For the story to fade into oblivion as quickly as the posts on everyone's Facebook feeds.

But Adam.

Adam is teased, the new joke around the lockers, the boy who got his cock out and made himself a ridiculous, public, sexual failure.

It's miserable. He is miserable. I am miserable.

And his humiliation is one hundred percent on me.

So, I plan a grand gesture. Because it happens in the movies, and I think small actions will never ever be enough. I've tried. They are not enough.

But I have absolutely no clue what that gesture should be.

Chapter twenty

I say, "God, I've had the worst day."

Lizobeth2000 says, "Tell me about it. Utterly awful. I don't want to think about it, really."

"Alright then. Tell me something good that's happened to you this week."

Liz pauses. "Something happened to me that I think you'll find entertaining. Will that do?"

"If it brings you joy."

"Retrospectively, I guess. I was in the supermarket the other day and I noticed that in nearly every aisle, I got what can only be described as a suggestive smile from a passing customer."

"Suggestive how?"

"As in, *let's shag out back between the dumpsters* suggestive."

"That sounds like a massive delusion of grandeur, my friend. Do you look in the mirror and the first thought that comes into your head is '*I'd* fuck me'."

She laughs. "I was not imagining it! I got the same look from a number of people, and none of them seemed to be doing much in the way of shopping."

"What were you wearing?"

"My arseless chaps. It was Wednesday."

"You wer-her not," I say through a laugh.

"I was wearing boring work clothes that in no way said, 'I'm available. Take me now'."

"So, was there anything special or unusual actually going on in the world outside your brain?"

"Apparently so. After I'd made my way to the bread aisle and circled back to get the stuff I missed, I noticed they all had wedges of vegan cheese in their carts, pointy end up."

"Every single one of them?"

"Every single one."

"What does that mean?"

"That vegan cheese is the new bananas."

"Ah, I'm pretty sure vegan cheese bears little resemblance to bananas. Unless it's actually made out of bananas, which it could be. It has a similar consistency."

"*You know* – if you're single and on the hunt, you go to a certain supermarket on a particular day at a certain time and you turn a bunch of bananas up in your cart to indicate your status."

"That is not a thing."

"It absolutely is a thing. Or was a thing. The new thing is vegan cheese, apparently."

"I take it you had a wedge of vegan cheese in your cart pointy end up?"

"I happened to have a wedge of vegan cheese pointy end up in my cart."

"And did you…?"

"No! I tipped my cheese over and made a run for the checkouts."

"Why vegan cheese? I suppose the code food would have to be something innocuous so you don't offend any ethical eaters." I scratch my nose, which to Liz probably looks like I'm poking myself in the face. "I'm thinking this has to be Marks and Spencer level of supermarket you're talking about. I can't imagine it happening at Aldi."

"I'm not sure there's anything suggestive you can do with a twenty pack of no brand baked beans."

"Not without opening them."

"Which has to beg the question, what do you do with your baked beans?"

"I don't need a twenty pack. You'd be surprised at the versatility of a single can."

"Um. Just give me a sec while my mind does some boggling."

"Take your time."

Liz doesn't say anything for a few seconds. "Aaaaand, we're back."

"Did you locate all the body parts that offer the best bean ski jumps?"

"I…have now."

I haven't actually done anything with baked beans apart from eating them.

And now flirt with them.

But I wouldn't want to ruin the moment by owning up to that.

Liz's hands form 'C's in front of her eyes, which means she's adjusting the goggles on her headset. Letting the steam out perhaps? "It, um, got me thinking. About how some people are perfectly comfortable putting themselves in a situation where they're vulnerable and how I very much am not that person. Do you ever worry about people judging you?"

"I get judged all the time, but I pretend like I don't give two shits. I don't think anyone would notice I suffer from crippling self-doubt."

"Really? Crippling?"

"Okay, maybe not *crippling*, but a lot more than I'd prefer to have."

"I've never been good at wearing my vulnerabilities, owning up to them and being brave in spite of them. Like, I've never told anyone I'm a raging *Pride and Prejudice and Aliens* gamer. Probably no one would ridicule me, but I can't bring myself to allow the possibility that they might."

"Do you think the worrying about what they might think of you is a reflection of self-doubt, that you're projecting your own judgement of yourself onto other people?"

Liz is quiet. "I've never thought about that before. Maybe. But where does the self-doubt and self-judgement come from? It has to be an external factor."

"I think mine is from the judgement of others, or one person in particular. If you hear a certain narrative often enough, you begin to believe it."

"And what's that narrative?"

"That I'm totally self-interested and never think of others."

She leans forward. "That's bullshit. All you've done in this chatroom is give to me. You've never once asked anything of me and have devoted a phenomenal amount of energy to easing my worries. You are the least self-interested person. Reject that narrative right now."

"I can when I'm in here with you. It's when I have to venture back into meatspace that the doubts come back."

"I'm sorry you have doubts about yourself. I really don't think you have reason to."

I shrug. Not that Liz can see it. "People can be dicks, but thanks." I know I sound flippant, but I do mean it. Her reassurance is something I need quite badly because of the anxiety I have over my decision to go to court. I want to feel at ease with it, but the thought of what might lie in wait for Max and the reality of being in front of a judge are both terrifying. "What's your self-doubt?"

She sighs. "That I'm too sensitive. That I let situations get to me when I probably just need to develop a sense of humour and not read too much into things. I wish I had thicker skin."

"I absolutely get that. It's taken me a long time to learn not to read too much into things."

"How'd you do it?"

"By reminding myself it's wasted energy imagining what's happening in other people's brains when I don't know."

"That, Mister D'Arsy, is very good advice." She slides her hand towards me and it rests, hovering above the simulated tabletop. "You know, I never have this issue with you. At least, I haven't for a long time."

I slide my hand towards hers. My table is lower and so when I turn it over, it looks as if her hand is resting in my upturned palm. "Why do you think that is?"

Liz answers quietly, "You understand me. At least, I think you understand me."

"I think I understand you, too. And...actually...I've never felt better understood by anyone other than you."

We are quiet for a moment, a moment in which we are basking in the glow of those declarations rather than being awkward about it. Or at least I am.

"So," says Liz eventually, retracting her hand, "are you going to Austencon?"

Austencon is not just for *Pride and Prejudice and Aliens* gaming fans, it's for all Austen fans, which means it's a massive event on the Austen calendar.

Yes. I was *so* going to Austencon and I kind of desperately hoped Lizobeth2000 was also going to Austencon.

I play it cool. "When is it?"

Liz laughs. "As if you don't know. You're a game master in the only decent Jane Austen computer game to have been created. You're going."

"Then why are you asking?"

"Because…. Because despite my conviction you're going, I still want to check, so I can buy a ticket."

My heart rate picks up.

"You'll go if I'm going?"

"Yeah. I thought, if you're comfortable with it, we could meet up and…share gaming tips in person. Or something."

I don't say anything, because I am too busy simultaneously mentally fist pumping and freaking out.

Liz fiddles with something on her real world tabletop. "You know, maybe we could have a…a friendship in real life, and if we meet and hate each other. All good. We walk away. No hard feelings."

Hate Lizobeth2000? I know her well enough by now, seen into her head, felt the way we mentally spark for that to be impossible.

I guess there's a very real chance we won't have a physical spark, but it's worth a shot. I've never connected with anybody as well as I connect with her. "Okay."

"Great. How will we know each other?"

"Will you be wearing a dress?" My tone is teasing, because Liz is a man. And then I wish I hadn't said that teasingly, because it is closed minded. He could be into drag for all I know.

Liz "Ffft"s. "I don't think they make empire-line frocks in my size. I'll be wearing an army uniform."

Bestill my beating heart. *Regimentals*. "I was hoping for Mr Collins."

"It's not too late. I saw a whole rack of Mr Collins costumes at the hire place due to the demand."

"You did not," I laugh.

"So what will you be wearing?"

Good question. I had debated long and hard about this. Whether *I* should go in drag as my gaming avatar, but swords are not allowed in the convention centre, for obvious reasons, so I'd just be an ordinary Darcy, which is very very boring.

"I *will* be wearing a dress."

"And how will I know you?"

"I'll be the one riding the horse."

Liz laughs. "You are joking, right? Or are hobby horses the new rage in Austen accessories this year?"

"*Or*," I say by way of answer, "I'll probably just have on a hot pink shawl and a yellow bonnet." Because I can never do anything in an ordinary fashion. "I'll be easy to spot."

"That sounds...authentic."

"It's authentic for me, the person behind Mister D'Arsy."

"Intriguing."

I want to know what's in her head. In my head, the person behind Lizobeth2000 has kind eyes and a permanently amused smile on his handsome face. And hair. Because I never thought I'd actually meet him and so my mind has been at liberty to entertain ideals. Other than that, I assume he's white because white men are the biggest demographic in the gaming world, but I'm happy to be wrong.

So.

How has he imagined me?

Chapter twenty-one

Fourteen years ago

It is the end of the school year and the end of my school career. As Head Girl, I am required to give a speech at prize giving, which is held at the final assembly for the year.

I listen to the Head Boy, Christian, give an entirely generic speech about how true success is in the trying and not the achieving that he probably downloaded from the internet the night before.

I have written an original speech, but wish I'd had the thought to just rip one off a website. It was really hard to write. It is designed to motivate the outliers, the kids that don't quite fit, but that is just as yawn-worthy as the Head Boy's speech and the Headteacher's speech before that. I know that even if I give it my full enthusiasm, the audience has long-since tuned out. They've been sitting in their seats listening and clapping and listening and clapping for an hour and a half now.

I take the podium.

Adam is sitting five rows from the back. He sits low and peers down at his lap.

I stare at him, but he doesn't look up. He doesn't want to look at me, at the source of his misery.

That is when I know this is the moment for my grand gesture. To prove my feelings, that the fallout from merely wanting to physically express those feelings is inconsequential. And fuck everyone else. They don't matter.

I open my mouth, not exactly knowing what will come out, but having a firm grip on the sentiment I want, that I need to deliver.

"This year, I got to know someone I'd been around for the last couple of years, but properly, truly. I saw into their heart and their soul and really liked what I saw."

Adam's head pops up and he shifts in his seat.

"I was incredibly lucky to have that person see who I am, too. To appreciate my thoughts and feelings, my terrible jokes, my fears. And was unlucky enough to have it all taken away because of a stupid, stupid thing that happened and everyone felt they needed to have an opinion about."

The students nearest Adam are now turning to look at him.

He doesn't seem to notice. He stares at me, and I stare at him and let the words tumble out. "And so I stand before you, my heart laid bare. I want things to go back to the way they were before, but I can't change what happened. I can only tell you how much I miss you."

It isn't enough. I need to go further, give more proof about what he meant to me.

And then the opening words to Taylor Swift's 'Love Story' spill onto my tongue and I begin to sing.

Titters break out around the hall. I ignore them. This is about me and Adam and nobody else.

I get to the part about Adam being Romeo and the titters and sniggers grow into laughter. People in the front of the hall crane their necks to try and find Adam. The people towards the back already have.

Christian, who's a rugby-head, but a decent guy shouts, "Shut up, you wankers."

The Headteacher tells him off and stands, presumably to shut the whole shit show down, but Christian beats him to it.

He steps around the Headteacher, grabs my hands, and shouts, "Thank you, Sarah, I feel exactly the same." Then he proceeds to kiss me.

I don't know what to do. So I do nothing and let him kiss me.

When he pulls away, he says, "That should shut their holes," like he has actually rescued me and not made everything a whole lot worse.

I look at the audience who are either closing their dropped jaws, "Ooh"ing, or watching Adam run out of the school hall.

And I know if Adam wasn't a total laughing stock before, Christian and I have made doubly sure that he is now.

Chapter twenty-two

The morning of Austencon dawns grey and drizzly, which has absolutely no bearing on my mood because I am bubbling with nerves and excitement and not even a bit of miserable London weather can stop the fizzing in my veins.

My worry about what the press can do to Max once word of my court case gets out, after what they did to Adam six months ago, might just be enough to bring me back to earth. But I tamp it down because I don't want anything to ruin this day.

Max is away doing ministerial PR at a union for care workers, so he doesn't get to witness my transformation into a Regency punkster.

Olympia comes round at 8 am to help shape my hair into something resembling Austen lady fashion. Most of it will be hidden under my bonnet, but the bits that do show need to be artfully arranged and I have very little experience with any kind of delicate placement of hair because I've never been terribly interested.

To compliment my hot pink shawl and pale-yellow bonnet, I have a deep teal dress, and have coordinated the remainder of my accessories with pale yellow gloves and my pink Doc Martens.

Were I in a black and white photo I might look authentic, but my outfit is deliberately a one hundred percent Sarah Fulton adaptation. I want to give Liz the right impression about me so there are no surprises or disappointments later.

Olympia takes one look at me and says, "You remind me of when I was courting Mr Bingley."

Naturally, I hesitate before asking, "I remind you of *what*?"

"I used to date a man called Leonard Bingley who preferred me in long dresses and petticoats. The more petticoats the better, so he had to really work for it, if you know what I mean."

I have a fair idea of what she means.

"At least I *think* his name was Bingley. Could have been Brinkley. Or Bingham, for that matter."

Her confusion is understandable given it takes three mimosas to get my hair to do what it needs to. I have one more hour left to get to the venue at the time Liz and I agreed to meet.

Knocking back a syrupy coffee to counteract all the mimosas and allow myself to question my decision-making about the need to drink that many, I nip into Sainsbury's on the way to the Tube and buy a wedge of vegan cheese.

I pin it in place on the crown of my yellow bonnet. I hope the joke is appreciated and not taken as presumptuous, and am then plagued with doubt that it will absolutely be taken as presumptuous and have to fight the urge to take it off again.

I do my best to forget it's there, but the few odd looks and the occasional laugh I get on the street make my palms sweat and I'm thankful I'm wearing gloves to soak up all the extra moisture.

I get a reprieve on the Tube due to everyone ignoring me per normal Tube etiquette, as if a woman dressed in a rainbow regency costume with a cheese bonnet adornment is nothing out of the ordinary.

A couple of other people in my carriage are dressed in regency outfits and that number swells as I disembark onto the station platform.

Once we've reached the damp air above ground, the stream of Austenites becomes a torrent. People hustle towards the venue, impatient to be first inside, to see the exhibits first, to head the queues at the book signing tables for spin off and adapted publications, to meet Keira Knightley first, who is rumoured to be in attendance, though I highly doubt it.

And I am overwhelmed by a simultaneous need to strip all my hot layers of clothing off and to empty the contents of my stomach. I hope my freak out has leant an attractive flush to my cheeks, but I suspect I just look pale and sweaty.

However, I don't have time to either strip or vomit, or even run away. I am jostled forward by the tide of excited fans, funnelled through the ticket check and deposited next to a man in regimentals.

And then I am standing on the face of the sun, burning up into a pile of dusty pathetic-ness, and I can't work my tongue to get his attention.

He turns and –

– I am back on planet earth inside a convention centre.

He is not Lizobeth2000 judging by the amount of pimples angrily decorating his very young, brown face. At least, I'm fairly certain I haven't been duped by a teen posing as a life-experienced adult.

I don't give him the benefit of the doubt and walk past him to exit the foyer and enter the enormous exhibition centre.

The vastness of the displays, the riot of signs and colours and noise almost *almost* makes me forget the kaleidoscope of butterflies fighting for freedom in my stomach.

Their wing beats intensify as I scan the crowd and see the number of people dressed in red.

It's all I see. Everyone else pales to grey, and there's *so many* and I've only managed to cross one off the list.

My only hope is to sensibly follow Liz's suggestion and meet at the signing stand for the author of *Pride and Prejudice and Zombies.* In all practicality, it's probably easier to just allow him to find me.

A short man in a red jacket pushes past me and I blurt, "Lizobeth2000?" before I miss my moment.

He turns and I see he is in fact a woman.

She gives me a blank look and turns back again to push through the next cluster of people.

Two down.

Even though it's a meeting point, I do actually have my paperback copy of *Pride and Prejudice and Zombies* in my bag and very much want to see Seth Graham-Smith in the flesh and stutter out a request for a signature.

When I get to his table, however, the queue is already snaking past five other exhibits and I know that with all the coffee I've drunk, I will need to pee before I get to him.

I don't want to lose my place in the line or risk missing my opportunity to meet up with Lizobeth2000.

So, I shout, "Oh my God," loud enough so most of the line can hear me. And then, "It's Keira Knightley. *Oh my God* it's totally Keira Knightley!" I point back the way I've come and several people break away from the line to head off in that direction.

I get to move up two exhibitions-worth of space and just see the top of Seth's head in the middle distance.

I wait and shuffle forward a pace, then another one.

Pulling my phone out of my bag, I check the time.

Liz is ten minutes late, which equates to ten years in Nervousland.

I try to surreptitiously sniff the damp patches under my arms as I shuffle forward another step.

I smell fine, if a little desperate.

I check my phone again. The time is still the same as when I last checked.

A bray of laughter erupts from near the head of the line and I hope it's Seth joking with fans and that he'll be just as cool with me when I don't manage to keep my shit together, and start gushing.

I pat my head to check the cheese is still there, even though I already know by the weight of it.

And check the time again.

One minute has elapsed.

I emit a sigh and behind me, a deep voice says, "It is a truth universally acknowledged that a woman in possession of a wedge of vegan cheese, must be in want of an alien hunter."

My heart stops beating for a second, then kicks back into life with a vicious palpitation.

I know that voice.

But.

It can't be.

Christ.

It is, isn't it?

It is unmistakeably him.

My brain boils and melts and a roar of angry insects builds and builds in my ear canals.

"Mister D'Arsy?"

I'm turned away from him. My hair and face are obscured by my bonnet, which means only one of us is aware of this new turd-soaked reality.

So.

There's only one thing for it.

I pick up my skirts and run.

Chapter twenty-three

Fourteen years ago

Adam blocks my number after that. He unfriends me on Facebook. I am told he doesn't want to see me when I go around to his house to talk to him. Max says Adam refuses to talk to him about me and he doesn't want to get involved anyway.

I am utterly, devastatingly heartbroken.

Chapter twenty-four

Adam doesn't come into the cafeteria for the next week, which I am entirely grateful for.

I think.

Mainly because I have absolutely no idea how to feel about the Austencon bombshell, apart from "Aaaaaaaaaaaaaaaaaaaaaaaaaaaargh", which is not an emotion that's particularly constructive.

I've made an attempt to analyse it, by which I mean I've stood at a safe distance and poked at it with a very long stick to see which dangerous animal will rear its head, and so far the only creature I'm willing to entertain is disbelief.

Namely, that in a world where random order reigns, the chances are so ridiculously slim that I'd know a person on the other end of their avatar in the chatroom, and even more infinitesimal that that person would be Adam Stringer.

I mean, *come on*! How is that fair?

There's also a significant portion of *on what planet does Adam-rod-up-the-butt-Stringer spend his free time murdering aliens while dressed in an empire-line frock?*

That Adam belongs to the boy I knew fourteen years ago.

Does this mean the old Adam is still there? I didn't ruin it? I didn't destroy his sense of self when I humiliated him so, so completely in front of a lot of people?

And –

– I don't know what this means.

I mean, it doesn't mean anything, because it can't. Just because I entertained the idea of a real-life romantic attachment to Liz and I now know Liz is Adam, only means that there will be no further entertaining. Ever.

And yet –

I haven't been able to bloody-well switch those feelings off, have I? I wish I could, but they're still there, swirling and undulating like storm clouds, and refusing to settle into anything concrete because I also have all these other feelings from before, which of course means I'm absolutely terrified of seeing him. I have no confidence I won't betray the truth of the chatroom in one tongue-before-brain blurt, or that I won't become more of a confused mess.

The fact he doesn't come into the cafeteria each day only makes my inner storm roil more violently.

When Sergeant Bowman comes in to lean against the coffee machine and wait for whatever surprise Simone produces in his coffee foam, I ask him where Adam is.

"Keeping to his office. He's been very quiet these last few days."

"Oh."

"Maybe I shouldn't have run that betting ring."

"No," I agree, knowing the betting ring is only one part of a Sarah Fulton-induced picture. Poor Adam.

He's been made to feel a laughingstock at work.

And the person he'd developed a romantic attachment to deserted him.

"Mind you," says the sergeant, "it's not as bad as that thing in the press about him six months ago."

"What thing?" asks Simone over the squeal of the milk frother.

"It doesn't matter," I answer, because it was awful but it's dealt with and not worth rehashing.

It doesn't make the effect of it all go away, though.

I look out at the table he normally sits at.

It's just like all the others. Square, plastic-laminated, beige, unremarkable.

But it looks wrong, like it has no right to be empty.

Christ. Do I...miss him?

The twenty minutes he insists on spending are usually a total pain in the arse, because I have to do my job while pretending I don't exist. Surely, I can't miss that incredible inconvenience.

A customer pulls my attention away from the empty table, and I smile and ask them how their day is going and take their money.

Then I stare at the table and stir the storm clouds a bit more, feeling the guilt build again, because, as it turns out, Mister D'Arsy is a complete arsehole.

Not only did he run away from Liz, but immediately after Austencon, he resigned from being a game master.

It was a pretty shitty move, but what other choice did I have? I couldn't answer the "why?" Liz would throw at me, and I couldn't behave as if I didn't know who she was.

The special thing Mister D'Arsy and Lizobeth2000 had going is ruined and will never be gotten back.

The sergeant tells a story about someone who mistakenly got arrested for soliciting and everyone laughs on cue.

I am only half listening and do not.

"You're very quiet today, Ms Fulton," he says.

I am.

I am thinking about how I should resign from my job and find another one so Adam never ever has to cross paths with me.

It's a big call. I might not be able to find another job, but I should give him that.

"Yeah. Sorry," I say distractedly, because the desire to be generous towards Adam is not something I've felt in a very very long time.

And I know why it's there. It's as if the Adam who looks down his nose at me is doing mortal battle in my brain with the chatroom Adam who's funny and self-effacing and thinks I'm wonderful and talks to me about anything and everything.

I just –

– can't reconcile the two. No matter how hard I try. They're two completely different people.

And then there's the fact I recognise chatroom Adam from all those years ago, which suggests, perhaps, that could possibly be the real Adam.

God it's a mind fuck.

Sergeant Bowman licks froth from his top lip. "You seem overly concerned for someone I didn't think you liked very much."

"I..." I start, then stop. I can't even refute it. I don't like that Adam very much. The one who comes in to the cafeteria.

But Lizobeth2000? I couldn't get enough of her. An hour or two in a chatroom was never enough to slake my thirst for her company.

There's only one thing for it. I laugh.

Strip away all our troubled history, our present frictions, and we still have an essential connection. The one we found fourteen years ago.

"What's funny?" asks Jas.

"Nothing. Absolutely nothing at all. It's really rather sad, actually." And I mean it. Ours is a tragic tale. It's one hundred percent saddening.

I hope he's okay.

I *really* hope he's okay.

A couple of days later, during a Sergeant Bowman coffee break, Adam rounds the corner into the cafeteria and a hot flush rolls over my skin, quickly followed by a cold one.

I drop to the floor.

He's reading some papers so I don't think he's seen me, but I have to be sure he doesn't.

I crawl towards Jas' station and hide behind it.

She peers down at me with a frown. "What are you doing?"

"Hiding."

"Why?" she says as she looks up and spots Adam. "Ah ha." She looks down at me again. "What's wrong with the castle?"

Nothing's wrong with the castle. Except it's made of paper and isn't a real castle and can't offer the psychological protection I need.

She turns her wrist over to look at her watch. "It's only ten."

That's right. Adam has never come into the cafeteria before his lunch hour since I've been working here. It's highly unusual behaviour.

"So." Jas punctuates this with a *thock* as she slices through something on her chopping board. "What have you done this time?"

"Nothing."

As far as Adam's concerned.

As far as I'm concerned, a very very big thing, that's probably also a very very bad thing.

Ash and Ian turn to look at me, crouched by Jas' feet.

"Don't look at me," I hiss. "I'm not here."

They turn their faces towards the cafeteria floor.

Ash looks at his watch and offers an unhelpful "ominous".

Ian says, "I reckon so," with a grin that suggests he's joyously buckling up for the ride.

"Shut up," I whisper.

"He's coming to the counter," says Jas.

Christ. Why is he coming to the counter?

He knows, doesn't he? He's going to accuse me of playing another sick game with him. Of being the worst kind of human being and toying with his emotions.

I didn't. But I *feel* like the worst kind of human being anyway.

"He's reading something." Jas is still talking at her normal volume, which is two notches higher on the dial than anyone else's.

"Lower your voice," I hiss at her. "You're a foghorn."

The fact he's still reading whatever he has in his hand, slows my racing heart slightly. If he is on the war path, he won't be working on route.

Would he?

This is Adam, who only allows himself a twenty-minute break a day. Maybe he would be shoehorning in some work on the way to bringing someone a large reckoning.

"Does he look angry?"

"He's reading."

I try not to sigh, even though her response is perfectly reasonable. "Is he *walking* like he's entertaining an anger fest?"

"Like all jerky and fast paced?"

"Yeah?"

"Not really."

I crawl over her feet, forcing her to shuffle back with a "Get-toff!" and poke my head around the end of her station.

His head appears in my limited field of vision as he nears the counter and my treacherous, treacherous heart stutters and kicks up its already elevated rate to a thundering gallop.

He stops in front of the coffee machine. "Double shot long black, please," he says without looking up.

Sergeant Bowman throws out an "Alright, Adam?"

Adam replies, "Fine, thank you, sergeant," with a politeness Sergeant Bowman probably doesn't deserve.

He's not fine. He looks terrible.

A surge of concern pushes up from my stomach towards my tongue and I have to bite down on it to stop myself from blurting something that could be considered caring and giving myself away.

He has bags under his eyes and the hand holding the paper shakes so the edges of the sheets quiver.

He's not reading it. His eyes don't move. He's simply staring at it.

Jas, perhaps noticing this, too, says, "She's not here. You can stop hiding in your piece of paper."

His shoulders drop a centimetre and I shuffle back before he spots me when he looks up.

Things must be really bad if he's come in wanting coffee. He's never come in wanting coffee before.

Simone bangs out the grinds from the previous coffee and flicks the thing that releases the beans from the grinder into the thing with the handle that clips into the machine.

And I can't bear it any longer.

"Ask him how he is," I tell Jas.

Jas, who is dicing at half her usual pace, clucks her tongue. "Sarah wants to know how you are," she calls out.

I elbow her calf and she steps away from me.

There is a pause before Adam says, "I thought you said she wasn't here."

"She isn't. I just know she'll want to know."

The tone of Adam's "Right" is dubious and I don't blame him. I wouldn't trust the sincerity behind me asking him how he is, either.

I whisper, "Ask him if he's taking breaks and not working through his lunch hour."

There's an almost imperceptible pause before Jas calls out, "She'll also want to know if you're deliberately avoiding the caf."

"Tell Sarah she can take an educated guess on that one."

Jas looks down at me. "You can take an educated guess on that one."

I freeze.

I don't know whether to entertain my fury at Jas for callously giving me away, my self-reproach for ever trusting her, or my mortification that Adam knows I am actually here, am hiding and am asking questions via a double-crossing proxy.

Adam's voice is a mix of resignation and anger. "Christ, Sarah. Stop playing games."

I'm not.

Am I?

I don't want to be. And I don't want Adam to think that I am.

"I'm not trying to play games," I call out. "I'm trying to make things easier for you by pretending I'm not here."

"Probably shouldn't have asked all those questions, then, yeah?" says Sergeant Bowman with an amused lilt.

"Well, not via Jas, anyway," laughs Simone.

It is not at all funny.

It's every way of awful.

I know that far from making things easier for him, I'm making everything a whole lot worse. He doesn't look like he can handle worse. He looks like he's one bad thing away from the straw breaking the camel's back.

"I'm resigning," I blurt.

Jas, Ash and Ian stop what they're doing and look at me.

"You're what?" says Simone.

Jas says, "No, you're not," in a tone suited for talking down a child wielding clippers and the desire to give the cat a haircut.

"Why...would you do that?" asks Adam, his voice betraying the shock I can't see in his face.

Simone adds, "Yeah, why would you do that? I like you. I want you to stay my front counter buddy."

"Because it's best."

Adam sounds at the point of exhaustion when he says, "Sarah, for God's sake, come out so you can talk to me properly."

He's right. I should.

I crawl out from behind the workstation and slowly push myself to my feet. Then, not knowing what to do with myself, I sidestep over to my castle. It doesn't offer a barrier between us due to where we are standing, but it offers a small amount of comfort, which I need in this very very awkward moment.

I pick up the table cleaning cloth and say to it, "Sergeant Bowman's been a complete nobstick. He's really sorry about the whole betting ring thing." I raise my eyes and glare at the sergeant, who puts his coffee down and stands upright.

"Um, yes." He turns to Adam and arranges his features into a mostly convincing expression of contriteness. "I was a *total* nobstick. Sorry, Adam."

I shift my gaze to Adam and can't bring myself to meet his eyes.

His face might look terrible, but nothing else does.

Have his shoulders broadened since I last saw him?

I tell myself not to be so ridiculous and then wonder when his suits became so well-tailored to his athletic frame. I can't remember them ever suggesting the musculature of his arms before.

Or thighs.

Christ, it's hot in here.

"Why is it so hot in here?" I say aloud and then wish I'd kept it in my brain.

"Four ovens, a steriliser and bain-marie?" ventures Ian.

And Ash helpfully adds, "It's no hotter than normal, Sarah. You feeling okay?"

Jas grins and flicks her eyes to Adam. "Sarah's feeling just fiiiine. Aren't you, Sarah?"

"It might be really hard for you to find another job," says Adam.

This...is not what I was expecting. I thought Adam would rejoice at the thought of me being out of his life for good.

"I'll find another one," I say with a certainty I in no way feel.

Adam gives a glimpse of the decent guy I know him to be. "I can't pretend it's not going to make my life easier, but it's only twenty minutes of my day. I can probably put up with twenty minutes of my day in your at-a-distance presence."

I don't want him to be that decent guy. It's not helping the tempest of emotions that are refusing to separate themselves out and offer any clarity.

"No, you probably can't. Look at you." I raise my eyes to his and his frown has a question mark in it, like he is genuinely confused as to why I might do this thing, and not high-five-ing himself on the inside.

He doesn't say anything for a beat and I can't look away.

There are things working in his brain that I want desperately to have an insight to and can only guess at.

I am overwhelmed –

– *God*, by a desire to hug him?

Wow.

I don't know what to do with it.

Our mutual gaze goes on for one second longer than it should and –

Actually, yes, I do know what to do with it.

I need to throw it on the ground and stomp on it, before I breathe life into it, because Adam most definitely *does not* want me to take him into my arms and offer him comfort.

He confirms this when the question mark disappears and he says, "I don't need you to martyr yourself for my sake," and we're back to the usual angry, resentful Adam.

"I'm not martyring myself. I'm resigning because it's the right thing to do and we both know it."

Simone holds out Adam's coffee and says, "Here you are, love," as if the whole few minutes happened in another universe.

Adam pulls a note from his pocket, slaps it on the counter, and turns to walk out of the cafeteria. "Don't resign, Sarah. That's a really stupid thing to do."

I do it anyway.

Chapter twenty-five

Adam then comes into the cafeteria every day and eats his lunch as if to prove he can put up with twenty minutes a day of my at-a-distance presence. He can't know I've already made my decision official and am seeing out my two weeks' notice.

He rounds the corner of the cafeteria at precisely 12.35 pm, which means at 12.30 pm I glance compulsively at the space he'll appear in until he does, and my stomach rotates like I'm on a roller coaster ride.

I hate it. I hate that I now have that reaction to him.

It's precisely how my body reacted to him when I was a seventeen, then eighteen-year-old.

I don't need to be reminded of that time, because it was spectacularly awful. And it was very sweet and wonderful.

I also don't need this added complication. The level of fuck-up-ery in my life is already at maximum and I don't have the energy or space to allow myself to fall for my brother's friend. Again. Especially when he doesn't like me very much.

God how can things be this unfair. I'd trade lives with anyone, even Simone with her pack of snot-missile-armed children.

And yet, without fail, when Adam rounds that corner with his long-legged stride and broad shoulders, I turn into the same nervous-excited girl-woman I was the first time around.

My final day of work can't come fast enough.

And then, a few days later, I get some news.

Max comes home during my final week of work to find me furiously pulling everything out of the pantry and on to the floor.

He watches me for several moments. "Everything okay?"

"No. I'm making teriyaki tofu with sesame slaw and garlic-steamed edamame, and I can't find my Kishibori Shoyu." I place a bag of flour on the floor with a little too much force and flour jets out one corner. "Fuck!" Throwing my head back, I let out a growl of frustration, then I shout at the bag, "Where the *fucking fuck* is my soy sauce?"

I look up at Max, who's peering at me with both concern and bemusement.

"I can only find the supermarket brand. How can I make decent teriyaki sauce with supermarket brand soy sauce?" I resume my search. "I *can't* make decent teriyaki sauce with supermarket brand soy sauce, because it's *shit* and beneath my teriyaki sauce-making sensibilities."

Max gingerly steps in between the contents of the pantry and opens the fridge. "Is this it?" He holds out my bottle of Kishibori Shoyu.

I stare at it. Then I look at Max, before refocusing on the bottle. "It doesn't go in the fridge! Soy sauce needs to be kept at room temperature."

"Okay." Max hands it to me. "You were the last one to use it, though."

I growl again in lieu of saying thanks and take the bottle. He's right. Max wouldn't dream of using my special artisan soy sauce.

I move to where my other ingredients are laid out and measure the sauce by eye into a bowl.

"Should we clean this up?"

"Yes. I don't feel like it right now, though. I just want to get on with making dinner." I hope my words shut this whole thing down. That Max will quietly put everything back and say nothing to me because he knows cooking is my happy place and I need some alone time there.

He does put everything back, but he doesn't do it quietly. "What's going on?"

I don't say anything.

"Sarah?"

After a pause, I say, "I'm just really stressed out right now, okay?"

"I can see that. Why?"

I give the contents of the bowl a vigorous stir. "Two reasons."

The flat's buzzer announces Olympia's arrival and after Max lets her in, bottle of wine in hand, she says, "Why is there food all over the floor?"

Max puts a box of baby potatoes on the bottom of the pantry. "Because Sarah has two things to tell us."

Olympia, happy to ignore the logic of his answer, says, "Oh goodie. Let me guess. You've been named as the new face of Victoria's Secret. Or the new boobs, as it were."

I can't help myself. "Yes."

She whoops then shoots her hands upwards, before clasping them to her chest. "I've never been right on the first guess before. Usually I'm wildly off the mark, like aiming for Chichester by shooting at Mars. You said that, Sarah."

"Did I?" I say with feigned mildness.

Max says, "Well done, Olympia," and eyes my A cup breasts with raised eyebrows and a quirk of his lips.

"Thank you."

I place pieces of floured tofu in a pan while she cracks the bottle of wine. When the silence stretches past her third glass pour, she says, "Oh. You're not really the new boobs of Victoria's Secret, are you?"

"No, Olympia. I'm about ten years too old for a start. Then there's the fact they tend to choose someone who actually has breasts."

"You have breasts."

"Not ones with the prerequisite ability to swell alluringly when stuffed into a push up bra."

"Well, my other guess was that you've been notified you didn't get your name withheld by the courts, but that's just ludicrous given the inefficiencies of all things English and administrative, so I decided to put my money on Victoria's Secret instead."

I pick up my 7-inch chef knife and vigorously slice cabbage by way of answer.

"Oh," says Max. "That's a bugger. But not unexpected."

It's not unexpected and it shouldn't be the kick in the guts that it is. But with the press not having the ability to print my name, my connection with Max would have remained unknown.

Olympia says, "But you said you had two bits of news. Are you sure the other thing isn't that you're a Victoria's Secret model?"

"Yes, Olympia. I am one hundred percent sure I'm never ever going to be paid for wearing designer underwear."

"Oh. Shame. I bet the buffets they have on those shoots are utterly scrumptious."

"And the fact Sarah could do with the exorbitant fee they'd pay her," adds Max.

I snort. "They don't feed models."

"They feed boob models, Squimpy. Breasts require a high diet of protein and powdered collagen, taken whichever way you want." She places a thumb to her right nostril and sniffs as if clearing cocaine residue, then winks at me. "I read about it in an interview with Miranda Kerr in *Vanity Fair*."

"Boy, it's a real tragedy I'll be missing out on that."

"Isn't it?"

Max, sensibly moving the conversation on, asks, "So, what's the other thing?"

The other thing is so big and scary, I don't want to acknowledge it, let alone think about it. I pull the letter out of my back pocket and slap it into Max's hands before returning to the hob to poke at the tofu.

The paper crinkles and after several seconds, Max says, "You've got a court date."

I do indeed.

"It's...quite soon."

"Yes." A mere six weeks' time.

"Don't those things take months?" asks Olympia.

"It's just so she can enter her plea."

I set the edamame to steam and take a long slug of wine.

Max comes over to me and pulls me into a hug. "I'd be scared too, but I'm sure the thought of it is more frightening than the reality."

"You can't be sure, Max. You've never had to go to court."

"No, but I've been scared of things happening in my future that I don't actually know much about."

I know he's trying to be reassuring, but all he sounds is patronising. And minimising.

I turn back to the hob. "I don't really want to think about it."

Olympia, helpful as always, says, "So, how are you going to do that for six weeks if you haven't got a job to distract you?"

"Work my way chronologically backwards through Max's wine cellar and cry myself to sleep watching *The Notebook*?"

"I can see two things wrong with that picture," says Max. "One, I don't have a wine cellar."

"And two," adds Olympia, "the best movie to cry yourself to sleep over is *John Wick* not *The Notebook*."

"Why would you cry yourself to sleep over *John Wick*?"

"All that violence for the love of a dog. It's really rather beautiful."

I laugh, because while what she's said is more disturbing than it is funny, I need the release. And laughing is preferable to crying.

"Sarah," says Max. "It's going to be okay. Focus on what *you* need, because I'm prepared for whatever's about to come my way."

"Because you're a wizard," says Olympia.

"That's right. And as everyone knows, the best skill a wizard can have is to be ready for all scenarios. I can handle it."

"But what if you can't?"

"But I can."

I know Max is strong, but I'm not sure I believe him.

"Chin up, Squimpy. Remember, what doesn't kill us –" Olympia waves a hand in the air. "– and all that."

It's a stupid saying and I say so. "There's a good chance coming close to death makes you weaker. I bet someone who survives a car accident only to be paralysed doesn't come out of it saying, 'Oh well. I'll never be able to walk again but the whole thing was really good for my character'."

"Don't be dramatic, Sarah," says Max. "It won't be anything like a car wreck. I've got a seatbelt and airbags and can deflect any flying glass."

"You're speaking metaphorically, aren't you, because you don't own a car."

"Yes," Max says through a smile. "I've had media training. A lot of it. And because I'm a politician, I have a finely honed skill of redirection and answering questions without actually answering them. Please don't worry about me. You need to focus all your energy on you right now."

I answer with an ambiguous, "Hmm," as the intercom chimes someone's presence at the main door.

Max opens the intercom app on his phone and I glance at it to see Adam's face looming large on his screen. "Do you know what your sister's done?"

Max pauses before saying, "Come on up."

When he hangs up, I say, "I haven't done anything. I don't think." Unless Adam has somehow found out I'm Mister D'Arsy. In which case, I absolutely have done something.

I have an urge to run away and hide under my bed, because even without a confirmed court date, Adam discovering that would be too much to handle.

Instead, I gather my strength through plating up the food, while Max goes to open the front door. I have approximately thirty seconds to get my shit together.

I take a deep gulp of wine, then three deep breaths, then another gulp of wine.

I raise my eyes to see Olympia watching me.

She gives me a wink and Max enters the room, followed by Adam.

"Adam," I say far too loudly. "Join us for dinner."

"I'm not staying."

"Yes, you are," says Max calmly. "Sarah made plenty and it'd be really good to see you." He points to a chair at the table. "Sit. You're staying."

Adam complies, because it's hard to deny Max, who can effortlessly mix charming and commanding, while I dish him up a bowl and wish the others hadn't seated themselves so Adam is directly in my eye line.

"Now," says Max. "What's Sarah done?"

"Can I guess?" asks Olympia.

"No," says Max as Adam says, "She's resigned from her job."

Relief rushes through me. This? This I can handle.

Max blinks at him.

I place Adam's bowl in front of him and sit down.

"I already knew that," says Max.

"But it's a foolish and rash decision."

"Which you should be pleased about, surely."

Adam looks at me as I stand to retrieve a wine glass for him. "I told you not to. I said it would be fine. But I found out today you did it anyway." His words are clipped.

"It won't be fine, Adam. It never was fine."

"How easy do you think it's going to be to find another job when you have to disclose you have a court case for assault coming up?"

"Not very easy," I admit. "But I'm going to try very hard." My hand hovers over the glass in the cupboard, because something alarming has occurred to me and I don't know whether I should entertain it or not.

It sounds like Adam...cares.

"Why don't you start your own consultancy?" says Olympia. "Everyone I know does it. Mostly for the sake of flashing a shiny business card, but you can make yours a real business and not just a pet you bring out for the sake of convo."

Max places his chopsticks in his bowl and turns to me. "That's a bloody good idea. You've worked in Michelin-star restaurants. Couldn't you do menu consulting or artisanal ingredient sourcing, or something you can own and control? Why hasn't anyone thought of this option before?"

I had. But I'm a coward, so I had quickly unthunk it. "Because it's a terrifying idea. I have to convince other people I'm an expert they should feel privileged enough to pay, and do my own taxes and stuff."

"You only have to convince people you're an expert just like in every job interview you've ever had. You were very good at it at the last one, I hear. The top candidate." Max winks at me.

I don't take any comfort in his wink. "But I don't know anything about starting a business."

"Then learn," says Adam. "You're going to have plenty of time on your hands soon it would seem."

Wow. That was *almost* nice. Brusque and sarcastic, as usual, but it kind of sounded like he was on my side. It was better than being accused of sympathy-seeking martyrdom.

"I'll help you swot up," says Olympia. "I adore research. I didn't get my first in Theatre Studies through skimping on the details."

"Thank you, Ollie." I mean it. This is not something I feel capable of tackling on my own. I tell everyone I'll think about it, then a thought rides in that could scupper everything anyway. "Would I...have to disclose my conviction if I get one?"

"I don't think that would be necessary," says Adam. "It's not relevant."

Olympia claps her hands together. "Right. That's one problem solved."

It's more a solution *started*, if we're going for accuracy, which of course Olympia wasn't because she never is.

"Wish I could say the same for my ish. Ottilie Harpoole's blocked my number because I went on a date with her step-brother, which is against some mysterious dating etiquette known only to her. It would never have happened if we were men. What is it about having a penis that gives you the power of frankly-speaking your way to a solution in a fraction of the time it does when I have a spat with one of my gal pals?"

"Less brain room to over think it," says Max. "Half our faculties are stored in our underpants."

"Speak for yourself," says Adam.

"Well, you know what they say – high intellection, small ..." Max holds up a pinkie finger.

Olympia showers us with her tinkly laugh. "That's the kind of emasculating wit I would expect from Squimpy, but you've hardly said a word since we railroaded you into starting a business." She reaches across the table and places a hand on mine, and says, "You feeling alright?" like she hadn't witnessed the pantry chaos of my earlier meltdown.

Max says, "Actually, outside news of her court date, she's been pretty monosyllabic since Austencon," and I whip my head around to look at him.

There's only room in my brain for one thought.

Whyyyyyyyyyyyyyyyy?

Why did he have to go and mention Austencon?

I flick my eyes to Adam and he's frowning at me. As usual. But this time instead of it urging me to rise to his censure, it urges me to clamp my sphincter shut and climb under the table to hide.

I don't of course, because I'm pretending to be an adult and I've already run away from this situation once.

I have no choice but to face up to inevitability. There is only one way this is ending, and it's going to be a disaster of epic proportions.

"You went to Austencon?" he asks.

I can't speak. I can't move. I can only look and will those words, that thought back into his head with a dose of amnesia for the last two minutes of conversation for good measure.

"Oh yes," says Olympia and I mentally scream at her to *shut the fuck up*. "She went in her rainbow regency outfit in typical Sarah fashion. Hot pink shawl and everything."

No.

No, no, no, no, no, no, no, please, no.

It takes two seconds for the colour in Adam's face to drain.

Chapter twenty-six

I stand up at the exact moment as Adam does.

He's looking at me with the same wild eyes as that night six months ago.

"I didn't know. I swear I didn't know until I got to AustenCon and you talked to me." My words are rushed and high pitched.

With a "No" he takes a step backwards and knocks his chair over.

Max and Olympia say stuff, but I don't really hear them. I'm too busy thinking about how to patch the damage from this bombshell and I can't think of any way. The blast radius is too big.

Adam places his palms to his temples, his elbows sticking straight out. "I can't..." His eyes are still locked on mine. He looks like a terrified fawn facing a lion and I feel wretched.

"I couldn't tell you," I say. "How could I tell you?"

He drops his hands and slowly shakes his head, backing around the fallen chair.

I wait for him to accuse me of being typical Sarah. Of crashing into his life to ruin it.

But it doesn't come.

He snaps out of his moment of internal panic and with an "I have to go", marches out of the room.

Max chases him but comes back twenty seconds later.

I am slumped over the table with my head in my arms.

"He quietly thanked me for dinner without looking me in the eye and left with...insistence," says Max. "I don't want to say 'what have you done?', but what have you done, Sarah?"

"It's awful," I say into the crook of my arm.

"More or less awful than that thing that happened six months ago?" asks Olympia.

I sigh. "More. I think."

"Oh, Sarah," says Max, which is very generous given I continually make his friend very unhappy and Max's life therefore difficult.

I sit up and finish my glass of wine in one long glug.

When I emerge, Olympia is looking at me like I have an exciting story to tell about a funpark ride I just went on, and Max is trying not to glower at me.

"Austencon," Max says as if I had miraculously forgotten that enormous shit show. "Tell us about Austencon."

So, I do tell them about Austencon and we are all quiet for a few moments while this next level of *how complicated and shitty can Sarah and Adam's lives get?* sinks in.

"He's going to need a while to process it," I say into the silence.

"No wonder I've hardly been able to get a word out of you for the last week."

"I'm still in the process of processing it."

"Adam didn't tell me," Max says. "I mean, I knew he played the game, but he didn't tell me the extent to which he played it, or that he'd met someone in one of the game master chatrooms, or I might have had alarm bells ringing." He laughs, but there's no humour in it. "I didn't even think to tell each of you the other played the game. Why would I? Neither of you would be interested in that information, because you're not, supposedly, interested in each other."

"It's alright, Max. Nobody could have predicted this."

"So," says Olympia. "What are you going to do now that you're in love with him?"

"I am not in love with him!" I shout, because I'm not. The notion is ridiculous and deserves a shouted, emphatic denial.

Max pours himself another glass of wine and takes two torturous sips before he chooses to impart his wisdom, or censure, or agreement with Olympia. "You know, I'm not surprised you would find your connection again in a situation where all your other crap was stripped away. What happened when you were teenagers was unfortunate, and the reason it happened was because you were both immature and made stupid by that immaturity. Your decision to do what you did at that assembly, and his decision to react the way he did was the result of emotionally underdeveloped brains."

"I agree," says Olympia as if she was there.

Max places a hand on my shoulder. "But you have the emotional intelligence now to navigate this if you choose to. And it's my advice that you do, so you both don't have to live the next few years in the perpetual hate-dance you two do."

"I don't have the emotional intelligence. I have tried to tease this thing out and all I've done is made a bigger knot of emotions. I have no idea what I'm feeling." Just because Adam had an attachment to a person behind a Mr Darcy avatar, doesn't mean he can just switch on his feelings for me again, or vice versa. "Hate is a very big emotion to overcome."

Max withdraws his hand. "Don't be so ridiculous, Sarah. Neither of you hate each other."

"You just said so yourself. You called it a 'hate dance'."

"Yeah, because that's how you *behave*. It's not how you feel. Neither of you is capable of that destructive emotion. And if Adam hates you, why would he come around tonight to express his concern for a decision you've made?"

Why indeed? "I don't understand why he would be so generous about the job situation when he made it very clear to me working there was making his work life impossible."

"Because he's a decent guy, and when push came to shove – you threatening to resign – he would have realised his reaction was unfair and your need for a job was greater than his need for a comfortable lunch hour."

I sit with that for a bit. I know Adam is a decent guy outside of his interactions with me.

"You know what I like about Adam?" says Olympia. "He is so grumpy around you and it makes your light shine brighter. He's funny with his cutting remarks and you are effervescent in response. It's like he taps into your essence and amplifies it with his grouchiness. I very much like your essence. And I think he secretly likes your essence too, otherwise he wouldn't keep encouraging you."

I snort. "I don't secretly like him being a dick to me."

"Nonsense. You love playing that game. Otherwise you just –" she flaps a hand. "– wouldn't."

Maybe. Maybe I do enjoy the game, but it's not a healthy way for people to interact.

Max scrapes up the last of his dinner from his bowl and says through his mouthful, "You two will work it out. Or not. To be honest, it's not going to make my life more difficult. I've been pretty much separating my Sarah and Adam lives for the last year, so it's not going to be much different."

"No," Olympia laughs.

I do not laugh.

God. It's going to be painful.

Perhaps Adam was right that night six months ago when he said he couldn't have anything more to do with me.

I think –

It's better if we never ever see each other again.

Chapter twenty-even

Six months before the arrest

It's Max's thirtieth birthday. Ordinarily, Max might have thrown a party, got fairly inebriated and had the kind of time you wake up from half wishing you didn't have quite so good a time and half regretting nothing.

But due to Max not being willing to tempt any tabloid fate and not wanting the kind of big do that would warrant hiring a private venue, he settles for dinner out with Olympia, me, and

–

– Adam.

It's a few months or so since Max properly reconnected with him. The rekindling of their relationship has been fairly intensive and joyful to see on the odd occasion I've witnessed it.

Mine and Adam's has not.

The choice of company is understandable, but if I was Max, I wouldn't want to go out with me and Adam. Sure, we'll be on our best behaviour, but the undercurrent of Adam's resentment for all the things he blames me for when our paths have crossed over the years might be palpable enough to bring the mood down.

I, for one, am not going to be responsible for that. Let Adam be the one to sour the evening.

I mean, I hope he doesn't, but I'm just saying, it won't be me who ruins Max's birthday.

I'm wearing a navy-blue, long-sleeved shirt with yellow polka dots, dress shorts with turned up cuffs, and my pink Doc Martens.

Max is wearing a suit. It's not the usual suit he wears on the job. It's black and is tailored to fit his lean frame fairly snugly. Underneath he wears an open-collared black shirt. It's a swoon suit. Which would not be appropriate in the backbenches of the parliamentary debating chamber.

He looks extraordinarily handsome. But then I am his sister and my bias is a given.

The restaurant specialises in vegan tapas and Adam is already there when we arrive.

He stands up from the table and is wearing a matching swoon suit to Max's, only being broader, he fills his out a little more and I'm annoyed that I've noticed.

They laugh and give each other a hug.

Adam does a bit of back slapping and I say, "Did you guys not ring each other and ask 'What are you wearing?'"

Adam's eyes traverse my body. "Bet you never had to do that to avoid accidental coordination."

I select one of the chairs adjacent to Adam so I don't have to spend the meal looking at him, and sit down. "Nope. Because I have two things going for me. Imagination and lack of fear."

"Hey," says Max. "I have imagination. I just have the fear."

"Fear is good," says Adam. "Keeps you on the path to sensible decision-making."

I want to ask him if his sphincter ever gets tired from holding the rod in, but it would be mean and wouldn't be conducive to starting the evening on the right foot.

To be fair, if Adam weren't sitting next to me casting righteous judgement on me thirty seconds into the evening, I would admit to myself that better decision-making due to consideration of the risks is something I need to work on. But he is, so I choose to remain fearless.

So, fuck you, Adam.

The waiter takes our drinks orders and Adam asks Max how it feels to have reached his fourth decade.

"It was scary as hell on approach, but now I'm here, I'm glad to have shed the stigma of being a politician in their twenties. I think I've just gained some gravitas."

I scoff. "People took you seriously before and have always respected the hell out of you because of your intelligence and drive and everything you've accomplished at a young age. Even the ones who cast aspersions do, because you were already high on the political ladder at the age when they were still wanking off to page three of *The Sun* and trying to imagine what a real woman feels like. They're just culturally obliged to be dickheads about it."

"I agree," says Adam, which is the nicest thing he's said regarding me in...fourteen years? "Although I wouldn't have expressed it in such a crude fashion."

Max takes each of our hands and says, "Thanks guys. If I said 'you're familiarly obliged to say stuff like that', you'd take it back, right?"

"That's right," Adam says, "any false modesty and I'm not saying anything else nice to you all evening."

"Are you...doubting your abilities?" I ask Max.

"All the time. I've chosen one of the toughest jobs you can. My imposter syndrome has been an arsehole lately. *Who am I to think I have the knowledge and experience and expertise to be the voice of my community? To make decisions on their behalf?* It waxes and wanes. I'm just at the bottom of a particularly vicious cycle."

I grip his hand again. "God. I had no idea. You do know you are very effective at what you do? Your popularity speaks for itself."

Adam looks at me with an expression that could be interpreted as *almost* approving, then refocuses on Max. "Max, you are *incredibly* good at what you do. Not many people get into parliament at the age you did. There's only one reason for that and it's not chance. It's because you are the right person to do that job and that has nothing to do with age."

Olympia is late. Olympia is often late, so when the waiter brings our drinks, I don't wait to propose a toast. "To Max, who has categorically earned his stripes, and is about to embark on the exciting adventure of entering a new decade."

We drink and Max says he has to go to the toilet and I direct a *No. Don't leave me alone with Adam* thought at him, but he doesn't receive it and I can't very well accompany him. I mean, I could, but it wouldn't be a very good look for a brother and sister.

Adam and I pick up our menus and peruse them, and I'm thankful there's an excuse to ignore each other without being impolite.

The items on offer sound interesting, the flavour combinations unusual and perhaps a little ambitious, but I've not explored vegan cuisine with any dedication, so I'm keen to try with an open mind.

Placing the menu back on the table, I glance at Adam.

He flicks his paper over to look at the dessert menu.

I eye the direction Max went in and will him to pee faster.

Adam places his menu on the table and takes a sip of his drink.

I take a sip of mine.

Then we gaze at the tables in our line of vision.

A woman in front of me laughs at something her boyfriend or husband has said and strokes his arm.

Christ, this is painful.

"How's work?" I venture.

"Good." It's not quite surly, but it's said in a tone designed to shut that line of questioning down. Or perhaps any line of questioning.

I lick my finger and pass it through the flame of the candle in the centre of the table. It hisses.

"Don't do that," says Adam.

Olympia's voice cuts through the restaurant hubbub like the heel of Gucci stilettos in a croquet lawn and I couldn't be more grateful. "Sorry I'm late, my lovelies."

Through unwrapping herself from several outer layers of clothing, Olympia says, "I was absolutely planning to be here punctually, but as I was leaving my new beau, Seb's, apartment, his parents arrived and I went in to air kiss his mother with a bit too much velocity because I didn't want to be late here and she went in for the right cheek first, when everyone knows it's always *always* the left cheek first." She sits down heavily, picks up my wine glass, and sticks her nose into it, inhaling deeply. "So I delivered a rather forceful kiss to her left nostril and sent her toppling backwards into the Jacobean grandmother clock, which toppled backwards onto the Tiffany Peacock lamp, which toppled off the table and onto her miniature Schnauzer." She takes a sip and smacks her lips. "It was a frightful mess. Bits everywhere."

Adam says through a down turned mouth, "Bits of...dog?"

"Bits of glass and mahogany. Brutus just got a nasty fright and a jolly good bruising." Handing the glass back to me, she emits a sigh. "I expect I'll be Seb's *old* beau now."

Max returns to the table and gives Olympia a kiss.

After she's signalled to the waiter and requested a bottle of Dom Perignon, she says, "So what are we celebrating?"

"Ah, my birthday, Ollie? I said that in the text I sent?"

She tips her head to one side. "Wasn't your birthday in April? We had that thing where you staged your murder and ended up burning the Mona Lisa."

Max's eyes flick to mine. "That was a movie. Ed Norton ended up burning the Mona Lisa."

"Was it?" Olympia fixes her gaze on the ceiling. "Oh, yes. Onion something. *God* it was clever. You know that thing when you're never sure if something happened or you dreamed it?"

"Yes, but I've never confused a movie for my real life."

"Haven't you? Happens to me all the time. It really doesn't happen to you?"

"No."

"Huh. That is bizarre."

Adam says, "Sarah confuses her life for a Monty Python sketch."

I want to retort *Adam confuses his life for an empty white room* and invite ruin before the evening's really begun, but Olympia saves the situation by throwing back her head and laughing. "That must be a riot."

"We haven't had a riot yet, but there's still time," says Adam.

"I'm hoping for a riot against the patriarchy," I say. "You with me, Ollie?"

"I'm always up for gal power, as long as it doesn't clash with my Louis Vuitton's."

"It might," says Max. "Depending on the height of your heel."

Olympia flaps a hand. "Oh, I never go over six inches. Any more than that and it's awfully difficult not to topple headfirst into people's crotches."

The Dom Perignon is delivered in an ice bucket and the waiter pours us all a glass, which, because champagne etiquette mysteriously requires the glass not to be tilted to avoid foam build up, takes an hour for a decent measure to be dribbled.

We watch in silence and I marvel at the waiter's ability not to collapse into a pile of red-faced steam under our collective scrutiny.

Olympia lifts her glass. "Happy birthday, Maximillian." She adds, "Love you a squillion," with a silvery giggle and I bask again in how much I adore her.

She's completely fearless. She never worries about the judgement of others, that her eccentricities might come across as ditziness, or that the world she was shaped by is up for ridicule by others. She loudly and unashamedly wears her self for all to see.

"Now, if we're having tapas," she continues. "We have to go for baby octopus. The Spanish know how to cook the proverbial out of an intelligent species. Like the Japanese and whales. It's not very ethical, but you have to try it once before you die."

"This is a vegan tapas restaurant, Ollie," says Max.

Olympia picks up her unbleached, unlaminated paper menu. "Oh? Is veganism still a thing? I thought it would die a natural death, like that fashion where grown men wear backward caps."

"Grown men still wear backward caps," I say.

"It's still a thing," says Max. "It's why I ask you to pick up vegetarian Thai take-aways, because I'm vegan. I've been vegan for three years now. How have you not noticed?"

"I just thought you were going through a very long Thai food phase."

"No. It's just the tastiest vegan takeaway option that's easiest to cater for everyone's preferences."

"What's wrong with wearing a backwards cap?" asks Adam.

"Everything," I say. "The purpose of a cap is to protect your face from the sun. Wearing it backwards renders it completely pointless. Also, the acceptable age for it to be a fashion statement is twelve, so you just look like a sad excuse for someone suffering Peter Pan syndrome."

Olympia puts a hand on Adam's arm. "But not if you're black. You get away with simply looking street and a bit gangster."

Max says, "So, if I wear a backwards cap, I'll end up looking like a sad excuse for a white man suffering Peter Pan syndrome?"

"Yes," says Olympia with a smile.

He looks at Adam. "How is it fair that you get all the cool stuff? Superior sporting ability, musical ability, dancing ability, innate coolness?"

"If we're going to talk about privilege of race, I think you'll win hands down, so let's not start that game."

Max puts his hands in the air, palms outwards. "Fair enough, brother."

Adam laughs. "Did you just call me 'brother'"?

"Yeah. Does it suit me?"

Adam chuckles out the remainder of his laughter. "Yes. Call me 'brother' as much as you want."

Max grins. "You're lying so you can laugh at me."

"Yes I am."

I shouldn't wonder at the ability of the two of them to be at such a stage in their relationship that teasing is a pleasure. They were best friends as teenagers, and despite everything, I can't help but feel the missed opportunity at not being able to participate, to add a third corner to their inner circle. So to speak.

We used to have it, many many years ago, but that time is long since gone.

Still, I'm glad Max has Adam, even if he is a judgy dick to me.

We eat and talk and drink our way through several plates, and by the time the dessert is delivered, we all have an alcohol-infused shine to our eyes.

Max and Adam are already on to the scotch, while Olympia and I have stuck to champagne.

I decide it's time for a group selfie, because how have we got this far into the evening without taking one?

I make everyone gather round and lean in, and take a smiley shot, then a silly shot, and as we move onto a serious shot, a woman from somewhere in the restaurant, shrieks, "Oh my Go'." The pitch of the last word is so high, the final consonant is lost to the realm of an undetectable frequency. "The table's on fire!"

"Who's table?" asks Olympia as a flame rises behind us in my phone's screen like a cobra readying to strike.

I whirl around, spot the paper menu that has been discarded onto the candle in the centre of the table and is now fuelling a fire on the synthetic tablecloth.

I drop my phone, grab the closest liquid in reach and throw it over the flames as Adam yells, "No" and clasps my hand.

It's too late. I already have momentum and the whisky sends a jet of flame into the air and I am engulfed in heat and the astringent scent of singed hair.

"I feel like my nostrils have been epilated." I rub at them, trying to massage the soreness out of them.

"That's what happens when you snort fire," says Max. "Might pay to stick to blow like an ordinary person."

"I was inhaling at the moment I tried to put the flames out."

Adam glares at me from his wingback chair. He looks utterly ridiculous. His eyebrows are gone and the front of his hair has shrivelled in on itself.

I don't laugh. I look pretty much the same, except, being a woman, my lack of eyebrows is more pronounced, and the shrivelled hair is at the side of my head.

We are in a private club Olympia insisted on taking us to so we can recuperate without spectators.

I've never been inside a members' only club, which is understandable. I don't have the money to pay the fees, and it's not something that has ever interested me, due to the aversion to extreme privilege I inherited from my mother.

It looks exactly as the ones on television. Oak panelled walls, open fire, leather-bound books and oil paintings adorning the walls, and penguin-suited wait staff addressing people as "sir" and "madam".

All my disapproval has been superseded by the novelty of it.

I've also never sat in a wing-backed chair before or drunk brandy from a fishbowl.

"There was water on the table, Sarah. Why did you have to go for the whisky?" asks Adam under a scowl that is not as nearly effective were he to still have eyebrows with which to scowl under.

"It was nearest to hand. I didn't think. I just did."

"No. You never think before you act, which just means a whole pile of crap for the rest of us."

"That's not fair," says Olympia. "Sarah can be very good at making considered decisions. Look at her outfit."

"Case in point," mutters Adam.

"Look," says Max, "apart from a bit of missing hair that'll grow back, it was funny. No one got hurt, we got a voucher for free meals from the restaurant, and I get to enjoy the weirdness of your faces for a couple of weeks."

"Precisely," says Olympia. "Chin up, Adders. No harm done." Her phone chimes with the resonant gongs of Big Ben and she wiggles her fingers in the air. "Goodie. A Max Sawyer Google alert."

She pulls her phone out of her Saint Laurent handbag and thumbs it open. "Ooh. That is not a good camera angle."

"What isn't?" says surly Adam.

Olympia hands her phone to Max who reads and sighs. "At least it's not considered as newsworthy as –" he scrolls up to read "– *woman who made love to Nelson statue shock pregnancy* or *Princess Anne ate my gerbil.*"

"Whatwhatwhat?" I rattle out and reach for the phone as Adam does.

We peer at it together, our singed heads almost touching.

Under the headline *HEROINE SAVES MP FROM FRENZIED GAY-HATE ATTACK* is a tele-photo picture of the moment the whisky catches fire as it reaches the flames in the centre of the table. Adam's back is to the camera, but because his hand is covering mine to prevent me from smothering the flames in a flammable substance, it looks as if he's throwing it.

I *am* facing the camera. The look of outrage on my face is directed at Adam and my free arm is slung across Max's middle like I'm pushing him out of harm's way. I don't even remember doing that.

This is very very bad.

Adam scrolls to the article underneath and stands abruptly. "They've named me. They know it was me in that picture and they've bloody well named me and my profession."

"How could they possibly know it was you?" I say unhelpfully, because they do and the 'how?' is the least of Adam's worries.

Adam paces while we make placating noises that only have the effect of increasing his tempo.

He stops, one hand gripping his fire-frizzled hair, and turns to me. "How do you do it?" His eyes are wide, his features slack. "How do you manage to constantly take a dump on my life and come out smelling of roses? Does anything ever go on in your brain apart from 'Do this thing without thinking. See how much it ruins Adam's life? What fun!'"

"Adam," says Max in an even, mollifying tone. "You must see Sarah was acting out of the best of intentions. She's not to blame for the willing and ludicrous misinterpretation by a media parasite."

"They *named me*, Max. I'm going to be the subject of vicious online censure, because trolls feed off this stuff. Christ, they could easily find out where I work, or where I live. And then there's the damage this might do to my professional reputation."

"Take down your social media profiles," says Olympia. "Everyone does that when they run into a bit of a bother. Celebs do it all the time."

I try to offer something and manage, "I'm sure it won't come to that, Adam." I'm not at all sure. I know just how savage people can be online.

Adam pulls out his phone, taps at it and reads. His features pinch and he turns his phone around to show us the screen. "It's already reached Threads. Look!"

We can't look because his hand is shaking so much. He turns his phone around again and reads, "@rollomylolo calls me a *black cunt*. Wonderful. Calling out supposed bigotry with actual bigotry. Or look, here –" he flips his phone around for us to see, and back again. "–@ourprophetess says I should step in front of a bus to save punishing my parents for the abomination of my birth."

Jesus.

That is truly truly despicable.

With an "Adam", Max stands, his hands reaching for him.

Adam steps back and points a finger at me. "This is too much. It's too much." He looks at me. "I'm backing out of having anything to do with you before you break me."

Max follows him as Adam continues to back away. "Adam. Come on, brother. I know this is really upsetting, but I'll put out a media statement tomorrow and it'll be forgotten by Tuesday. The tabloids will be on to the next imagined sensation and so will the trolls."

Adam shakes his head and mutters, "Uh uh." He catches his heal on the leg of a chair and stumbles. "I'm going now. It's best. It's the best thing to do."

Adam disappears out the door and Max stills.

Well, shit. This is truly truly awful. Whatever my feelings for Adam, I would never wish this on him. "Fuck, Max. I'm so sorry."

"What?" he says still looking at the empty doorway, then fixes an unfocused gaze on me.

"I'm really sorry that happened and I kind of made it happen."

Max walks back to his chair and collapses into it. He places his elbows on his knees and rubs his face. "You didn't make it happen, Sarah. The unregulated freedom of the press made it happen. Adam is just the latest collateral damage."

Chapter twenty-eight

Adam doesn't come into the cafeteria during my last few days of work.

I can't blame him. The awful truth of the identity of Mister D'Arsy is a big one for him to get his head around.

I watch every day for his appearance. I anticipate it. I –

God.

I look forward to it.

And that tells me that the feelings I developed for Lizobeth2000 outweigh the ones I had for disapproving, judgemental Adam.

I can feel its intensity swelling and bubbling its way to the surface.

I don't like it.

And I especially don't like that I can't help wondering if Adam's absence means he is also struggling, or that he's simply horrified by it all.

Does he miss my presence in the cafeteria?

Does he want to come in and turn his back and pretend I'm not there while being acutely aware I am?

I guess I'll never know.

I mark my departure from the cafeteria with a planned drink with my co-workers later, following a visit to my lawyer.

I open the door to Bob's rooms to find him pacing with his hands behind his back, head nodding and chest puffed out like a pigeon.

I sit as Bob stops, leans against his desk and sucks in air like he's just finished a sprint.

"Are you alright?"

He picks up a glass of water from his desk and drains half of it, before walking to his chair and collapsing into it. "I've just had some cross-examination training."

"Right. You don't need cross examination training, Bob. I'm pleading guilty, remember?"

I'd made that very clear on my last visit. I don't want to go to trial, because if I want Jeffrey Wainwright to take responsibility for his actions, I have to do the same. And I absolutely am guilty of committing assault.

"I've been told the old 'pace and nod' has the magical duality of being disconcerting and patronising. So, if you can't confuse the defendant into a corner, you offend them into a corner. Either is just as effective."

"If we went to trial, *I'd* be the defendant, Bob."

"Do you think I could prop a hand on the barrier between the defendant and the floor, instead? Lean against it and seem casual and friendly? Then I could lure them into a false sense of sharing with a confidante, a pal. And WHAM." He claps his hands together. "I strike with the question that undermines everything he's already said."

Bob doesn't wait for an answer. He shuffles over to one of his bookshelves and leans against it with one leg crossed over the ankle of his other. He immediately loses his balance.

"Sitting can be just as intimidating," I say.

"My thoughts exactly," he says, returning to his chair.

Bob blinks at me behind his glasses and I can almost hear the lashes slapping on each other. Then he reaches for his water and takes a long drink with a shaky hand.

"I don't think you should take up barristry, Bob."

"Nonsense," he says when he's emerged from behind his glass. "I just need to strengthen the cross-examination muscle."

He needs to strengthen everything. Including his ability to stand for longer than a minute.

He blinks at me a bit more.

"Do you...need to talk to me about my case?" I prompt.

His attention snaps to the scattered contents of his desk surface. "Oh yes, that's right."

"Last time we talked about getting evidence of Jeffrey Wainwright's character that we could include in the statement I'll be giving. What have you found out about him?"

Bob sits up straighter in his chair and pushes his glasses up his nose. "Quite a bit, actually. I think you'll be really happy."

My heartbeat quickens. If we can prove Jeff's a predator and a position-abuser, maybe the judge will factor that in to my sentence.

He spends thirty seconds locating the information he's found and begins to read from the piece of paper. "His full name is Jeffrey Harris Wainwright, he is thirty-seven years of age, he was born in Ashford, Kent, to Peter and Marion Wainwright, he attended Highworth Grammar School in his final year of schooling, received a BComm from the University of Kent, he is unmarried, his NHS number is 229-070-3545, and he's been working at executive level for Hachet for two years and three months." Bob looks up at me with a smile and several blinks.

"So...you've basically just found a whole lot of demographic information about him." That probably anybody could with a bit of persistent Googling.

He looks back at his piece of paper, still looking proud of himself. "It's pretty thorough."

I sigh. "Indeed." Then I issue a thank you because I am British.

I am so fucked.

Chapter twenty-nine

J as wends her way through the tables in the garden bar and places three pints on the sticky surface of our tabletop.

"Amstel's fifty p more here than my local. Daylight wanking robbery." She settles in between me and Ian and pulls her container of leftover beef stroganoff towards her. "Makes me not want to patronise this place again."

True to form, Ian and Jas have over-catered a couple of the lunch dishes for a mythical late rush, which means the poorly paid cafeteria staff get to take home an evening meal or two.

I point at her food. "You're not really patronising it anyway."

Through a mouthful, she says, "Yeah well, who's got an extra fifteen pounds, ninety-nine for stuff we make just as well?"

"True that," I say, because apparently I have a need to be a middle-class nobhat trying to sound street. I can't argue with the quality of their food, or the rising price of everything thanks to record rates of inflation.

I take the lid off my container and inhale the mouth-watering aroma of beef and cream and sherry. "Thank you, Ian."

"Pleasure, pet."

"Keep an eye out for someone collecting glasses," I tell Ash, who sits facing the door next to Simone.

Ash and Simone have Jas' leftover bean hotpot. Somehow we have arranged ourselves so the meat eaters face off against the vegetarians.

"Dolphin or eagle?" asks Jas.

Simone rolls her eyes. "We're not discussing which we'd rather do again, are we?"

"No! Jesus. When did we even have the first discussion about inter-species sex?"

"Dolphin," I answer.

Simone nods. "They're the only other species that do it face to face."

"I would rather *be* a dolphin than an eagle, which, I believe, was what Jas was asking."

"I'd rather be a centaur," says Ian.

"They're not real," says Ash.

"Neither is becoming a dolphin or an eagle. If I'm going to choose something it's impossible for me to be, I choose a centaur. I think I'd quite like the body of a horse."

"By which you mean 'schlong'," says Jas. "Do centaurs even come in beer-gut model?"

Ian wraps an arm around Jas' neck and rubs the top of her hair with his knuckles.

She extracts herself with a "Gerroff" and then says, "I'd be King Kong. Taking it to the little people, letting them know who's boss."

"Until they kill you," Ash says.

"I'd be immortal. Because this is a make-believe game, which gives me license to modify the fuck out of my imagined alternative self."

"He's pretty big. That's a lot of nits," Simone says with the knowledge of someone who has to deal with a lot of nits. She blows air through pursed lips at the enormity of it. "You'd need another Kong to eat all the nits."

Jas rolls her eyes. "I'll be a *nitless* immortal King Kong."

Olympia materialises at the end of the table. "Sorry I'm late, everyone. If I didn't have a digital personal assistant, I wouldn't know which way was Tuesday." She squeezes in between Ash and Simone and turns the beam of her smile on everyone.

No one says anything.

"Not to be rude or nothing," says Jas, "but, like, who the fuck are you?"

I slap my forehead. "God, sorry. I forgot to tell you my cousin, Olympia, was coming to join us."

Olympia's smile doesn't waiver. "That's right. I'm Olympia, Sarah's cousin."

"You're very posh," says Simone.

"Yes."

"Distant cousin three times removed?" asks Ian.

"No," I say. "We're the no times removed sort. *Cousin* cousins. Olympia's dad is my mother's brother."

"*You're* not posh," says Simone.

"No."

"So." Olympia slaps the table. "What are you all having? Shall we order a bottle of Taittinger, or are we doing things like 'rustic' and 'charm'?" By which she means whatever beer's on tap.

Simone's mouth drops open. "*I'll* have a glass of Taittinger."

"Me too," says Jas.

"Sarah?" Olympia asks.

Well, I'm hardly going to say 'no'. "Yes, please."

"Excellent. I'll get a couple of bottles."

When she leaves the table, Jas asks, "How did you come to work at a bottom feeder job when you come from that?" She points behind her to where Olympia has disappeared inside.

"I don't come from that. Not really. My mum turned her back on that and made her own way in the world, and I guess I have the same ethos. I couldn't get another job and was incredibly grateful when the cafeteria became an option."

"So," Jas' frown deepens, "you're on the bones of your arse like the rest of us, when all you have to do is swallow your pride?"

God. I sound incredibly spoilt in front of these people, who likely do not have a wealthy family to fall back on. And even though I haven't fallen back on them, living in Max's flat is hardly doing it rough.

"Yes."

Nobody says anything and I wonder if I should apologise for sounding like such a spoilt twat.

Jas continues to frown and glare at me.

Then Ian says, "Good on you, girl," and I relax a little bit. Not much, but I probably shouldn't have brought Olympia here to rub my twattery in their faces.

"God," says Simone. "What I'd give for a rich cousin. Do you make her buy you champagne all the time?"

"I never have to make her buy champagne."

"I'd be milking that totty for all she's willing to give if I were you," says Jas, who's dropped the glare but not the frown.

"Thank you for your advice. Don't be offended when I ignore it."

She shovels in a mouthful of stroganoff and says through it, "I notice you didn't say, 'No thank you. Just get me the house white'."

"Of which you are benefiting. Shall I run after her and get her to change the order?"

"Don't you dare!" says Simone. "I've never had real stuff before. Probably tastes like gold leaf."

"Gold leaf doesn't have a flavour," says Ash.

"I meant it metaphorically." She sips her beer. "Obviously."

"Staff!" says Ash and we pull our containers onto our laps.

Olympia reappears and places an ice bucket on the table, while the bar staff removes champagne flutes from a tray. She thanks them once they are done and says, "Exciting news, Squimpy," while she pours out the Taittinger.

I give a neutral, "Oh yeah?" Exciting news for Olympia could be anything from having her rubbish bag ripped open by a fox, to seeing a cloud in the shape of a coconut macaron.

"I just got a Google alert about your man."

"What man?" Did I have a man? Surely, she's not referring to Adam, who most definitely is not my man. And I don't think Olympia knows about the primary school teacher I snuck into Max's flat a few weeks ago and then kicked out before he crossed paths with Max, or saw a photo of Max, or even smelled Max. And if she does, why would she have a Google alert on him? Even I barely remember his name.

"That Jeffrey fellow."

My coordination fails and I freeze, glass halfway to my mouth. "Why would you want to do that?"

"To see what juicy stuff there might be out there to use against him. Google's a good sort like that. Tell you anything about anyone if you know how to ask nicely."

"Who's Jeffrey and why are you blackmailing him?" asks Ian.

"Oh, we're hoping it won't come to blackmail," says Olympia. "Some good old red facing in front of the stiff in the wig should do it."

Simone looks at me. "I know she's speaking English, but that last sentence just sounded like words picked at random."

Olympia isn't offended. She sits up straight, draws in a breath and says cheerily, "Jeffrey's the chap whose nose Sarah broke, which means she's up for assault."

Every head swivels from Olympia to me.

A bubble rises up my glass to burst aggressively into the sudden quiet.

"*Sarah Fulton*," says Ash in a tone somewhere between surprise and horror. "No wonder you were very evasive when we asked what you got done for."

"Wow," says Ian. "I'm surprised Sergeant Bowman didn't blab."

"Hold up," says Simone. "You broke some poor bloke's nose and now you want to blackmail him as well? I thought Jas was the gangster of our lot, but she's got nothing on you."

"I'm *not* going to blackmail him, and I broke his nose because he didn't give me a job when I was skint and scraping chewing gum up off the pavement for food, because he wanted to have sex with me instead."

"He got that wrong," says Jas. "He should have only withheld giving you the job *until* you had sex with him if you were that desperate. Dangled it in front of you like a carrot."

"Jasmeena Shah," says Simone. "I am ashamed to call you a fellow woman. Go inside and give your mouth a good scrub out with the foaming soap."

"I'm not saying I agree with him being a perve. I'm just saying he was asking for a decent face kicking due to being a *stupid* perve."

"As opposed to a semi-decent face kicking?" says Ash.

I say, "There shouldn't have been any face kicking. I shouldn't have done it."

"Bet it felt good at the time, though," says Ian.

"Sometimes, when I think I'm going to lose my bladder function over the thought of being in court, I imagine that moment when his face bounced off the bar and his tie jerked out of my hand, and I feel a little braver."

"Shame the twonks in my neighbourhood don't wear suits," says Jas. "Would make the face to knee action a lot cleaner."

"You are very very dark," says Ash.

"You try growing up small, brown and female in an estate in Dagenham."

"What does your Google alert say?" I ask.

"Oh, right. Yes," Olympia says brightly and fishes her phone out of her Prada handbag. "It says there's a new charity for single mothers whose ex-partners have defaulted on child support blahblahblah." She scrolls and says, "Here we are. *Jeffrey Wainwright from Hachet Hotel Group is co-chair of the charity. Wainwright describes himself as a feminist. 'I always have been. I have a strong empathy with women and the challenges they face due to inequity in our society. It's a crying shame that well into the twenty-first century, women are still having to fight to be respected by men, to have the same opportunities as men. When I was invited to help lead this charity, I didn't hesitate'.*"

There's only one possible way for me to react after I reposition my jaw from agape to clenched. "That hypocritical...smug...arsefaced...fucker!"

"I wouldn't worry, Squimpy. It's not going to look too good for him when he gets accused of skirt lifting in front of the paploids who'll no doubt be at the hearing."

"It's not going to look too good for Max, either."

Olympia flaps a hand. "He's a politician. He's going to have to weather worse storms."

"Who's Max the politician?" asks Jas.

"My brother," I say on a sigh. "He's the Associate Minister for Social Care."

There's a disquieting pause before Jas says, "So, you have a filthy rich, posh cousin and an MP brother. I don't understand this." She waves a hand between me and the rest of the cafeteria staff and raises her voice. "You had a choice to not be scraping by, to not work in a shitty job for minimum wage, and you *turned it down*? None of us have ever had the luxury of a *choice*." She throws her hands in the air. "God, you probably could have got off the charges if you wanted."

"Steady on, Jas," says Ian, despite us all knowing she's right. My choice *is* a luxury, and yes, if I'd been willing to pay what Jeffrey Wainwright wanted, I would have got off the charges as well.

Jas crosses her arms and narrows her eyes at me. Her resentment is entirely fair, as is the shame I can feel spreading across my skin in a fierce flush.

"I don't think you have any understanding of the privilege you have of being white and coming from that." She jabs a finger in Olympia's direction.

"I do."

"No you don't. You can't, because you've never been anything else. You've never experienced true poverty, or being called a Paki bitch, or being racially profiled. You have no fucking clue."

The table is quiet, as it should be. I don't deserve for anybody to leap to my defense.

"I know," I say softly. "You have every right to be angry."

After a moment, Ian clears his throat and Olympia says, "I didn't finish the article, Squimpy, there's another para or two."

I jump at this reprieve, such as it is. "I don't need to hear more about what a fucking chivalrous hero he's pretending to be. I'd rather keep my stroganoff on the inside."

"I think you'll want to hear this next bit, actually. But down your glass of fizzy first."

"Why?" I say slowly as my hair ripples into standing upright across my scalp in an unnerving Mexican wave.

"Fortification."

I stare at her for a beat, then down my drink and reach across the table to down hers as well. "Get on with it. I'd prefer a quick death, please."

She reads, "*Wainwright, who was the victim of a female-led brutal assault several weeks ago, says the experience has only strengthened his conviction women need extra support in these difficult economic times. 'Women are under extra pressure to be full-time caregivers for their families and to earn full-time livings in order to provide for their families, often in jobs that are underpaid. No wonder some of them give in to that pressure and snap. I don't hold my experience of violence against that woman. I feel sorry for her'."*

Olympia looks up at me, her lips downturned in a small grimace.

I am paralysed by my warring reactions, not sure which one will break to the surface first – my anger at his complete insincerity and his deeply patronising bullshit about feeling sorry for me, or my terror that someone, a journalist, might look into the details of that 'brutal assault'.

I stand and pace while the others discuss the cheek of the man, but in less polite terms.

When I've worn a groove into the pavers and quaffed another glass of Taittinger, Olympia's phone starts pinging like an arcade game.

She looks at it and gives an "Ah" that has the stroganoff rolling over in my stomach with a painful lurch.

She peers up at me. "I also have Google alerts about your name in the media."

Well, fuck.

Chapter thirty

It takes less than half an hour for the press to discover who my brother is and set up camp outside Max's constituency office, the Houses of Parliament, and his flat.

The first two I learn from Max, who also warns me the last one is likely. And then I find out for myself when I try to enter the apartment building once everyone called it a night at the pub.

Thankfully, Olympia had offered to accompany me and leads me through the flashing of cameras and the cacophony of shouted questions with several calmly delivered "No comment"s.

I try to close my ears to it, but it's impossible, despite the earplugs Olympia bought at a Boots on the way home for this very eventuality. Once upon a time, the press would have put up a pretence of showing respect by referring to me as "Ms Fulton". Now they assume anybody is ripe for the taking. There are no barriers and no standards with which to lower.

It's "Sarah" this and "Sarah" that, their assumed intimacy making their questions hit home harder, which, of course, is the point. They want to provoke me into a reaction.

"Sarah, do you enjoy assaulting men?"

"Sarah, are you going to issue a statement?"

"Sarah, do you think your brother should resign?"

"Sarah, do you come from an abusive family?"

"Sarah, did Jeffrey Wainwright deserve what you did to him?"

"Sarah, how do you feel knowing you've ruined your brother's career?"

"Sarah."

"Sarah."

"Sarah."

"Sarah."

Jesus Christ, it's horrible.

Olympia pushes me through the door to the lobby and turns to wave to the press with a "Thanks everyone. Have a good evening".

I shouldn't be surprised. She treated the situation with the same emotional calm she treats everything else. Olympia doesn't live. She wafts. And she does it very gracefully.

She points up the stairs. "Up you go. They're still watching. Have your crisis when Max's front door is closed behind us."

I do. As soon as the door is closed, I let out the pent up "FUCK OFF!" I refrained from screaming at the pack of journos at the apartment door. It feels good, so I shout it again while I jump up and down in large, thumping leaps.

Then I turn to Olympia and collapse tearfully into her arms.

"There, there, Squimpy." She pats my hair and says, "It'll all come out in the wash," which isn't very comforting, because while I'm familiar with the saying, I'm not familiar with it being used in this context.

"I haven't, have I?"

"You haven't what?" asks Olympia.

"Ruined Max's career."

Olympia tsks. "Only Max can ruin his own career. And unless he's silly enough to get caught attempting to give an undercover policeman a hand job in a public loo, like that George Martin fellow, God rest his soul, he's not going to."

"Michael," I say, then add, "But he's the Associate Minister for Social Care. He can't hold that portfolio while his sister faces an assault charge."

She gives me a final pat and pushes me off her, but keeps her hands on my shoulders.

I attempt to suck up the snot that is rapidly seeking exit out my nostrils.

"Look. He might have to sit in the backbenches for a bit, until the next ministerial scandal shifts attention away from him, but it won't critically damage his career. And if it does, ex-ministers can make a packet becoming lobbyists. A scandal like this could turn out to be very lucrative for him in the end."

"A *lobbyist*? I'll have forced him into corporate prostitution." I cry harder and Olympia pulls me into another hug.

"I have to stop this from happening," I say into her shoulder. "How do I stop this from happening?"

I have to save Max.

"The genie's already out of the bottle, Squimpy. You can't stop the press running their stories." She turns towards the kitchen, pulling me along with her. "You need a big glass of water, and then an equally big cup of tea."

I sit on one of the stools at the kitchen island with my head in my hands, willing a plan for preventing Max from having to find another career to pop into my head. I can't. The journalists' questions are still pinballing around my brain, stopping any coherent thought from forming.

Selfishly, another fear rises. "Adam will be furious."

"Adam will be worried."

"He'll be worried, then he'll be furious." I don't know why I care. I shouldn't. Adam should be the least of my worries now.

Except I do know.

Olympia places a glass before me and turns to put the kettle on. "About the situation."

"No, no. He'll be furious at me. He always is. And to be honest, he has every right to be."

"Squimpy, it was fairly inevitable this would happen. It doesn't make it easier that it has, but nobody is surprised, and nobody is furious at you now it has happened."

"Apart from Adam."

She sighs and smiles. "It's very cute that you care so much about what he thinks."

"It's not cute, Olympia. It's a royal fuck up that my old feelings for him are resurfacing on top of an already great, big steaming pile of royal fuck ups. I need to be worrying about Max, not him."

She gets two cups out of the cupboard. "I know exactly what you need to take your mind off everything."

I'm genuinely afraid to ask, but I do anyway because curiosity wins out.

And so it is that after negotiating the scrum of journalists outside his place of work, and a second one outside his home, Max arrives to find his cousin and his sister doing strip karaoke to Rihanna.

Max doesn't seem the least surprised. Olympia's favourite pastime is adding a strip element to anything innocuous that might carry it off.

I am down to one sock and my underwear after dressing myself in everything I could find in my wardrobe while still allowing me some freedom of movement.

Olympia's rules are to pick a song we both know and love and take an item of clothing off when you muff up the words.

Olympia didn't bother to add any extra clothing and has only lost her shoes and cardigan.

God she's got an amazing memory for lyrics.

Max simply sits on the couch and watches us like we're playing a game of monopoly, instead of gyrating and singing about umbrellas at the top of our lungs.

When I lose the sock, I decide it's probably time to admit defeat. I turn the music off and sit on the couch beside Max.

We both stare at the blank TV screen.

I blow air between my lips. "Quite a day."

"Quite a day," he agrees.

"Do you know Olympia has a remarkable memory for song lyrics?"

"I didn't know that. Judging by the amount of clothes scattered on the floor, you don't?"

"I thought I did."

"Huh."

We fall silent.

"Cup of tea, Maxy?" asks Olympia.

"Yes, please."

She moves to the kitchen and I chance a glance at him. He's still staring ahead.

"Are you still an associate minister?"

He places a hand on my knee and gives it a pat. "I'm still an associate minister. Whether I'll still be Associate Minister of Social Care tomorrow, I don't know, but portfolios are constantly shuffled around and lost. The Prime Minister values me too highly to lose me altogether. This is nothing I can't come back from."

Max could mean it. Or he could just be saying this to stop me worrying. It doesn't stop me worrying. "When are you next in the debating chamber?"

"Day after tomorrow."

God. It's going to be savage. "What's your plan?"

He squeezes my leg. "Ignore, deflect and not sink to their level. It's unlikely to be the last time. Might as well get the first bit of vitriolic stupidity hurled at me over and done with."

"I'm really sorry, Max." I throw myself at him and hug him with all the strength I have left after the shitty end to my day.

"I know. It'll be okay."

It's not okay.

I watch the live parliamentary channel over the internet and shrink in on myself as question after question about Max's integrity-compromising sister is hurled at the Prime Minister during her question time. The Speaker struggles to maintain order as the opposition resort to shouting at Max to stand down. They boo when the Prime Minister refuses to make a decision on it.

I knew it would be vicious.

It's nowhere near Max's first time in the parliamentary debating chamber, but it is his first experience being the target of the appalling behaviour typical of it, and I wish it was not as a result of something his sister has done.

I mean, he shouldn't have to experience it at all, but for it to be because of me –

My shame resurfaces with as much aggression shown by the opposite benches and I allow myself the indulgence of another cry, because despite my best efforts, I haven't yet thought of a way to make any of this better.

I try to find consolation in the fact that while there are still journalists camped outside the flat, there are a few less than the previous day. I hope it's a sign it's already yesterday's news.

That hope crashes and burns when I watch the six o'clock headlines. There are scenes from the debating chamber interspersed with a solemn "Here's what we know about the case" from a reporter outside the Houses of Parliament. The story cuts to a shot of Jeffrey Wainwright exiting a building and being asked about it. He offers a small smile and apologises for not being able to talk about something that is yet to go before the courts, and naturally looks magnanimous and humble and stoic in the face of his injustice, like the great, big arsehole he is.

I think about building an effigy in his likeness and burning it on the roof, of standing there and howling his name and pedigree into the city air.

But I don't, not least because I don't fancy making another tabloid headline, but because most of all, I'm furious at me. For choosing to react the way I did to Jeffrey Wainwright and not walking away.

Why couldn't I have just walked away?

I have one comfort, however temporary. Mum and Dad are currently on an Antarctic cruise and are well away from the risk of media attention being turned on them. They probably don't even know about it, given their warning they would only have sporadic internet access. I hope it's not too much of a shock when they come back into the world of digital communication.

Needless to say, I don't leave the flat. I execute a complete withdrawal from the outside world by deleting every app on my phone that might tempt me to look at the news, at social media, or receive communication from people. Eventually, I turn my phone off for good when the twelfth unknown number rings.

On the third day of being barricaded in Max's flat, things die down a bit. I only get twenty-four calls from unknown numbers and the journalists waiting outside dwindle to one.

Then Max is dropped from his portfolio and it all starts back up again.

Why? *Why* did the judge not see that withholding my name was necessary? That not having it would only lead to trial by popular media and public opinion and the most powerful bullies in the country?

Two newspapers publish pictures of me. Thanks to Google and social media tags, they're not hard to find. Which is simply *brilliant* and increases my fear of leaving the bubble of Max's flat at an exponential pace.

A great lump of lead settles into my stomach. I don't want to be that person who thinks everyone, everywhere is judging them wherever they go, but I suspect I probably will be.

Max goes up north to attend some very important conference in Chester about something very worthy, and we run out of toilet paper.

I think about calling Olympia to bring some around, and then decide it's time I do something, anything, about the media attention, even if it's just braving a walk to the shops. In a hat and sunglasses.

It doesn't fool the journalists lying in wait, but I pull my hoodie over the top of the cap to form blinkers, which gives me the psychological fortification I need to tune out their questions, and I emerge from the scrum without resorting to violence.

Two follow me and lose interest after I reach the end of the street and then the universe feels –

Normal.

No one pays me a blind bit of attention. Cars drive past, birds chatter in trees, a woman walks by me pushing a toddler in a stroller.

It is the most beautiful reprieve.

And then I round the end of the next street and am greeted by a three-foot-high picture of my face.

The corner shop has poster-sized covers of the major newspapers and tabloids displayed on either side of the door and my face is on every single one of them. And Max's. And little insets of Jeff's.

My heart races, and my lungs won't work, and everything, even the soles of my feet, break into a sweat.

The reality of the entire nation being alerted to my stupidity, being handed a mandate to judge Max's worthiness based on something he had nothing to do with, comes home with a savage kick.

I pull my hoodie back up, stalk into the shop, grab a packet of toilet rolls, and then have to wait in fucking line because I didn't think to bring a five pound note I could slap on the counter to allow myself a quick exit. I only have my bank card.

The man in line in front of me taps the newspaper he's placed on the counter and says, "What's this world coming to, eh?" His finger hammers my right eyeball. "I used to think nothing could surprise me anymore, but this silly cow..."

I pull my cap lower.

The man behind the counter doesn't agree or offer further censure. He does something far worse.

He looks at me and points to the "No caps and sunglasses" sign, which is in place presumably for the benefit of the CCTV system and due to the high rates of aggravated robbery in convenience stores.

The man in front of me shuffles off and I'm next and I can't move.

"I can't serve you until I can see your face, love. Hat and glasses off."

My skin reignites the fever that struck me at the shop entrance.

I have to be able to do it. If I can't do something as simple as buy some loo paper, how am I going to be able to stand in a courtroom and face the judgement of the law?

I tug my hood back, then I slide the cap off, and push my glasses to the top of my head. The whole thing takes five years.

I keep my chin lowered, my eyes to the floor and place the toilet rolls on the counter with a shaking hand. If I could curl in on myself, I would.

I know my behaviour must be drawing attention, but I can't find it within myself to do anything better, braver.

"Two pounds, nineteen."

I wave my card over the terminal and clutch the toilet paper to my chest while I wait for the payment to be accepted.

Sweat gathers in the hairline above my temple and I wipe at it before it gives me away.

And then the payment is through and I push my sunglasses back onto my face as I turn to exit the shop.

The eyes of the woman behind me flick from my face to the tabloids by the counter. She gasps and whispers, "That's the woman in the papers!"

I scurry past her and out the door, but I'm not fast enough to avoid hearing her, "Shame on you."

Pushing my way through the journalists outside the flat's lobby is almost preferable. At least they have reasons outside of their own convictions to cast judgement on me. It's their job. The public has no such motivation and so their condemnation is far worse.

I don't want to ever have to do that again. But I have no time to lick my wounds. Half an hour later, I have to run the gauntlet again when I get the phone call from Max that he's dying.

Chapter thirty-one

Max writhes on the hotel bed and groans.

I want to call him a baby, but he looks to be in serious pain.

"I thought it was food poisoning, but nobody else got it."

I put my bag down and place a hand on his forehead. It's hotter than it should be. "You should see a doctor."

"No. I am not sitting in a waiting room with a clamped sphincter and a bowl in my lap, guessing which end is going to erupt first."

I wrinkle my nose. "Don't you have a personal assistant who can hold your hair back for you?"

"I am not subjecting anybody I'm not related to to this."

Awesome.

"I am humbled and privileged you chose me above any of our other relatives." It's sarcastic, of course, but I do owe him. A lot. So, if I have to be a nurse maid while whatever's in his system works its way out of it, I will be. "Guess this means I'm your favourite."

"They couldn't spare any helicopters to get mum off the boat."

"You checked?"

"No, I didn't check." Max clutches his stomach and curls in on himself. His pale lips are drawn back in a grimace and I feel utterly helpless.

"What can I do for you?" I say softly.

His face relaxes and he pants through pursed lips as if he's giving birth. Eventually, he says, "Help me to the bathroom?"

When I envisaged making up for all the trouble I've caused and am probably yet to cause Max, I'd imagined spa treatments and a Hebridean knitting holiday in a little bothy.

Considering both of those require money I don't have and may never have if I remain unemployable or too cowardly to start a business, maybe this act of propping up my weak, clammy, vomit-smelling brother while he staggers towards the toilet bowl, is actually the long end of the stick. It'll be over in twenty-four or forty-eight hours and I will never ever have to owe him anything ever again.

After I've helped him in to the shower, and we decide it's better he shivers in the stream of hot water from the shower tray rather than standing and adding a cracked skull to his list of ailments, I unpack the extra clothes I've brought him and wonder where I'll be sleeping.

There's a couch, but it's short and will only accommodate a curled position. I test the cushions to see if they're removable and can be laid out on the floor. They are, but my legs from the knees down will have to make do with the carpet.

I walk back into the bathroom. "Do you think the hotel has a trundle bed I can use?"

Max doesn't open his eyes when he says, "I don't know, Sarah. Ring and ask them."

He's right. How could Max know that and why am I bothering him with that triviality? I try to do better.

"You need medication. Will you be okay if I find a pharmacy and get some electrolytes and anything else that might help and doesn't need a prescription?"

Max turns his head towards me but keeps his eyes closed. "Actually, that's all taken care of."

"By who?"

A man's voice calls out, "Max?" from the other room and the steam in the bathroom becomes cloying. It coats my skin and my lungs and my brain.

I turn towards the door as Adam steps into the bathroom.

"Sarah!" he says as I say, "What are you doing here?"

Chapter thirty-two

"Um," Adam says. He hasn't said "Um" to me in fourteen years. He is always certain of his words when casting disapproval on Sarah Fulton.

I turn back to Max. "You called *me*."

"You didn't reply, Sarah." Max sounds exhausted and exasperated and maybe a little bit pissed off.

"My phone ran out of charge. I had just enough juice to listen to your message, then I hopped on a train." My tone is defensive, and I know that in the face of Adam standing next to me and doing a better job of nursing duties than I have so far, and because Max has a right to be annoyed for me not managing a simple thing as recharging a phone, I am being entirely unreasonable.

"Can we have this conversation once I'm out of the shower please? It's weird you two standing over me while I'm crumpled in a naked heap in here."

Adam and I shuffle off to the other room.

He smells of cinnamon.

I really wish he didn't smell of cinnamon, because it makes me want to stand near him and keep breathing him in.

Cinnamon has never had that effect on me before.

He places his shopping bag on the kitchenette countertop and I crouch to riffle in my bag for my phone charger.

"I was up this way visiting Nan," says Adam as he empties a sachet into a glass.

"Ah." I'd completely forgotten he had a grandparent in Cheshire, and when my phone beeps with nine missed call alerts from Max, I can't blame him for seeing if his friend was available to help him out.

I should probably extract myself from my phone, or at least stop pretending I'm absorbed by it, and thank him for being available to help out. But this situation is as awkward as fuck and just as overwhelming, and I have no idea how to deal with it.

The glass *tink tink*s as Adam stirs the contents.

I pretend to look for something else in my bag.

The paper shopping bag *crinkle*s. And stops.

I chance a look at Adam.

He is leaning over the bench, arms locked into straightness, and his head gives a series of small nods.

Is he…giving himself a pep-talk? Willing himself to turn around and talk to me? Reassuring himself this situation will be okay?

I stand to straighten the bed covers that will only be rumpled again when Max is finished in the shower, because it's something to do that doesn't involve talking to Adam.

Adam turns and looks at me. I know because a line of heat tracks its way up my spine as if my body is attuned to the direction of his eyeballs.

I have to look back. It's impossible not to.

Adam's mouth is slightly ajar like he's paused on the edge of saying something.

There's a loud squeak of body on shower plastic and Adam turns his head to look towards the bathroom. "How long has he been in there?"

"Long enough."

He says, "I'll help him out," without looking at me and strides towards the bathroom.

My eyes follow him because they have a will independent of my brain, and as he turns to close the door behind him, he raises his eyes and meets mine.

For the briefest of moments, before I look away in a panic, a thrill courses its way over my skin. Every hair follicle on my body contracts. Even, God help me, the tiny hairs on my fingers are standing on end.

Fuck.

I collapse on to the bed and have the ridiculous urge to laugh. Adam and I were always going to cross paths again, and whatever the circumstances it would have been challenging, but I could never have imagined this.

Bless Max and his ability to catch whatever bug's on trend.

I don't want to be stuck in a hotel room with Adam.

But I do.

But mostly I don't. I think.

Hopefully I won't be for long. Max doesn't need both of us here. I check the time on my phone. It's nearing 6 pm, which means there's no way I'll be getting a train back to London. It took me the good part of a day to get here.

Surely Adam can go back to his nana's.

I feel more confident with the thought. I can ride out the awkward remaining time here, which won't be much longer, and both of us can carry on as if there won't be another awkward encounter sometime in our near future.

I stand and pull down the covers on one side of the bed for ease of access.

Then I twitch the curtains open to peer at the Tudor buildings Chester is known for.

There is a low rumble of male voices behind the bathroom door and my focus narrows in on it. I can't hear what's being said, but the fact one of them belongs to Adam means the only thing making a meaningful connection between my senses and my brain is not the gorgeous architecture outside the window.

I sigh and walk over to the kitchenette to peruse Adam's selection of non-prescription medicine.

Electrolytes. Naturally.

Crackers, which I know from childhood stomach-bug experience is the simplest way to get something neutral into the stomach.

Diarrhoea stopping tablets.

Huh. I didn't know they existed.

Ginger tea, presumably to help with the nausea.

I wouldn't have thought of that.

God. Adam is a way better nurse than I am.

Maybe *I* should go back to his nana's.

The bathroom door opens and I drop the packet of tea to whip around and try to act as if I haven't been snooping.

My elbow collects the edge of the glass full of electrolyte water and I have to whip around again to catch it before it topples over and smashes into the sink.

I take the opportunity to hide my embarrassment by putting the kettle on.

When I have sufficient confidence that I won't do anything else that might tempt disaster, I emerge from the safety of watching the little blue "on" light of the kettle and turn to hand Max the glass.

He's propped up in bed with his eyes closed.

"You need to drink this."

"I can't." His voice is flat, the energy required to put any inflection into the words, unavailable.

"Three sips."

Adam and I watch as Max takes the demanded number of sips.

And vomits them back up again.

"Told you," he whispers hoarsely and Adam takes the bowl off him to wash it out in the bathroom.

"You need to keep trying."

"I really don't."

"You really do."

Max sucks in a deep breath and exhales slowly.

I watch him take four more breaths and know he has either fallen asleep or is being his usual stubborn self.

When Adam appears from the bathroom, he places the bowl in easy reach and looks up at me. "We both don't need to be here," he says at the same time I say, "There's no point us both being here."

It might be the second thing we've agreed on in fourteen years, but I choose not to take this moment to point it out lest it be misconstrued as snark and we fall into our old patterns, which would not be conducive to Max feeling better.

"I doubt there's any trains back to London tonight, but I haven't checked."

"No." Adam runs a hand down his face. "And the last bus from Macclesfield to Nan's village left forty minutes ago."

"You could...Uber?"

"I *could*. It took me nearly two hours to get here by bus and train."

"Oh."

Oh indeed. It looks like Adam and I will be spending the night together, in the same room, for hours. A whole night of hours.

My stomach sinks, then bounces like a cork rising to the surface of an undulating sea.

I wait for it to sink again, for my body to thrash against itself in confusion, but my stomach settles on buoyant. Which is just –

Great.

I wipe my palms on my jeans and turn to look at the diminutive couch again. One seat cushion apiece might not be so bad. "I'll ring reception and see if they have two trundle beds."

Max pulls his lips open with a pop. His eyes remain closed. "Or you could just get another couple of rooms. Put it on my bill."

"I thought you were asleep," I accuse him.

"It's really hard to lose consciousness with the palpable awkwardness between you two. It's like smelling salts."

"I...don't know what to do about that, sorry," I say and hope Max doesn't come back with a suggestion for us to shag already.

Before he can, Adam says, "We only need one extra room. One of us needs to be with you. We can take turns."

I try not to have a reaction to the thought of sleeping in the same bed as Adam, even if it's not at the same time, but a hum issues from my bones and settles just beneath the surface of my skin.

Brilliant.

"The tax payer won't care, Adam. Get a room each. Now please shut up so I don't have to waste energy talking sense into you."

Adam looks down at Max, hands in pockets, then turns towards the door and says without looking at me, "I'll go sort it at reception."

And then I am left in his cinnamon-smelling wake to ponder the reality of being trapped in the same building as Adam for a night.

I pick up the room service menu, willing myself to prefer food as the occupier of my thought space.

I *am* hungry.

I read *Carbonara* and Adam's surprised face as he entered the bathroom superimposes itself over the cramped writing, which isn't very useful. I can't very well have Adam for dinner.

And even though I didn't mean that how it sounds, my skin bubbles from the intensity of the heat suddenly issuing from it.

I fan myself with the menu instead.

By the time Adam returns and announces we have a – meaning one – room across the hall, Max is sound asleep and I have categorically imagined all the ways I could, in fact, have Adam for dinner.

I thrust the menu at him and turn around as I say, "Are you hungry?" before he can detect the blush sweeping up my neck to settle incriminatingly in my face.

Adam reclines on the couch and I pull a chair up to Max's bed and we wait for our ordered meals to arrive in excruciating silence.

There is a conversation lurking around the two of us. It hangs over us, weighted and threatening to fall at any moment. It's only Max's presence that prevents it from emerging, cautiously into the open.

I don't know whether to be relieved or frustrated.

Max saves us from our inertia by waking and vomiting at the smell of our food when it arrives, and condemns us to further excruciating silence without the tenuous protection of his presence by evicting us to the other suite.

After three mouthfuls of Vietnamese Beef Salad, Adam clears his throat. "This is not the circumstances I had imagined when we revisit the chatroom situation."

I swallow my mouthful of Four Cheese Gnocchi. "No." And spoon in another one.

Adam turns his salad over with his fork. His brow is creased in thought or displeasure or both.

"We could...not revisit it and spend the rest of our lives pretending it never happened," I say.

He looks up at me then. "I think we have to. Revisit it, I mean."

I find I am unable to look away from him and surprise myself by saying, "That's not the thing we need to talk about first."

The frown deepens. "What do we need to talk about first?"

Oh God. Why am I doing this to myself?

It has to happen. After fourteen years, the weight of its inevitability has given it a velocity that's too fast to outrun any more. I gird my loins and let the words tumble out. "Max says what happened fourteen years ago was the result of emotionally underdeveloped brains." I stuff a large spoonful of gnocchi into my mouth as if to stopper other incendiary thoughts from emerging.

Adam's fork hovers halfway between bowl and face. A piece of beef falls off and onto his lap. He looks down at it in surprise.

Then he looks back up at me without removing it. He says, "I presume he's talking about the school assembly and not us...forming an attachment to each other," and thereby categorically denies any opportunity to backtrack from here.

I wash my mouthful down with some water and rub at the potato-y lip mark on the glass. "What I chose to do at the assembly and how you chose to react to it."

I can't bring myself to look at him.

He doesn't say anything, which only serves to urge me forward. "You know I tried to apologise after, that I knew it was a stupid thing to do after I'd done it. It just felt like the right thing to do at the time, to do some grand gesture to prove how I felt."

With the next words, I can't help but look at him. "I didn't want to lose you and I felt I'd already lost you and I was made stupid in my desperation to get you back."

The frown is gone, which should be a good thing, but at least it gave me some indication of what he's thinking. With his tongue refusing to shed enlightenment, I can only guess.

I put my half-eaten bowl of gnocchi onto the coffee table between us. "I know why you couldn't forgive me. I made your life even more miserable in that moment with my thoughtlessness. I get it. But we never ever talked about it. You never gave me a chance."

Adam's phone issues a long groan. Before we left Max, Adam insisted on a monitoring system. A phone call with Adam's phone on mute so Max can't hear us talking, but we can hear him if he needs us.

Adam stands. He strides towards the door with a rigidity it is hard not to read into.

He's angry. He's still angry after all these years.

When he returns from Max's room, his movements are purposeful, but there's no aggression in them. He pulls his bowl onto his lap and scoops up a forkful of salad, before putting it back in the plate. "You know, I've revisited that day, that time a lot in the last few days."

My "Oh" comes out as half question, half exclamation. I had kind of expected Adam to dismiss the whole chatroom thing as yet another disaster on the Sarah/Adam tragi-comedy of errors.

He picks up his fork again. "I think Max is right." He slides it into his mouth before there's any chance for elaboration.

I stand up.

Because I'm shocked and because a ripple of anger courses through that shock. How, after fourteen years of resentment, can Adam so casually dismiss a moment that has been detrimentally pivotal to our relationship?

Adam looks up at me, mouth mid-chew. He frowns and gives his head a minute shake. "You don't get to be angry about that."

"I have every right to be angry about that."

Adam doesn't break eye contact as he finishes chewing and swallows. "Even if we had the maturity to talk it through a couple of years later, every time you've come into my life since that event, you've made it incredibly challenging. It's like I'm being continually punished for being that immature, heartbroken kid."

And we're back in the familiar territory of the blame game. I shouldn't be surprised. It was always going to be the destination we'd end up in. "I'm not jinxed, Adam. That is an utterly ridiculous notion, and surprisingly illogical from a man who, and I quote from the chatroom, 'believes in science'."

Adam carefully places his bowl on the coffee table and leans back in his chair with his fingers interlaced over his stomach. He looks like he's settling in for battle armed with the smug conviction he's right.

I walk around my chair and lean on its back. I'm not sure if this action is to brace for what's to come, or to be poised for attack. Perhaps both.

"It's a pretty convincing data set, Sarah." Adam's voice is calm, mild. It doesn't fool me for an instant. "If you make my life fairly miserable with the regularity you have over the years, I'm actually glad things imploded when we were teenagers. I can't imagine the extent to which you would have destroyed my life if we'd stayed together."

I snort. "*Destroyed your life*? Don't be absurd. That is unfair and, frankly, melodramatic."

"You do know I lost my job over the 'gay-hate attack' article?"

"Yes, I know."

"The firm said it wasn't a good look for them and paid me just enough severance that I wouldn't take them to court over unfair dismissal."

"And that was really shitty of them." If Adam wants me to take responsibility for it, I absolutely refuse.

He leans towards me and his voice notches up in volume. "*My job*. If Max wasn't in a power to issue a statement and force the paper to print a retraction under threat of libel action, it would have cost my professional reputation as well. I'd have never got another job again."

"But he was, and you did get another job."

"Don't minimise the seriousness of it, Sarah. Do you know what comes up when you Google my name? All that bullshit. Not the work I do now, not the pro bono work I did in the past for people who couldn't afford a lawyer, not my social media accounts because I'm too scared to start them up again. It's marked me. I'll forever be tainted by it, and all thanks to your usual, unthinking actions that invite disaster with open arms."

I push away from the chair and stand up straight. "You know, Adam, I'm really sick of you continually laying blame at my door like I'm some kind of malicious person who's deliberately set out to ruin your life." I could say things like, "Get over yourself," or, "And you call *me* self-interested," but I don't want to *actually* be malicious. "I'm really sorry you had to go through all that – it was absolutely awful and unfair, but it was the result of an opportunistic tabloid photographer, nothing else. All I did was choose the wrong glass on the table. The rest was entirely up to that arsehole and his editorial team."

I have to exit this situation before it descends into territory we can't get back from. "I'm exhausted by it and I don't have the energy to refute your convictions any more." I walk towards the door. "I'm going to check on Max."

Chapter thirty-three

I sit in the dimness of Max's room. The only light is a free-standing lamp in the corner furthest from the bed.

"You okay?" croaks Max.

No. "Completely chipper."

"Where's Adam?"

"Digesting." I'm referring to the food, but I hope he's also considering the last words I fired at him.

Max doesn't ask for clarification. He's probably aware, as I am, that anything we say will be heard by Adam in the other room.

"You want to watch telly?" Max asks.

"What's on?"

"Does it matter?"

Nope. I'd be happy to watch the train wreck of complete strangers marry each other if it meant I didn't have to spend any energy thinking about Adam and which part of the roller coaster ride we're now navigating.

The last few weeks have been tiring enough as it is.

Max finds an episode of *Antiques Roadshow* and we settle in to watch people learn the history of their possessions and then invite a coronary by greeting the news it's worth several thousand pounds with composed restraint.

Half an hour later the door opens. Adam stands on the threshold, one hand on the frame, one on the doorknob. "Sarah, can we...continue our conversation?" He doesn't sound like he's entertaining a smug conviction he's right any more.

Any residual anger dissipates in the face of it.

I kind of don't want to, but I should probably continue the conversation with him, because it's the adult thing to do. So I get up from my chair without saying anything and follow him back to the other room.

"Your dinner's cold," he says as I sit down. He plucks the bowl from the table and puts it in the microwave.

It is a conciliatory action. Not quite an apology or an admission that he has been wrong all these years to believe I'm either bad luck or have deliberately set out to bring disaster into his life, but it's something.

Perhaps he's still working through it all. Holding a belief for fourteen years is a long time. It's going to take a lot of mental manoeuvring to shift. If he wants to try.

As he's invited me back to continue the conversation, I wait for him to reopen it.

He remains leaning against the kitchenette counter, which feels less ominous than if he were to sit down. I think. "We should probably address the elephant in the room before it gets any bigger."

Ah.

The chatroom.

"I think we should forget the romantic aspirations of Lizobeth2000 and Mister D'Arsy and see this as an opportunity to build a friendship."

The microwave beeps, but Adam doesn't make a move to open the door and retrieve the gnocchi.

Even though I say, "Agreed," the relief I thought I'd feel at voicing a categorical "no" to the idea of picking up where we left off in the chatroom is not as great as I imagined.

My stomach dips with what only can be an equal measure of disappointment.

"It's too..." Adam trails off, but there are any number of sentiments he could have finished that sentence with.

Messy? Risky? Terrifying?

"It is," I concur.

"It would be good for Max if we could actually enjoy being in the same room as each other."

"Yes."

"And didn't complicate things."

"No."

He turns and pulls out my dinner from the microwave, and as he places it in front of me, he says, "But I want to straighten out one thing first."

My, "Okay," has a question mark at the end of it. I have no idea what's coming and if I need to prepare for entering another battle ground.

I spear a piece of gnocchi and look at him to invite him to continue.

He's sitting back in his chair and is staring at his hands in his lap. "When you said in the chatroom that you'd begun to believe the narrative, set by someone who constantly judges you, that you're self-interested and never think of others, I suppose that was me."

"Yes," I say and fork the gnocchi into my mouth. I'd almost forgotten I had something to be angry about, too.

Adam nods and raises his eyes. "I've come to see, over the course of our chatroom conversations, that you are not, in fact, a self-interested person, who's unable to think of anyone else's feelings."

Well.

Good.

"All you ever did in there was support me and help me through my problems. And...I'm really sorry if I made you doubt yourself. That's –" he runs his fingers over his short curls. "– Christ, that's truly awful. You always seem so sure of yourself. So larger than life. Impervious."

The small flare of anger that had ignited on his reminder of how he's treated me dies under the earnestness of his apology. It's disarming, this humility. For just this moment it feels like a gift.

So, I give something back. An admission.

"I played it up as an up yours to your judgementalism."

Adam gives a small laugh, hopefully because judgementalism is not actually a word, and not because my actions were laughable.

It breaks the tension.

"Max told me you were going to pay Jeffrey Wainwright off and he put a lot of pressure on you not to."

"Yes. Although the fact the prick wanted one hundred and fifty thousand pounds also motivated me to go to court."

"*One hundred and fifty?*"

"Yep."

"The idiot should have bargained. Now he's risking exposing himself in a public hearing."

"Yes, well, everything rests on that really. Otherwise it will have been for nothing and I'm not sure I'm going to be able to do it effectively."

Adam is quiet and I concentrate on the food in my bowl.

"You know, as much as I think paying Wainwright off is the better option for both you and Max, I do admire you for making a stand."

I jerk my head up. "Really?"

"Yes. You're refusing to let an injustice lie. You're fighting to be heard. It's an incredibly brave thing to do."

Something hums just behind my breastbone. I refuse to look at it closely, to analyse what that feeling might be. There's no point.

Instead, I fork in another mouthful, and Adam gets up to refill my water glass.

The phone quietly transmits the next episode of *Antiques Roadshow*.

My brain does not quietly transmit my thoughts.

I don't know how to navigate this new territory. The landscape of our relationship has changed. It's smoother underfoot, the air is easier to breathe.

It's absolutely terrifying and feels incredibly fragile. Because if the last fourteen years is anything to go by, one of us, probably me, will fuck it up.

Chapter thirty-four

After dinner and an hour of co-managing Max, his room's phone rings.

Reception lets me know there's a large package waiting for me and Adam from an Olympia Fulton.

Adam disappears off to retrieve it while I marvel at her ability to bend the universe to her will. She can't have known for more than a few hours that Adam and I were both here, looking after Max, and yet she, or someone she'd paid, had shopped for us and managed to get it couriered door to door in a tiny time frame.

Reception didn't exaggerate with their description of the box. Adam can barely see over the top of it when he shoulders the door open.

Max manages a weak, "What have you got there?" and I say I don't know, that it's from Olympia and that I'm therefore a little scared at what might pop out of it.

It's big enough to house a toddler, or several lion cubs, neither of which I'd put past her putting in the post.

Adam collapses onto the couch and says he doesn't feel brave enough to open it.

So I kneel at his feet, hold my breath and peel off the wide sticky tape.

Inside is a note in Olympia's untidy scrawl. *My <u>darling</u> darlings. You are doing a most important job of caring for Max and so I shall look after you. Mucho kisses xxxxx O.*

Underneath is a selection of luxury chocolate bars. I pull them out one by one and place them in Adam's hands.

There's a cryptic crossword book, which must be for Adam, because I have neither the intelligence nor the patience to know what to do with one of those. I am, however, happy to claim the adult colouring book and accompanying set of pencils.

Adam laughs when I pull out a game of Twister.

Towards the bottom of the box is a Rubik's Cube with a *For Adam* label on it and underneath that, a vacuum-packed bag of clothes of the cube's six colours for me. The instructions read: *Sarah must dress in the six colours of the cube and race Adam to solve a side.* I'm not sure what she means until I see the amount of clothes of each colour she's managed to stuff into the bag.

"How does she know I'm a former Rubik's Cube geek?" asks Adam.

"It was what brought you and Max together. How could she not know that?" Two skinny, shy thirteen-year-olds brought together by their mutual love of a retro multi-coloured cube.

"I don't know if this is sweet or extremely weird and inappropriate." He gestures towards the clothes.

"It's one hundred percent Olympia." I open the bag and pull out a red cardigan, hoping she hasn't included underwear as a game prop, but resigned to the reality that it's a distinct possibility.

If I'd known she was going to be sending a care package, I would have made some requests. Like the pyjamas I didn't pack. And horse blinkers, so I didn't have to be constantly focused on where Adam was in relation to me at all times.

"Do you think Max will mind if we crack a block of chocolate?" I ask.

"Yes." Max is propped up in bed watching a black and white Western on the telly with the sound so low as to be barely audible. He has managed his three sips of electrolytes and kept them down. The ginger tea he is nursing between his hands is steadily turning cold, however.

I tilt the box towards Adam for him to deposit everything back inside and glance at the TV. I do not want to watch a black and white Western, even one I can hear, so I riffle in the box. "I think I'll do some colouring in. You want the crossword book?"

Adam's "Sure," rumbles close to my ear. He is leaning down, arm extended to extract it, and our heads are closer than they've been since we made out like the world was coming to an end and we'd never have another opportunity.

I am at the mercy of a blow torch.

It is the proximity, the flashback to the press of our mouths and bodies.

I stand and head across the room to the chair beside Max's bed, as far away from Adam as I can get without fleeing to the other suite.

Choosing a picture of a jungle scene, I will myself to be lost in the task of applying colour in an unorthodox fashion. My jungle is a rainbow-scape.

When I am half finished, I look up.

Adam is watching me. "You purse your lips when you're colouring. You look like a duck."

I do not look like a duck.

"You do look like a duck," confirms Max.

Awesome.

Max groans.

I take the tea out of his hands and he clutches at his stomach. "Don't make me put anything else in my stomach, you evil doers."

And so begins another half hour of bathroom assistance and trying to keep Max as comfortable as we can make him.

When he drifts off into a fitful sleep, and I can't bear to be in a room with Adam that is silent, I suggest a game of Twister out of complete desperation.

Adam laughs. "Not on your life."

"Scared I'll out bend you?"

"Yes."

"You have the advantage of longer limbs."

Adam's eyes scan my body and he blinks and looks away.

I wonder if the reason he's not so keen is the reason I'm not so keen. That it would put us in close proximity of each other. With body parts touching.

I'm not sure what it will do to me, but I have a suspicion any effect might accumulate in my vagina. Which is probably why Olympia thought to include it.

An image of Adam hovering over me while I am in a table-top position on the Twister board surges forward from some wicked corner of my brain and while one part of me would quite like to dwell on it, most of me knows it's probably not a good idea and makes me say, "In your head, am I now the same person as the one you met fourteen years ago?" as a subject changer. I screw up my face. "That's a really stupid question. Don't answer it." *Of course* I'm not the same person as I was fourteen years ago. Also, it brings us dangerously close to discussing the chatroom.

Should either of us feel brave enough to do that, here is not where it should happen, with my sweaty, leaky brother in a bed between us.

Adam stops everything. Blinking, breathing. I have no idea what he's thinking. He doesn't look alarmed, exactly, but the cogs are certainly whirring. He inhales. "What about you? Am I the same person in your head now?"

Ah. Now I know why he froze. It's a loaded question. If I say "yes", I'm pretty much admitting to having feelings for him. If I say "no", it would be mostly untruthful and could take us back several steps in this fragile new world we've entered into since dinner.

But his stall and deflect *I think* gives me my answer.

Something releases in my chest and I feel like I'm riding an air bubble towards the ocean's surface. I don't know if it's relief or elation or something else I'm yet to put a name to. It feels good, whatever it is.

So, I decide to be generous with my answer. "The pieces have settled into place. The personality behind Lizobeth2000 matches the boy I knew fourteen years ago, but you are different. Not in essence. You're just...older. More world-weary, you carry experience now."

"You make me sound like a cynic."

"No. You're still an idealist. Or at the very least an optimist. Otherwise you wouldn't love what you do."

And besides, I couldn't love a cynic.

Fuck.

Where did *that* come from?

I mentally shove a fist in my mouth, and twitch the curtains open to look at the rain-glistening street below the window.

The ancient buildings glow in the yellow streetlight. People step over puddles, umbrellas folded and hoods pulled back now the rain has stopped.

I better fucking mean "love" theoretically.

Because I cannot love Adam. I do not love Adam.

I hope my abrupt interest in the world outside does not give away my inner crisis, that Adam has no idea what terrifying thing is playing out in my brain. It will make our having to sit together in close proximity for however long it takes for one of us to need the bed next door somewhat awkward.

Or at least a whole lot more awkward than it has already been.

"It makes sense to me, too." Adam says it very quietly, but I hear him perfectly, because everything else is quiet in the room.

I shift my gaze from the street to him.

He's peering down at his hands in his lap. "Mister D'Arsy could only ever be you now I know who he is." He smiles and his teeth are very white, and then gone again. "It's funny how easy it can be to pick up where you left off with someone you know very very well, even after fourteen years."

When he looks up and meets my eyes, a pulse of energy rushes through me like I've been shot with one of *Pride and Prejudice and Aliens'* lasers.

I'm tethered to him.

I can't, *Goddamn it*, I can't look away.

I feel like there's a whole conversation happening right now, but it's being held on either side of a glass wall. I think I know what's being said, but I don't know if I'm ready to hear it and am fearful I'm getting it wrong.

Adam turns his head towards Max and I suck in a deep breath.

Then he laughs. Which is confusing given the intensity of the last few moments.

"How ninja were we?"

I have no idea where his brain is at. "What?"

"To not let anything slip that might have given the other person a clue." Adam's gaze is back on me now and all the eye-talk is gone.

"Well, you know. I guess all those horror stories of creeps in chatrooms have made an impact."

"But we talked for hours over a period of weeks. We talked about stuff happening in our real lives and neither of us got anywhere near to connecting the dots."

"You're right. We were total ninjas. Not even you being clueless about a singles' aid gave me a clue."

Adam laughs. "Might I point out that you stuck said aid to your bonnet. Which suggests you were so sure of the person you were about to meet but had never seen that you wanted to signal your availability."

"It was a joke."

"It wasn't just a joke."

No. It wasn't. A blush gathers at the base of my neck and I will it to recede. I turn my head towards the window and open the curtains again.

"Don't be embarrassed. I think it was sweet. In fact, I believe I saw a wedge of vegan cheese in the box." He starts riffling through it.

"You did not," I laugh out.

"I hope she's not trying to tell us something." As soon as Adam realises what he's said, his smile fades and he retracts his arms from the box. "I mean, you know." His eyes flick to mine and he settles back into his chair.

"*Don't be embarrassed*," I say with glee. "It was almost a good joke."

He snorts and doesn't say anything else. He is either wallowing in mortification or is unwilling to venture further into the chatroom minefield.

Adam is too in control of himself to wallow, so I put my money on the latter.

Whatever is going on inside him, his comment has raised the already reasonably high tension bar to lofty heights.

I have no idea what to say to break it, and neither, it would appear, does Adam.

The silence stretches.

And stretches.

And stretches.

I think about offering a critique of the, frankly, completely tasteful decor, which is superbly dull, so I don't.

I think about saying how nice Chester seems from my limited exposure to it. Also dull.

I even consider dredging the depths of conversational desperation and talking about the rain.

Maybe I could feign sleep.

I eye the colouring book.

"Rubik's Cube-off?" Adam says.

"God, yes please."

Chapter thirty-five

"Go," I whisper so as not to wake Max.

Adam is turned away from me, his arms working as he races to solve a side of the cube.

I am dressed in its six colours and have to undress, swapping out each item for only one of the colours.

All I manage to achieve is to remove the red French bob wig and replace the orange mini skirt with green shorts when Adam says, "Done," drops the cube onto the chair in front of him and turns.

I have a white T-shirt bunched around my neck and my black, lace-trimmed bra on full display.

"Oh," says Adam, his eyes glued to my chest. He turns away and his Adam's apple bobs with a swallow.

My body thrums in the wake of his reaction to me and it takes me longer than it should to find the coordination to pull the T-shirt on properly. "One side isn't enough." My words are breathy, like I can't get enough air. "You're too quick. It has to be the whole cube."

"Okay." Rallying from his embarrassment, he says, "I'm pretty quick with that too. You sure you're up for this?"

"Up for handing your Rubik's-Cube-loving arse to you on a platter? I could have done it online. I can do it now."

He turns again and appraises me. "Big words from a little lady."

I refuse to rise to the provocation. "Yep. Here's some more." I rush out, "Three, two, one, go!" and I take a split-second advantage as Adam has to turn away from me before he begins.

This time I beat him well before his cube is complete.

"I think we need to even up the handicaps." He takes the bag of clothes and scatters the contents around the room.

"If you think you'll need all that help, I'll happily give it to you. A fair game's a fun game after all and I wouldn't want to accuse you of cheating."

"I have never cheated in my life."

I can believe it. "I have."

"And I wouldn't put it past you now."

I have my strategy worked out before Adam counts down. I've already located the position of all the yellow items around the room, and on "Go" move as fast as I can to dress myself in them.

I leave the yellow bell bottoms until last, because Adam has dropped them in his eye line, and I can't resist rising to the cheat challenge he set.

Possibly, if I allow myself to think about it a little harder, there is also a desire to chase that rush from before, when he found it very hard to remove his eyeballs from my breasts.

I bend over in front of him in my knickers that match the lace-edged bra and pick up the trousers. I hold them out in front of me and turn to make a show of fumbling with the button above the zip. "I just can't seem to undo this."

I look up.

Adam is frowning at my underwear. After a moment, he says, "I knew you'd cheat somehow."

"This isn't cheating. This is…distraction."

"It's working."

"Good." I hurriedly step into the trousers. When I straighten, Adam moves into the space that had been between us and I am eye to eye with the dip between his collar bones.

I swallow and look up.

Adam peers down at me, the frown gone, his eyes very dark, and I can't breathe. I can't move.

He shifts his head towards mine and –

Holy fuck!

He's going to kiss me.

My heart kicks into a gallop and my eyes are drawn to his lips.

Then a completed Rubik's Cube appears in front of my face. "Done."

He smirks and my hands fall away from where they'd failed to do up the flies because Adam had pulled a very damn good distraction himself.

"You fucker."

He laughs and steps away from me. "If that was best of three, I believe it was me who did the arse handing out."

He opens his mouth again and I point a finger at him. "Don't you call me 'little lady' again."

He raises his hands in surrender. "Okay."

I pick up the cube and sit in my chair, turning it over to examine its completed sides. "God, you're good. How did you master this as a child of the digital revolution?"

Adam shrugs. "I was late to puberty."

I have to think about this. "You got good at solving Rubik's Cubes because you hadn't discovered masturbation yet?"

"Maybe. Probably."

I laugh. "Thank you for trusting me with that information."

"You know I tell you that on pain of death?"

"There is literally nobody I can think of who would want to know that about you, so your secret's safe."

"Good." Adam pauses before saying, "Are you going to stay dressed like that?"

I look down at myself. Apart from the yellow bell bottoms, I have a yellow bikini top on underneath a yellow mesh tank top, a yellow headband with little pom poms bouncing on the end of long springs, a yellow tie and yellow fingerless gloves.

"Yes. I like looking like I'm about to keel over from kidney failure at any moment."

"You don't look jaundiced."

"I do. Yellow is not my colour."

"It's not the colour that's the most noticeable thing about your outfit."

Adam could be talking about the furry balls yo-yoing above my head. Or he could be talking about the amount of skin on display around the triangles covering my breasts.

I look at him to check and he quickly turns his head towards Max.

It is very hard to ignore the small creature unfurling into existence behind my belly button, but I try to by standing and announcing I am going for a walk. It sounds like running away from what Adam has just said. Which it is, but there's no point in hiding what we both know, so I take off the gloves and headband, and shrug on my jacket to venture into the night life of Chester.

I exit through a rear entrance the concierge directs me to so I can avoid the journalists I had to push past on my way into the hotel that afternoon.

Chester's just like any other town or city centre with pubs maintaining the heartbeat, but prettier.

I don't want to venture too far from people, because I am a woman on my own, so walk the same route twice through the central streets until an hour is gone and I feel bad for leaving Adam with Max while I indulge my inner crisis.

When I open the door to Max's room, it's dark, the only light coming from the dim wall lights above the bed.

Adam's head jerks up from where he has been sleeping with his long frame draped across the short couch, and then he rests it again on the junction between the couch's back and arm. "Nice walk?" he says sleepily.

"You should take the bed."

"No. I'm okay here."

"You won't be in another hour when you wake with a crook in your neck. I'm wide awake. Take the bed, Adam."

He draws in a deep breath and pushes himself upright. He looks at me before exiting the room, but whatever words play across his brain don't reach his tongue.

Adam wakes me with the news Max is feeling better.

I am buried deep within the bedclothes on the side of the bed Adam didn't sleep in, because I didn't want to get all weird and tempt myself to sniff the sheets for his smell, or something.

We'd had a change of guard at 3 am, which I was intensely grateful for given I'd exhausted all hope of finding a comfortable sleeping position on the couch and given Max's need for another shower and a change of sheets due to a violent bout of sweating the remainder of the virus out.

Thankfully, it sounded like it had worked.

Max's delicate disposition did mean he was happy to renege on his tendency to forgo his parliamentary fancy car privileges and use public transport instead, which was something he did to help the tax payers' wallet and the planet. A packed train is no place for an invalid.

The ministerial car couldn't have been any less typical. Dark with tinted windows and a memory of being in the back of another official vehicle on my way to a cell swims into clarity in my mind, followed by the fear that it might happen again if the judge sees fit.

I repress a shudder and try to force the thought out of my mind. I know jail time is unlikely. But fear isn't always rational.

Unfortunately, it is replaced by another less-problematic but more-immediate issue. I insisted Max sit in the front, but as soon as I clip my seatbelt in place, I see it's been a massive mistake.

The back seat is wide and I can see all of Adam. His body is turned towards me so his long legs can fit more easily behind Max's seat.

There is no escaping him. I have to sit for several hours with him in my peripheral vision. Hours in a car mean lots of thinking time. Being able to see him *and* think about him is not a good combination.

He says something to Max and my eyes are drawn to him. They hitch on the V neck of his jersey. There's only flesh visible, like he's not wearing anything underneath it and it sits against the swell of his pectorals, defining their shape. It's indecent.

And of course, this back seat hell being what it is means I can perve, but I can't touch.

I put my sunglasses on, despite the grey of the day. *Should* I want to perve, the least I can do is be less obvious about it.

I finally manage to look at Adam's face and my skin tingles in the knowledge Adam is having a similar problem.

I am wearing the green mini-dress from the Rubik's Cube game, because, well, it was there and bright green and calling to my inner rainbow.

Adam doesn't seem to be able to look anywhere else.

He raises his eyes to mine and quickly averts them to look out the window.

I do the same.

And that is how we spend the return journey. Between short bouts of inconsequential conversation because there's a driver and Max to eavesdrop on us, and because Adam is presumably feeling as self-conscious as I am, we catch each other's looks and then pretend it never happened.

It is torturous.

And utterly delicious.

It only takes one day for our paths to willingly cross again.

Adam appears outside Max's flat as I exit it to do some food shopping.

I have my usual cap/hoodie/sunglasses combo to help me brave the small pack of journalists still lying in wait, and I jump when I see Adam.

"Sorry," he says and pulls me inside, away from the chorus of shouted "Sarah"s.

"It's okay," I say as we stop just inside the closed door. Then follow it up with an "Um", while Adam says, "Ah."

So I wait to hear what he has to say.

And naturally, Adam waits to hear what I have to say.

Which forces us to both speak at once.

"I wanted to –" he says.

"Are you –" I say.

And then he says, "Sorry, you first," while I say, "Oops. You go," and chase it with, "No, no," as Adam says, "After you."

We are ridiculous.

I grin at Adam and he laughs.

His Adam's Apple bounces and I feel –

Wonderful.

Slapping a hand across my mouth, I urge Adam to speak through the universal language of raised eyebrows.

"I, um, wanted to talk to you about what we discussed in Chester."

"Oh?" I try not to sound hopeful, but the syllable emerges loud and round and shiny.

"Can we talk upstairs?"

I jerk my ahead around to peer in its direction, like a total idiot, then turn my head back to Adam. "Sure. Max isn't here. If that...is what you..." I don't want to commit to the words by voicing them in case they are wrong. *Were hoping for? Need?*

All Adam says is, "Yeah," which is reasonable indication they are not wrong.

I climb the stairs ahead of Adam whilst trying not to trip over any of them because I am acutely aware my arse is in his eye line and he's probably watching it.

Once we are inside the flat and jackets are removed, I turn to face Adam to ask him what he wants to talk about, but the words don't come.

On his face is an expression of desire, and hope, and *fuck*. If his figure-hugging jersey in the ride home from Chester couldn't bring me to my knees, that expression sure does.

An avalanche of lust picks me up and sweeps me forward. I take two steps towards him and Adam closes the gap between us.

Chapter thirty-six

His hands are in my hair and his mouth is hot.

I press my lips to his, wedging my glasses between us. They push into my cheek.

There is no tenderness, no finesse. There is no time. We are back in my bedroom, desperate with the urgency of our teenage selves.

Adam's tongue meets mine and my nipples tingle and my belly flip flops and my groin tightens and if I'd already lost control of my body, I absolutely lose my mind on that point of contact.

I place my palms on his back, pulling him to me.

I try to draw breath, but Adam sucks it out of me.

He walks me backwards and our teeth clash.

His fingers scrape against my scalp.

I moan.

Lord help me, we need to get naked. If I can't have him panting and writhing against me in the next five seconds, I am going to pop.

My bottom hits something. I stop abruptly and Adam crashes into me, which pushes the hard front of his jeans into my abdomen. The knowledge that he has been made desperate because of me amplifies the pulsing of blood between my legs.

We are at the kitchen island and there's only one way to go from here.

Adam lifts me up onto the countertop.

Then he slides my glasses off and he might as well have removed my knickers with his teeth, because it feels like that electric point of no return.

His face is slightly blurry, but I can still see the black of his enlarged pupils, the parting of his lips as I slip my hands under his top and run them over his warm skin.

And then we are kissing again and Adam pulls me forward so that we can grind and kiss and moan and kiss and pant and kiss.

And kiss.

And kiss.

His jersey is the first clothing to come off. Then my shirt.

He has sparse, tightly-curled hair he didn't have on his chest when I last saw him shirtless and desperate.

He sighs when I run my fingers through it and slides his hands up the outside of my thighs to gather my skirt at my waist.

He leaves a blaze of stars across my skin and *Jesus*.

My hands find the buckle of his belt and pop the domes of his jeans in the space of four rapid heartbeats. I push his jeans down his legs with my feet in the space of two.

I am ravenous.

I think *now* and *God* and *yes* and *now. Now. Now.*

Adam wants *now* too. He unclasps my bra and pulls it free to cup a breast. He squeezes and rolls the nipple with his thumb.

I gasp and run my palm over the swell of his cock inside his briefs.

He groans.

And then my knickers are being tugged down my thighs and over my shoes, and his boxer briefs are at his knees.

Both of us stop breathing when our fingers glide over each other's sensitive skin.

Adam's eyes are wide.

He draws a circle on my clit and with an "uh", I throw my head back and tighten my fingers on him.

His mouth is hot and wet on my neck and I croak, "Condom."

Adam retracts his head and looks at me like I've spoken under water, then he bends to pull out his wallet from the back pocket of his jeans.

I am half tempted to joke, "What are you? Seventeen?" but it would be a stupid thing to say in this moment, and besides, having a condom stashed in his wallet is incredibly convenient right now, so I shut up like the grateful person I am.

He presses his forehead to mine as he rolls it on, our eyes locked, our quickened breaths shared.

And then he hesitates, because after this, there is no going back.

I help him in his brief and mistaken moment of doubt by tilting my pelvis up and guiding him to the heat of my lips. When he is nestled in my entrance and his eyelids flutter closed, I pull on his buttocks and slide him in.

I bite my bottom lip and let the air hiss out of my lungs as I stretch around him.

Adam can't get his breath. He sucks in tiny sips of air and stops breathing completely when he has filled me.

Then he blinks and his hips rock forward.

Our centres meet, and it is the sweetest of collisions. We drive into each other and pause, the newness of each other, the intensity of the sensation powering our constraint.

And then our rhythm descends into frenzy.

With each thrust, a glorious ache spreads deep within me.

Adam says, "Fuck," into my mouth. I say, "Mff," and other unintelligible sounds that increase in volume as the pressure between my legs mounts.

This is going to end quickly.

It was only ever going to end quickly and I don't want it to, but I do because I am chasing release and everything feels so fucking good.

And Adam. *Christ* Adam.

Adam's grip on my buttocks intensifies and I wonder if I will have finger marks, before I am distracted by the knowledge that I am about to come.

I crush my mouth against Adam's and bite his lip as the liquid swell of pleasure crests and breaks with tsunamic force. I cry out as it breaks and breaks and breaks, and then I am a puddle of molten wax and Adam's hands shift to my scalp, cradling my head with tight fingers as he issues a series of gasps and shudders before sighing into a final couple of shallow thrusts.

I rest my head against his shoulder.

His rapid exhales blast hot across my neck.

When my breathing has steadied somewhat, I raise my head and look at him.

He isn't smiling at me, but his expression might be wonder, or *wow*, or a thing far far deeper.

Something builds in my core. It is warm and full of light and radiates out from my chest and through my veins.

I raise my hand and run my fingers down his cheek and smile into his eyes.

And I know in that precise moment what the thing is that's coursing through my system.

Love. I am in love with Adam.

He sees it too.

His eyes widen almost imperceptibly. And with a "No" he is pulling out of me and pulling up his pants. "What am I doing?"

"Adam?" I push myself off the bench and follow him as he finds his jersey and drags it over his head.

"I'm sorry. I…" I'm not exactly sure what I'm apologising for. Except I kind of do, but if anyone should be freaking out, it's me. I'm the one with the total loss of control over how I feel.

"This can't happen," he says, heading to the door. "You're going to wreck my life."

I'm not –

A life wrecker. I'm *not*.

Before I can form any further words, he's out the door, spent condom still sheathed, and gone.

Which is very very shitty.

Well fuck.

I didn't see that coming.

I don't know whether to laugh or cry.

I turn to face the place of the thing we just did, and swallow down the ball of *I'm an idiot* and *fuck you, Adam* that is rising up my gullet.

I shouldn't be surprised.

Because after what my actions have done to Max, after what they've done to *me* –

Maybe I am a life wrecker.

Chapter thirty-seven

I try to push the whole shitty experience aside. I already have *so much* on my plate that I need to focus my energy on, but I can't.

After fourteen years of resenting each other, Adam and I finally get our shit together over some gnocchi and a Vietnamese salad, and end up having frenzied sex on my brother's kitchen island.

That's a lot to process right there, not to mention making him run away because I shouted I was in love with him through my eyeballs and he had a moment of terror that I'd break him again. They are both very very big things to concentrate thought energy on.

And yet.

Falling back in love with Adam should not be the surprise it is. I practically got there in the chatroom, anyway. The only thing holding me back was making sure he wasn't an extremely eloquent thirteen-year-old girl.

Right now it feels oppressive rather than a release to acknowledge it. I will once again be emotionally tied to him, but it will be like I'm dragging an anchor. Unreciprocated love is like that. A thankless, energy-sapping weight you have to pull around with you.

It took me some time to cut the chains to that anchor fourteen years ago. Now I'll have to do it again, because only arseholes and people who realise they've made a massive mistake run immediately after having sex.

Clearly, Adam still thinks I'm unworthy of him.

Ugh.

I don't want to feel bereft all over again for the same person. It was totally shit the first time around, and it took me a long time to pull myself out of the pit I fell into. I do not want to find myself in that place again.

I refuse to revisit the dark.

I try to distract myself by looking for another job. I put in application after application for cleaning work, supermarket work, retail assistantry, anything and everything that might look past the fact I have an assault charge against my name and a court case pending.

I don't hear from anybody. I don't blame them. Any employer who values their business would do homework on the shortlisted candidates, and the assault charge thing fills the first five pages of a Google search on my name.

I know that because I looked and I really really shouldn't have. It does absolutely nothing for my aim to avoid any dark places.

I hear nothing from Adam.

Neither does Max. He arrives home one evening with his hair plastered down one side of his head and says, "Has Adam been in contact with you?"

"No." I try not to sound surly, but I manage a *fucked off* edge to my words anyway. "What happened to your hair?" I touch it and it crunches under my fingertips.

Max sighs and heads towards the fridge. "I got egged."

"You got *egged*?"

"By someone from a men's protection group." He pulls out the half bottle of pinot gris from the fridge door. "You want one?"

"They have *men's* protection groups?"

"Apparently." He grabs two glasses from the overhead cupboard without waiting for my reply.

My cheeks tingle and my mouth feels as if its been turned inside out, like I've just sucked a lemon, or am about to vomit. "I've made you a target."

Max doesn't say anything. He pours the wine into the glasses, emptying the bottle with a sequence of glugs that should sound satisfying at this point of the evening, but right now feels like a leitmotif for desperation and despair.

"What did they shout?" They would have shouted. They always shout something when making a symbolic protest.

"I don't know. 'Man hater' or something equally inane. The idiot couldn't see the irony of using a violent action on a man to protest about violence against men."

"Christ, Max. It could have been a bottle, or a brick."

"I think the irony on that is too apparent for them to throw something that could cause damage. Cheers." He raises his glass.

I refuse to pick mine up and clink it against his.

He clinks it against mine anyway.

"How can you be so nonchalant about this?"

Max takes a sip and smacks his lips. "Because it was an egg, Sarah. Also, the stupid bugger threw it at me outside the Houses of Parliament where there are police stationed. Got himself arrested before he could run away."

I take my glasses off, put the heel of my palms to my eyeballs and attempt to rub this new shitty reality out of my head.

"I wouldn't worry about it. Not many people are going to take a men's protection group very seriously when reported instances of rape and sexual assault against women and girls has quadrupled in the last fourteen years, not to mention violence against the LGBTQ+ community."

"They still have a point."

"Yes. But a point most people are going to laugh in the face of, because the overwhelming majority of violence against men is committed by other men, and the reality of violence against other genders by men is so much worse. Here." He picks up my glass of wine and places it in my hand. "I'm much more worried about Adam. I haven't been able to get hold of him and he's not making any effort to get in touch with me. Do you think he's reneged on the whole being cool with a best-friend politician thing again?"

I peer down at my wine and give it a swirl. "No."

Max pauses before saying, "You said that pretty authoritatively," and then adds, "What do you know?" which we both know means *What have you done now?*

"You must be starving." I push past him to open the fridge door. "I'll whip up some roasted artichoke tagliatelle. You want some roasted artichoke tagliatelle?"

"Sarah."

"Yes?" I say brightly and take four artichokes out of the fridge.

"Tell me."

I drop them on the bench, lean against it and inhale deeply. "We had sex." I turn to look at him.

His face slackens. "You and Adam *had sex*?"

"Yes."

Max's mouth closes with a snap. He pushes his fingers into his hair, forgetting he can't run them through it, then drops his hand. "Right. I didn't see that on the near horizon. When and where did you have sex?"

I turn around again to get a roasting tray out of the oven. "You don't really want to know that, Max."

He pauses before saying, "I don't understand. Why is Adam avoiding me because he slept with my sister? I'm not an overly protective brother. He knows I wouldn't have an issue with it. I think."

I'm not sure if his 'I think' refers to whether Adam would know that or if he's unsure if he has an issue with it.

"He's probably avoiding you, because I gave him love eyes immediately after we...you know...and he panicked about me bringing disaster to his life again. He couldn't leave fast enough."

"Ah."

"Yeah."

Max gives a series of nods. "He's having the mother of all freak outs."

"Most probably." Yet again, I've ruined everything and have made his relationship with Max difficult.

"I'm so sorry, Max. It's really muddied already very murky waters and added one more complication in your life you don't need. I'm making things difficult enough for you as it is and then I have to go and do something stupid like that."

"It's not stupid, Sarah. I don't know what it is...exactly. I'm still getting my head around it, but it's not stupid. If Adam was up for it, and he's one of the most measured guys I know, it can't have been a stupid thing to do. He's just not used to doing impulsive things and is taking time to recalibrate. Or something."

I mentally put the few hundred pounds I have in my anaemic bank account on the 'or something' and grab flour from the pantry to make the pasta.

"So, when you say you gave him love eyes, does that mean –" Max doesn't finish the sentence. He doesn't get the chance.

The undoubted fact of unrequitedness, plus my looming court date, plus Max being targetted, plus Jeffrey Wainwright winning over the press with some bullshit feminist posturing, plus the fact I am unemployable teams up against me and knocks me to the ground for a massive pile on.

I cut him off with a wailed, "I'm so scared," and collapse into a sobbing, snotting mess. Scared for Max, scared about the court case, scared about nurturing a broken heart again.

Max wraps his arms around me and says words meant to console, but that I don't hear. I'm too busy being desperately sorry for everything I've done and accepting the fact that even though I've been trying to run from the darkness, it has longer legs and better footwear than me.

When I've thoroughly soaked his shirt through and feel hollow and wrung out, he says, "Come on, we're going out for dinner. Let's do the local curry house. It's cheap and cheerful and nobody cares about who we are."

I nod. I don't have any energy to protest about not really wanting to have to interact with strangers.

"I'll see if Olympia wants to come. Then you don't have to talk if you don't want to and you can be distracted by the surrealness of her life."

Max calls her while I wash my face, but can't find the energy to change out of my tracksuit bottoms and T-shirt. Then he places my arm in the crook of his while we descend the stairs to the front door like I am an elderly woman at risk of breaking a hip. I find it reassuring anyway.

As soon as Max pushes the heavy door to the street open, a flash goes off.

"Sarah! How does it feel to have made your brother a target? That your violence against men has encouraged reactionary violence against your brother."

Max pulls me back inside and slams the door shut. "Fuck." His hand goes to his head to pat the dried egg he forgot to wash out and I forgot to remind him of because my mind was on other things. "I didn't even think."

I feel very light-headed and the world shifts on a backwards axis.

Max catches me before the floor does. His shouted, "Sarah!" snaps me back to my senses and I allow him to walk me slowly back up the stairs, my arm once again in the crook of his.

Forty minutes later, Olympia arrives with takeaways and a large candy-striped bag, which she opens to reveal a reel of garden hose. "You go ahead without me. I have something I need to do first," she announces and attaches one end of the hose to the kitchen tap. "Actually, Max, do you mind?" She gestures towards the sink and walks towards the balcony sliding door, the coil of hose unravelling.

Once the door is open, she says, "Now. Full throttle," and points the hose down towards the street.

There are yells and curses, which Olympia greets with a gleeful cackle.

After half a minute, she announces, "They've scuttled off like the cockroaches they are," and skips inside to turn the tap off.

I should be happy. I should be high-fiving Olympia and wreathed in mirth.

I just can't find it within me.

I also can't find it within me to turn off the television the next day when the news footage of a small protest held by members of the egg-thrower's group makes the slot after the first set of ads.

There are several placards showing a picture of me on them. On my head is a badly Photoshopped witch's hat, which is fairly clear in its vilifying and misogynistic message, but in case anyone is in any doubt, I am also tied to a stake and standing amid flames.

Ordinarily, I might have fled to empty the meagre contents of my stomach, but I am distracted by a shot of Jeffrey Wainwright standing on a small stage and addressing the crowd.

Christ. The man has made himself the face of female violence against men. And it's a seemingly worthy and empathetic face, too, given the bullshit charity work he's suddenly doing.

The sound bite they choose to air is when he asks why Max Sawyer won't publicly denounce his sister's actions, and if he won't, why hasn't the Prime Minister asked for his resignation?

"His silence is tantamount to advocating for female violence against men."

That's the moment I choose to vomit. Only I don't make it to the toilet and spend the next twenty minutes crying and scrubbing the carpet.

I pay little attention to what goes on around me after that. The days tick by in a haze.

I know Max gives a short speech in the debating chamber and a public statement, both of which denounce my actions without any buts or drawing attention to the terrible crime statistics about violence against women, and I give him my full support. It is a very hard thing for him to do, but something he has to, mostly because it is the right thing to do.

He says other stuff like he's proud of how I've owned my actions and am ready to face justice for what I've done, but that is the most "but" he can do in the position he's in. In the position I've put him in.

Other stuff happens.

Like, me being too anxious to brave the hostile world outside the flat and having to rely on Olympia and Max to get anything I need.

And the date of my court case getting closer.

Other stuff does not happen.

Like, hearing from Adam.

I feel numb to it. The aching, Adam-shaped hole inside merges with the rest of my abyss of despair.

When TalkTV air a supposed exposé on the extent of "society's violent female underbelly" and lead with my assault of Jeffrey Wainwright, I feel fed up with feeling impotent, of not having any control over what's happening, and very very angry.

It surges through my veins and I ride the swell of energy it unleashes, playing the Taylor Swift song I tried to sing to Adam at the school prize giving. I put it on repeat and with each playing, I sing a little louder, adding my own version of the lyrics by adding as many "fucking"s as rhythmically and syntactically possible.

By the time I've played it through six times, I am pumped with adrenaline. I shout out the song and punch the air.

For the first time in weeks, I feel like I have some power.

I think –

I am undergoing some sort of catharsis.

"This is happening," I shout at the dark TV screen. I am *so* catharsissing the shit out of all the black and worry inside me.

I can't do anything about what happens before the court case, but I can absolutely decide what happens after – what shape my life will take once I have my conviction.

I think back to the night Adam found out it was me at Austencon and the discussion about how if I can't find a job, I should make one.

This is how I get some control back. I am totally going to make a job and it's going to be ridiculously, disgustingly successful.

I celebrate by opening the bottle of wine in Max's fridge.

Chapter thirty-eight

"You look wankered," says Jas.

"Thanks," I say, not bothering to lift my head from my arm. My head has stubbornly clung on to a mild throb, but at least I don't feel like I have a terminal case of flu any more.

She throws a plastic container in front of me. "Vindaloo. Best thing for sweating the toxins out. Ian made it."

The most I can manage is raise my eyes to follow her as she sits down.

I've slept for half the day and still feel completely drained. I shouldn't have celebrated my catharsis with quite so much wine-loving enthusiasm.

"The others are on their way. They're just placing their orders at the bar so Olympia can pay for them."

"She's good like that," I croak.

"She's a keeper, alright," says Simone, who slides in beside me. Her vanilla perfume wafts out on the updraft as she sits down heavily.

"It's not in question, Simone. She's my cousin. I have to keep her."

"But you would, anyway."

"I would, anyway," I concede.

Ian arrives and pushes a glass of ginger ale and orange juice towards me. "Look lively, girl. Can't stage an intervention if you're half asleep."

"What intervention?"

"Olympia says you're a pathetic excuse for the sisterhood," says Jas, "and you need some boot insertion."

I peel the corner off the container of vindaloo and take a sniff. "Are you sure Olympia said that?"

"She's paraphrasing," says Ash, who sits between Jas and Ian.

"She said something about you being all maudlin, and us being needed to help with shifting some perspective," says Simone. "She might have added some 'jolly good's and 'terribly's in there, too."

I grunt. She probably did sprinkle some words last heard from very posh people from the 1950s, because that's how Olympia talks.

She emerges through the garden bar doors and exclaims, "Isn't this nice? The whole clan reunited. Just like in *Watership Down*." She sits down on the other side of me and I am obliged to get my head somewhat to vertical.

I prop it on a palm and pull my drink towards me. "Before they start dying, I'm guessing?"

"Spoilers!" says Simone. "I haven't seen that one yet. Is it any good?"

"No," says Jas. "I had to read it at school. Just a bunch of whiny rabbits."

"Speaking of," says Ian, placing containers on the table.

"You cooked rabbit?" I ask.

Ian frowns. "No. Why would you think that?"

"Because you just said 'speaking of' when I said 'rabbit'?" says Jas.

"Well, it's definitely not rabbit."

"I know. It's cannelloni. I saw you make it."

I take a mouthful of vindaloo and regret it almost instantly. Heat flares on my tongue, and up my nostrils, and across my lips. I take a greedy drink and Jas rolls her eyes.

"Here." She plonks two more containers in front of me that hold raita and roti.

I pour the whole mini container of raita over the vindaloo and gingerly poke strips of roti into it.

"Your replacement only lasted a week," says Ian.

"Why?" I say slowly. "What did you do to them?"

"Nothing," says Jas. "Couldn't handle the pace."

I laugh, then wish I hadn't as it turns the volume on my head-throb up several decibels.

"We think you should reapply," says Ash.

"For my old job?" I think of Adam sitting at one of the tables, eating his home-made tuna salad and reading an Austen novel. "No way."

"He's never there any more," says Simone, as if she's read my mind. "Hasn't come in for a while now. Since last Thursday, at least."

The day after he had me in the kitchen and then ran like his arse was on fire.

"I..." couldn't risk it? If Adam decided to show up again to eat his lunch, I'd have to watch him, knowing all the love energy I was pumping his way was unreciprocated. It would be really shit. "I'm actually going to start a business."

"Are you?" says Olympia.

"Yes."

She claps her hands. "Oh goodie. I'll do your branding."

"Which will be proofread first," I say.

"Are you going to start a restaurant?" says Ash.

"Maybe one day. I couldn't secure the capital at the moment." Nor am I prepared to take on that kind of debt, even if I could. "I'm going to start a consultancy. Designing menus and doing in-house workshops on flavour and prep technique and presentation and stuff."

"I think that's a great idea," says Simone. "If you won't work with us again, the least you can do is make us proud by working for yourself."

"Yeah, but there's a problem with that, isn't there?" says Jas. She shifts her gaze to me. "How are you going to start a business from jail?"

Ian snorts. "She's not going to go to jail for breaking a bloke's nose."

"She might. Get an unsympathetic judge who's been listening to what the media are saying. There are bigoted nobhats everywhere."

I sit up straight as a block of ice tracks its way down my spine. "They...won't pay attention to what's in the media. They have to be professional and not bring in personal bias."

"Oh, you think all sentences are handed out fairly? That every black man has had the same punishment as every white man who's done the same crime?"

She's right. God, she's absolutely right. Of course there's prejudice in courtrooms.

"Your best bet is to plead 'not guilty' and argue provocation. Then it's up to a whole jury and not just one person to decide if you go to jail. More people means better odds of having less dickheadery."

"But. That means I'm not taking responsibility for what I did."

"But you're increasing your chances of not going to jail. I know what I'd choose."

I pick up my drink and down half of it like it actually has alcohol in it. I really don't want to go to jail. But a trial means drawing out the media attention and keeping the political pressure on Max. Plus, if I lose, my sentence will be worse than if I'd pleaded "guilty" and jail that much likelier.

I wave a hand in the air to dismiss Jas' words with a confidence I in no way feel. "I'm a first offender. I won't be given a prison sentence."

"But will you?" says Jas.

Ash, bless him, changes direction before I can tumble further into the fear and uncertainty beginning to knot up my innards. "What were you planning to do?"

"Read a statement that explains why I resorted to violence and hope everyone believes me, especially the judge?"

Olympia chews and swallows. "It might work in terms of getting a bit of sympathy from the judge, Squimpy, but it would be good to categorically identify Jeffo as a sexual predator."

"How do I do that?"

"He's used the media to manipulate public opinion of him, and you. So, you just have to do the same back."

"Is that...ethical?" I don't want to resort to anything unethical, because I have a strong aversion to being a hypocrite.

"You don't have to do the manipulation part," says Ash. "It's not a closed court session, is it?"

"I don't think so."

"Then make sure there's plenty of journos there to bear witness to your statement," says Olympia.

"With the amount of interest I've held for them up until now, that shouldn't be a problem."

"I've got a mate works for a tabloid," says Ian. "I reckon I could get him to skew a piece in your favour."

"Thanks Ian, but it's hardly sensational stuff, is it? *Perpetrator claims retaliation for gross abuse of position*. It's my word against his."

"But he'll look like an exploitative arsehole, and you won't," says Ash. "I'd believe your word over his any day."

"Especially if you cry a bit while reading it," says Ian.

"You think I should…make myself cry?"

"It wouldn't hurt, Squimpy. Victim impact statements can be very powerful with a few tears."

"Except I'm not the victim. And he'll probably read a victim impact statement that undoes anything I said."

"Read yours last."

"I probably won't have control over that. I'm not going to stand there and say, 'No, no, Jeffrey, you first. I insist'."

Ian pats my arm. "Just make it good. Make it media worthy and the rest will look after itself."

"Maybe."

"We'll do our best to give it a little help." He gives a final pat and I am in no way reassured.

"So," Simone says chirpily, as if we are discussing holiday plans for Christmas, "when's your court date?"

"Tuesday."

"Tuesday, as in six days away, Tuesday?" asks Jas.

"Yup. The next Tuesday on the calendar."

"Wow," says Simone. "That's not far away, is it?"

I stand. I need to move, to push the energy roiling inside of me out. My head feels like a lead ball, but I find the coordination to walk to one end of the courtyard, then back again.

"Well," says Ian. "It'll be good to have it over and done with at the very least."

He's right, but it's hardly pep talk gold.

Simone elevates the level of motivational rhetoric by saying, "I have to say, your Jeff's doing a good job of making himself look good and all." She sighs. "It really is unfair."

I don't reply. I turn and retrace my steps.

"You know," says Jas, "there are other ways than the judicial system for taking him down if you're not into going to trial."

Ash narrows his eyes at her. "Like what?"

"No!" I say. "God. We are not entertaining the idea I get someone else to wreak more violence on him, or whatever it was you were thinking."

Jas shrugs. "It was all bluster anyway. Ninety percent of the time I'm just swagger and hot air."

"What happens the other ten percent?" Simone asks.

Jas winks at her and continues to eat her cannelloni, which could mean anything.

I walk back to the table and sit, collapsing on to my outstretched arm again. "I already feel so defeated. I have no faith I'm not just going to go into that courtroom, plead guilty and beg to be taken away."

"Not because Jeffrey Wainwright volunteers for a woman's charity?" says Simone.

"Because of being mobbed by the press, and turned into a witch, and my brother being egged and demoted and shouted at, and all the stuff on social media I haven't read but know is festering and breeding, and the fear of showing my face in public. It's been relentless."

"But you don't deserve any of that," says Simone.

"No. And yet it's still happened."

"You know," continues Simone, "I'm beginning to come round to Jas' idea. I think you should go to trial. I wouldn't want to see you in jail when you've already suffered enough."

"It's not –" I say, my stomach tight and heavy like I've swallowed a block of concrete. "I'm not going to go to jail. Probably."

"I agree," says Ash.

Jas leans over the table towards me. "But Jeff fronted a rally where a whole crowd of nobheads held up placards with you burning at the stake on them. He's an accessory to making you a public target of hate. Is all that stuff that's happened to you fair? Is what Jeffrey Wainwright doing fair?"

"No."

"Then don't accept this lying down," says Jas. "Put up a real fight. Reading a statement and crossing your fingers is lame."

"It's not lame. It takes strength to take responsibility for your own wrongdoing. Right?" I look at Ian.

He holds his palms up. "Switzerland."

I look at Olympia who smiles back at me. "I hear jail terms are the new tattoos. You'll be the envy of all your chums, Squimpy."

"Thank you, Olympia. That's very...helpful."

Christ. I have six days to decide to stick to the plan and definitely get a conviction by pleading "guilty", or regroup and wager my future on the rather limited criminal-trial abilities of Bob Sutton.

I pick up Olympia's glass of bubbly and drain it.

Chapter thirty-nine

The courtroom is small and not the wooden-panelled room I've seen on television and in movies. It is utilitarian in muted tones, and is no doubt meant for the quick, plea-entering procedures my appearance is scheduled to be.

Despite the lack of gallery for court reporters and other…news agency representatives, they are there, scattered around the public area of the room, audio recording devices in hand, notebooks being slapped against knees. They are the same ones that heckled me for comment on my entry to the building.

Olympia sits next to my parents and Max, and waves at me with a frenzied energy and a wide smile when I enter the chambers.

I do not return the wave or the smile. I take my seat and try to resist the urge to adjust the period pants Olympia gave me to wear. I'd like to think I'd keep my dignity throughout proceedings, but given the loosening of my insides when I entered the room, her gesture might have been well placed.

I do, however, adjust the toilet paper I'd stuffed under my arms when my copious amount of sweating wicked through my three layers of clothing.

The cafeteria staff are not present, it being a weekday and them having to work, but they are there in spirit, so they've said. I wonder which of the greasy-haired press is the one Ian lined up.

Jeffrey Wainwright is also present with a white man who is not the same one who turned up to Bob's office, and who looks sufficiently lawyer-y. He has papers in front of him, no doubt in preparation for my plea and the statement he will be invited to read.

Beside me, Bob adjusts his wig.

The other lawyer does not have a wig, so presumably wigs are not required at this type of proceedings, but Bob borrowed one from a colleague and is determined to wear it, despite the fact that it can't find purchase on his small, bald pate and keeps slipping over his eyes.

He has also tripped twice on his too-large gown while walking to the courtroom. I try not to interpret this as an omen for things that may happen as a result of his ability to be a liability.

We rise as the judge enters. He is a white, middle-aged man. I cross my fingers he is an open-minded white, middle-aged man aware of the privilege afforded to him and other white men, but I don't pin my hopes on him sympathising with my situation.

But it's okay, because I am a strong woman. I can handle what's coming my way. And I can pee my pants without fear of giving myself away.

We sit as he does and wait while he does some paper shuffling.

I wonder if I should also have brought in a sick bag as the thin contents of my stomach list to one side, then the other.

The judge looks up at me with an expression that is stern and soul-penetrating, and my intestines drop alarmingly close to the exit point.

"Sarah Fulton, please stand."

I stand.

"You are charged with Assault Occasioning Actual Bodily Harm against Mr Jeffrey Wainwright. You broke his nose on –" he looks down at his papers and reads the date, then looks back up. "How do you plead?"

Beside me, Bob pushes himself to his feet with a groan as I open my mouth. His wig *fallumps* on to the table and he hastily picks it up and replaces it on his head.

"Um," I say as Bob says, "My client pleads *not* guilty, your honour."

Murmuring sweeps through the courtroom and I shout in a high-pitched voice at the judge, "No! I plead guilty. I want to plead guilty!"

There is a laugh somewhere towards the back that is quickly stoppered by a glare from the judge. Then he swings his Eye of Sauron to us. "Mr Sutton, do you require time to consult with your client?"

"No," I say. "I definitely want to plead guilty. Because I am." I offer a little laugh as I add, "Guilty as sin," and mentally kick myself for laughing during my own court case for a serious offence and then voluntarily labelling myself an evil person.

"Are you quite sure?"

"One hundred percent, your honour." I resist the urge to turn around and shoot Dad with my eyeball lasers for saddling me with an incompetent, and grab Bob's hand and pull him down with me to sitting before anything else foolhardy can exit his mouth.

"I thought we wanted to go to trial," says Bob in a whisper that everyone in the room can hear.

"No," I answer through gritted teeth. "*You* wanted to go to trial and be all dramatic and shouty. I do not."

I look over the top of Bob's head to Max's concerned face and know I've made the right call after what I've already put him through.

I am taking responsibility for my actions and protecting my brother from more harm.

"Very well," says the judge. "Mr Wainwright, would you like to read a statement at this point?"

Of course Mr Wainwright does, because he is a wronged man and he has an audience. His statement is read by his lawyer and says things like, "loss of confidence" and "anxiety" and "post-traumatic stress", all of which sounds justified and I might have assumed responsibility for had Jeff not spoken at the Sarah Fulton hate rally with an eloquence and confidence and charm not normally seen on someone suffering from post-traumatic stress.

It is, quite frankly, highly offensive and disrespectful to people who do suffer from it.

I take some pleasure from the fact the judge does not seem moved. But then again, his expression hasn't changed from the stern mask he entered with, so it might not actually mean anything.

"Thank you, Mr Wainwright. Ms Fulton, do you have a statement you would like to read at this point?"

I wrestle the paper off Bob, not trusting him to not fuck this up as well and make myself ready to stand.

The public entrance doors at the back of the courtroom swing open and a wigged brown woman strides in, her barrister gowns flapping behind her. She sits next to me and asks the room, "Right, where were we?"

"Who are you?" asks the judge, not unreasonably. I'm wondering the exact same thing.

The woman stands. "Hazeema Javed, Ms Fulton's barrister, my lord." She sits back down.

"Ms Fulton already has a barrister, Ms Javed."

The woman stands again. "Mr Sutton is a solicitor, my lord." She sits back down again.

Bob slides the wig off and places it in his lap.

I want to say, "Since when are you my barrister?" but I'm guessing this unexpected development is a good thing?

I turn to look at the people sitting behind us.

At the back is Adam.

My heart stutters and trips and I whip my head back around to face the front.

Then I have to have another look to make sure he's not a mirage.

He isn't. He gives me a small smile and everything all at once seems quite a lot to deal with, really. I desperately want to know what the *fucking fuck* is going on.

I swallow, turn to Ms Javed and whisper, "Um. I was about to read my statement after pleading guilty. Mr Wainwright's already read his."

Ms Javed nods, says, "Good," and reaches for the paper in my hands before standing up with a set of her own.

Chapter forty

M s Javed clears her throat and reads. "*I would like to make clear my mortification, deep regret and whole-hearted remorse for my actions. I am incredibly sorry for the hurt I have caused Mr Wainwright and any trauma as a result of it.*

Violence of any form is not okay. I have never been violent prior to this incident with Mr Wainwright and am confident I will not be violent towards another person in future. And yet I was violent in that moment. So, I would like this opportunity to explain why I lost all reason and resorted to a violent act.

It is not intended as an excuse. There is no excuse for what I did. It is intended to give Mr Wainwright and the court the chance to understand why a previously non-violent woman would act in this way.

In May, I resigned from my executive chef position because my employer made my job untenable. Due to her profile in the industry, she was able to blacklist me and I was unable to find another job. I was unemployed for three months. By the time I had secured a demonstration and interview with Hachet, I couldn't afford to feed myself and was facing eviction from my flat.

Mr Wainwright was on the interview panel as the executive team representative. The interview went well, I had very encouraging feedback from Mr Wainwright and his colleagues and received a text message that afternoon from Mr Wainwright asking to meet at a bar a block away from where the interview took place."

There is movement from the area where Jeff sits, some fierce whispering, and his lawyer stands. "My lord, Mr Wainwright's character is not in question in this courtroom. Ms Fulton's is. Rehashing the events leading up to her crime is not helpful to the fragile state of my client."

The judge eyes him for two seconds longer than is necessary to convey his disdain at the interruption.

"Sit down, Mr Muirhead. Your client has had his uninterrupted chance to make his statement. It is now Ms Fulton's turn to make hers. I will not accept any further interference." He looks down at his papers and says, "Carry on, Ms Javed."

"Thank you, my lord." Ms Javed draws a breath and continues, *"I was led to believe, by the wording of his message, which used the words 'onboarding' and 'strategic fit', that he was meeting me to offer me the position. Not long after arrival at the bar, Mr Wainwright put his hand on my knee and admitted that although I was the top candidate, he decided not to employ me in favour of having sex with me so that he wouldn't be accused of having a conflict of interest."*

Jeff jumps to his feet. "That is a complete lie. I never touched her and she was not at any point considered for the position. The top candidate was someone else entirely different."

Once again the judge doesn't say anything. He doesn't have to. He allows the people present to wonder why Jeffrey Wainwright would ask to meet with me if it wasn't for sex or for a job offer. As the silence lengthens, Jeff's outrage shrivels in what I imagine to be a beautiful synchronicity with his ballsack.

He slowly sinks to his seat and the judge looks at Ms Javed to continue.

"Hungry and desperate, I lashed out at the abuse of the power he had to end the misery of my financial situation and which he chose not to for the sake of his own sexual gratification. I simply lost my head. I'd had a piece of bread that morning because that was the only food I had in the house, and I was overcome by the injustice of the situation. I was unable to act with any reason in that moment. And I am truly sorry for it."

Ms Javed shuffles my sheet of paper behind her own and continues, *"I am accepting of the consequences for my actions, but ask the judge to take into consideration during sentencing the impact the failure of having my name withdrawn from the courts has had on myself and my family.*

I have been harassed by the press, my brother has been harassed by the press, and even though he bears no responsibility for my actions, he has been demoted and subject to publicly broadcast vilification in his place of work. I have also been targeted in the most hateful and misogynistic manner by a group protesting female violence against men – a group to which Mr Wainwright publicly supported and addressed.

What's more, my lawyer has secured affidavits from the two other Hachet professionals on Ms Fulton's interview panel – "

Jeff gasps.

"– which confirm that Ms Fulton was the preferred candidate, but Mr Wainwright overturned the decision in favour of another one."

Jeff splutters out, "Can they do that?" to his lawyer and the judge asks Ms Javed to approach the bench with the affidavits.

I whip my head around to look at Adam and he glances at me, then looks at the judge, his face unreadable.

Jeff's lawyer jumps to his feet. "My lord."

"Yes, Mr Muirhead, I understand your objections," the judge intones impatiently. "However, you will be aware I am able to take into consideration any unusual duress suffered by Ms Fulton at the time the crime was committed and therefore need to evaluate whether the affidavits constitute evidence."

"But..."

"Yes?" The judge looks over the top of his glasses at Mr Muirhead while holding out his hand to Ms Javed, who deposits the papers into them.

Mr Muirhead sinks into his seat and the judge reads in silence. Eventually he looks up. "Is that the end of your statement, Ms Fulton?"

I have no idea.

I look up at Ms Javed as she stands. "Yes, my lord."

"Do you have copies of the text messages Mr Wainwright sent?"

"No!" says Jeff.

"I do, my lord." Ms Javed walks over to the judge and hands them over to him.

The judge's eyes skim over them with a "Hmm." When he looks up, his cold stare locks on to Jeff.

"It would appear, Mr Wainwright, that your character has, in fact, been called into question today just as much as Ms Fulton's. The difference is she has owned up to her actions and accepted responsibility."

Jeffrey opens his mouth, thinks better of it and closes it again.

"You have made a poor set of decisions, not least one to front a protest in which Ms Fulton was turned into an object of public hate with her image displayed in, itself, a grotesquely violent manner. Nobody has the right to cast judgement on an individual in the incredibly biased court of trial by media. You have no right to encourage them."

Holy shit. Not in my wildest dreams did I think the judge, *that* judge, with his carefully curated *no bullshit shall pass* face, would give Jeff a dressing down.

Jeff does not look at the judge. He glares at his lawyer as if the censure he is receiving is the fault of his legal counsel.

The judge then turns his eyes to me. "Ms Fulton, please stand for sentencing."

My blood retreats from all superfluous areas in order to drive the wild thumping of my heart. I have to grip the table to steady myself.

"There are several circumstances I have taken into consideration. You have no previous criminal convictions, there is no precedent for withdrawing names from the court outside of extremely sensitive cases in this country, which meant no possibility of that being granted to you. As a result, you and your family have been subject to harassment from the press, and significant public pressure and censure. What you did was a rash and senseless act, which you have, however, shown remorse for, and I am satisfied that due to your situation of unemployment and the unethical behaviour shown by Mr Wainwright prior to the assault, it was out of character."

That's good, right? It has to be good.

"I hereby sentence you to one hundred hours Community Payback and a fine of five thousand pounds. Court dismissed."

Holy shit.

I'm not going to jail. I'm nowhere near going to jail.

Collapsing against the back of my chair, I close my eyes against the prickle at the back of my eyeballs. This means it's nearly over for Max, too.

I push myself to standing, along with everyone else as the judge leaves the room, and as soon as the door closes, Jeffrey shouts at me, "This was not my trial. It was yours, you –"

"Mr Wainwright!" his lawyer interrupts.

Jeff turns on him. "She broke my face and I'm the one who gets the dressing down. How is this justice?"

"It wasn't her trial, Mr Wainwright," says Ms Javed mildly. "She pleaded guilty."

I look over the top of Bob's head to watch Ms Javed gather her papers. "Thank you. That was...I can't even..." Talk? Remember words? I know I'm overwhelmed with gratitude and relief, but surely I can push a few intelligible sounds across my tongue.

She smiles. "You're welcome. Adam put it all together. I just delivered it."

I whip my head in the direction he's sitting in, but people are pushing forward to speak to me and I can't see anything over the top of their heads.

There are shouts of "Sarah" from Olympia, from Mum, from the press and I can't see past them to the solitary figure at the back of the room.

Max voices the "I'm really proud of you" I'll never hear from our mother and envelopes me. Then he propels me towards the exit. "Don't say anything yet," he whispers into my ear.

Dad flanks my other side and kisses the side of my head but says nothing. Presumably Max has schooled everyone to wait until we are safely out of range of the press.

We burst through the bubble of journalists asking me for comment and there he is, looking at me. His hands are in his trouser pockets and he offers me a small, closed lipped smile.

I don't know what it means and I push down the hope blooming in my chest, because a half-commitment to smiling is not much of a promise. It's not much of anything.

He could have ridden in here on his white stallion for Max's sake, not mine, for all I know.

Max slaps him on the tricep as we sweep past, and then we are into a corridor, then a foyer, then out onto the front steps where cameras whir and click.

Chapter forty-one

Questions are thrown at me and deflected with Bob's imperiously delivered "no comment"s, which is honestly the only useful thing he's done in the last few months.

I look around for Adam, but he's not outside. Perhaps he and Ms Javed are debriefing or whatever it is lawyers do.

Dad leads us off to the safety of the nearest pub and the journalists keep pace, jostling to be in my or Max's eyeline and shouting our names.

Presumably Jeff has already run the gauntlet. If anybody's going to be provoked into a reaction, it's him in his current state of outrage. Perhaps he's already delivered all they need.

They stop at the threshold to the pub and when the first round of drinks are delivered, I say, "Are we...I feel bad for this kind of being a celebration."

"Don't be silly, Squimpy," says Olympia. "It's a champagne debrief. Absolutely everyone does it."

"Of course it's a celebration." Max wraps an arm around my shoulder. "For full justice being delivered – you getting an appropriate sentence after what you've been through, and Jeffrey Wainwright's character being publicly exposed. It couldn't have been a better outcome."

"I'm guessing thanks to Mr Delicious-face Adam," adds Olympia.

"Yes," I say. "Ms Javed said Adam did the leg work and put the statement together."

"Good," says Max. "He came through in the end. I was starting to doubt *his* character, but I think I'll keep him on as my very good friend for a bit longer."

"Where is he then?" I say. "He shows up with a hot-shot barrister, delivers a game-changing statement, and buggers off again. It seems to be his pattern at the moment. Give a mind-blowing moment, then run away."

Max tips his beer towards someone over my shoulder. "Hi, Adam."

I whip around, the top centimetre of my bubbly splashing onto Adam's chest.

"Oh my God. I'm so sorry." I step forward to wipe at it with my free hand, and the other one shakes so much it spills sparkling wine onto his leather shoes.

"Sarah, you're a menace." Max pulls me away from Adam as he extracts a handkerchief and wipes himself down.

"Adam!" my mother says and rushes in to thank him for all he's done for me before I get the chance.

Dad joins her and I am forced backwards to stand next to Bob, who is having a conversation with Olympia that is entirely at cross purposes.

"...skin sweats a lot when it can't breathe," says Olympia. "In my body art therapy classes, you have to powder down the armpits and crotch first so that five hours in, your creation doesn't look like a weeping Madonna with a sinus infection."

"I saw her once," answers Bob. "On her 1990 Blond Ambition world tour. She had very conical breasts. I don't recall her crying, though."

All I'm capable of doing is looking at Adam. He looks tall and broad in his tailored suit, and so handsome. *God* he's handsome.

His eyes keep flicking to mine as he talks to my parents.

And I no longer have to wonder where his head is at or his heart.

I nod towards the other side of the round bar, and hoping he saw and understood, walk towards it.

It only takes a minute for Adam to excuse himself and appear at my side.

I peruse the selection of liquors on the high shelf behind the bar as nonchalantly as I can. "You grand gestured me."

Adam's laugh is soft. "I did."

I turn to him then. "You must have felt really bad for shagging me and then scarpering."

"I did." His smile turns into a regretful press of lips. "I had a bit of a panic."

"I know."

"It was a terrible thing to do. Running on you like that. In that moment."

"It was pretty shitty."

"I've been really ashamed."

"Good."

"I saw the depth of emotion in you, and…recognised the same depth of emotion in me and it absolutely scared the shit out of me. Last time I felt like that about you, it ended up being reasonably traumatic."

Honeyed warmth pushes out from my chest with each of my heartbeats and fills all of the spaces made empty by events of the last few weeks. Adam feels deeply about me.

"But you're not worried about the luck see-saw? That I'll cause some dreadful accident and magnificently embarrass you in public?"

"A little bit, to be honest. But I think –" he runs his hand forward along the bar top to where mine is, and reaches out with his little finger to touch mine. "– my belief you invite disaster upon me is ultimately a false one and therefore not a fair one. I'm sorry I've blamed you for bringing ruin to me. I know none of it was the result of intention."

The warmth turns molten and I take a step towards him. "I'm pretty sure if you kissed me right now, my dad won't punch you."

He takes a step towards me. "Only pretty sure?"

Adam's body is a pint glass away from mine. I can smell the cinnamon of his soap.

I let out a shaky breath and can't find a witty comeback. Or any comeback at all.

The brown of his irises are almost black in the dim light at the back of the pub. Or it could just be because of me.

I drop my gaze to his lips. They are open slightly. Ready.

I stand on my tiptoes and he leans down and then we are falling.

Chapter forty-two

After we leave the post-court debrief at the pub, we take the Tube back to Adam's flat and sit pressed against each other, despite the carriage being half empty and there's no need to economise on space.

Our fingers are laced together and Adam runs his thumb over the back of my hand. "I wish I could go back and rewrite our narrative. I feel like I've wasted an awful amount of the wrong energy on you."

"I would have read the speech I'd actually written and serenaded you at your house instead."

Adam gives a low laugh. "You would. There still would have been some grand gesturing, even if done in private."

"*Relative* private."

"More private than a school assembly. I've never been much of a Swifty, but you have categorically ruined that song for me."

I sigh. "Yeah. Me too."

"If I could just –" Adam balls his free hand into a fist and issues a sharp exhale. "– hand that totally lost boy the perspective of time and age, things would have been so much different." He looks at me and smiles. "I can't though. I'm really sorry I can't."

I squeeze his hand. "It doesn't matter any more. It's done. You're just wasting a whole lot of energy anyway on the wrong thing."

"I'm hoping that means it's time to look towards our future?" Adam's smile is almost shy, like he isn't sure I've past the point of no return with him. How can he not know all I think about is our future?

I reassure him with a kiss and a "yes" whispered against his lips. Then I pull my head back. "Once we've ironed out the kinks."

Adam hesitates before saying, "Okay. Which kink do you want to address first?" He delivers it with a seriousness appropriate to the topic, but a smile plays on the corner of his lips.

"Do you really wear arseless chaps on Wednesdays?"

Adam's smile broadens. "I would never think of constraining my arseless chap habit to a particular day of the week."

"Just what I was hoping to hear."

The smile settles into a soft curve, ready for my real question.

"Do you really think I dress like a colour-blind clown?"

"I never said that."

"You inferred it."

Adam brushes my hair off my forehead. "I actually love that you're not afraid to stand out when so many people are. I think your dress sense is bold and considered and in no way clownish."

"What about when I do things like ride trolleys and build paper castles?"

He takes a deep breath before answering. "You know, despite the censure I might have issued over your ability to grab 'fun' and 'carefree' with both hands, behind those words are always *always* the wish I lacked the self-restraint and fear of judgement to be able to do them too."

"So when you purse your lips and frown at me like you disapprove, you actually mean to smile in admiration?"

Adam shrugs one shoulder. "I had a role to play that I'd forged over such a long time, I didn't know how to behave any different. Also, you did try to castrate me with a mop, so I think some semblance of disapproval was warranted."

"I notice it didn't handicap your performance in Max's kitchen."

"I noticed you noticing. Quite loudly, if I recall correctly."

I don't have a comeback. I can't refute it. I offer what I imagine is a simmering smile, an invitation to allow me to notice again.

It takes Adam five long seconds to extract himself from my look and gather his thoughts again. "What I want to know is, how do you feel about my wordiness now you know exactly who I am and how I feel, because if I remember right, you called me 'uppity' and a 'tosser' for being verbose whilst also claiming my use of language was sexier than French."

"I'm not sure. I think I need more exposure to make up my mind."

He dips his head. "I am disposed to articulate my meaning in an abstruse fashion for your aural pleasure, my lady."

"My what pleasure?"

"Aural."

"Oh good. For a moment there I could have sworn you said 'oral'."

"That's an altogether different type of tongue flapping, but I can always combine the two if you think you might be partial."

My breath is shaky when I say, "Yes please."

I wake to find myself wrapped in Adam's arms and my phone pinging with Google alerts.

"Hmph?" Adam says as I extract myself to get my phone from my jacket pocket and put my glasses on. I sit up and open the notifications.

There are a few articles on my plea sentencing and what this will mean for Max, which is to be expected. But there are other articles as well.

Women's charity drops Wainwright as spokesperson

Hachet executive suspended from job pending investigation

"Me too" says ex-employee after sexual misconduct allegations aimed at top executive

"Holy shit."

"What?" Adam murmurs.

I thrust the phone at him and he blinks rapidly at it. Eventually he just says, "Good," like he's being very careful with his reaction. "How do you feel about it?"

"Like the universe is in balance after all. That I'm no longer paying for his actions as well as mine."

Adam pulls me back down to lie next to him and I nestle my head into the junction between his neck and his shoulder.

"Do you think it'll all die down now? Things will go back to normal for Max?"

"I do. You're already yesterday's scandal. Wainwright will be in the news for another day or two, maybe, and then we'll never hear about him again."

"Great," I say on an exhale. "I want to put it all behind me."

Adam runs the flat of his hand from my shoulder down to my elbow and back again. "How are you planning on stepping into your bright new future?"

I grab my phone from where I've placed it on the bed behind me and wake it up. Then I navigate to cuisinelab.com and show him the screen. "There's this."

"You built a website? I thought the idea of starting a business terrified you."

"I needed a distraction on the days leading up to court." I thumb through the small number of pages to *About Me*. The photo is the one I have on my resumé. I look happy and approachable and hopefully not immediately recognisable as that woman in the papers.

I lower my hand. "I've even had my first enquiry about work. It's from someone Olympia knows, so it's pretty much based on nepotism, but I'll take what I can get."

"It's not nepotism. All start-ups need a hand up and lots of jobs are gotten by word of mouth. When you establish a reputation, you'll get lots of them."

"I hope so. It might take a while."

"It might. But that's the nature of starting a business." Adam's breath is hot against my scalp.

"In the meantime, the guys at the cafeteria want me to come back to work, so maybe I will now I don't have to hide from you any more."

"Those guys mean a lot to you, don't they?"

Yes, they absolutely do. "I needed a whole lot of medicine after my arrest and they gave it. Plus a whole lot of mostly unjudgemental support for everything going on in my life." I swivel my head to look at Adam and have to shuffle back on the pillow until he's in focus. "I've got a pub date with them tonight to debrief on the hearing."

"Okay."

"Do you...want to come?"

Adam snorts. "They probably all think I'm an uptight, angry, misery seeker. It might test their capacity for mostly unjudge-mental support."

"I'm not afraid of them. Not even Jas." I think about that. "Sometimes not even Jas. You can show them who you actually are – the funny, self-effacing guy who does like fun and thinks

I'm incredible. And we can tell them our origin story and they'll probably laugh and say they're not surprised that we're now romancing each other."

"Romancing each other?"

"Or I could tell them I just got boifed. If...you want to go all official. And stuff."

Adam pauses before saying, "I'm not sure saying you just got boifed sounds particularly official, especially if the meaning is hidden in some kind of esoteric teen speak."

"Fine", I sigh. "I'll introduce you as my boyfriend, like a plain speaking, mature person."

With a grin, Adam says, "I'll happily be your boyfriend, Sarah. You don't need to be awkward about asking me. I would have thought it was pretty obvious."

"When you did all those naughty things to me last night?"

"Yes. Also when I told you I loved you."

"Did you?"

He closes the gap between us and smiles against my lips. "Yes. I can say it again if you need me to. I love you, Sarah Fulton."

My chest fills with light, and he reaches down to sling my leg over his hip and slide his hand up my thigh to cup my buttock.

His "pretty obvious" presses into my stomach.

I plant a soft kiss on his mouth and whisper, "You want to say it, though, don't you?"

"Say what?"

"That you just got girlfed. You want to say it just once, to feel how edgy it is to do slang talk."

Adam laughs.

"You only live once. Go on. It'll feel really good."

Adam leans towards my ear, smiling. His voice is low and husky and shiver-inducing when he says, "You know, I think I have a can of baked beans in my cupboard," and I know he's not thinking of breakfast. Or not only of breakfast.

"You want to locate all the body parts that offer the best bean ski jumps?"

"God yes. I've been thinking about that for weeks. It's driven me to distraction."

I purse my lips and pretend to deliberate. "I'll help you with your locating. On one condition."

Adam sits up and peers down at me, his customary frown wedged between his brows.

"You have to shout it."

"I'm not shouting it, Sarah."

"Yes you are."

He takes a deep breath and his exhale takes an unnecessarily long time to exit his nostrils. Then he gets up, goes over to the window and slides it open. "I just got girlfed!" he hollers into the street below.

He slams the window home and turns with a grin.

It is delightful and I laugh delightedly.

I throw back the covers and hold my hand out to him. "Let the fun with beans begin."

Thanks for taking the time to read my book

My books are always a complete labour of love, so I hope you enjoyed it. Please consider taking the time to leave a review (it only needs to be a line or two). As an independent author, reviews help support my work by allowing more readers to discover me, which means I can produce more great novels for you to read! If you're not sure where to post a review, try the Goodreads website or your favourite online bookstore.

Acknowledgements

Factual stuff can sometimes be an inconvenience to the fiction writer, by which I mean to say that there's stuff (mostly the legal stuff) that happens in this book that I've taken liberty with. All inaccuracies are intentional. Mostly. Thank you poetic license!

Thanks very much to my first readers, Rachel Axcell, Fiona Baylis, and Sarah Gardiner. Your feedback was invaluable. Thanks also to my editor, Kura Carpenter, for making me work so so hard to get this book into the shape it needed to be in. I couldn't have done it without you.

Bailey McGinn, you have excelled yourself again. Thanks for the gorgeous cover design.

I want to acknowledge all the quirky, funny, and clever British chick lit and rom-com books that I've enjoyed over the years and that have helped shaped the world of this book. I would never have had the confidence to tackle this story without them.

About the Author

Merren Tait is the award-winning author of The Good Life series, a humorous exploration of kick-arse women changing gears and seeking a quieter life in the less-well travelled places of a (fictional) New Zealand.

Merren has lived a series of bookish lives. Her first incarnation was as a book-hungry child, then as a mildly pretentious English literature student. Her third life saw her teaching English to somewhat-willing high school students, and her fourth, sharing her love of books as a librarian. Now she has been reincarnated as a fiction creator.

She is of Scottish, Ngāti Apa ki te Rā Tō, English, Irish and German extraction and attributes her cross-cultural comedic flair to the enthusiastic interbreeding of her ancestors.

Merren lives in a small house on a large piece of land near Raglan, New Zealand, where she dreams up fabulous names for her chickens, like Princess Layer.

Find out more at merrentait.com

f facebook.com/merrentaitauthor/

◉ instagram.com/merrentaitauthor

BB bookbub.com/profile/merren-tait